H━━━━ ━━━━ NCH

SHIPMENT 1

The Rancher by Diana Palmer
Big Sky Standoff by B.J. Daniels
Branded by the Sheriff by Delores Fossen
Texas Lullaby by Tina Leonard
Cowboy for Hire by Marie Ferrarella
Her Rancher Rescuer by Donna Alward

SHIPMENT 2

Last Chance Cowboy by Cathy McDavid
Rancher Rescue by Barb Han
The Texan's Future Bride by Sheri WhiteFeather
A Texan on Her Doorstep by Stella Bagwell
The Rancher's Hired Fiancée by Judy Duarte
That Wild Cowboy by Lenora Worth

SHIPMENT 3

Lone Star Survivor by Colleen Thompson
A Cowboy's Duty by Marin Thomas
Protecting Their Child by Angi Morgan
The Cowboy's Bonus Baby by Tina Leonard
Claimed by a Cowboy by Tanya Michaels
Home to Wyoming by Rebecca Winters
One Brave Cowboy by Kathleen Eagle

SHIPMENT 4

Wearing the Rancher's Ring by Stella Bagwell
The Texas Rancher's Vow by Cathy Gillen Thacker
Wild for the Sheriff by Kathleen O'Brien
A Callahan Wedding by Tina Leonard
Rustling Up Trouble by Delores Fossen
The Cowboy's Family Plan by Judy Duarte

SHIPMENT 5

The Texan's Baby by Donna Alward
Not Just a Cowboy by Caro Carson
Cowboy in the Making by Julie Benson
The Renegade Rancher by Angi Morgan
A Family for Tyler by Angel Smits
The Prodigal Cowboy by Kathleen Eagle

SHIPMENT 6

The Rodeo Man's Daughter by Barbara White Daille
His Texas Wildflower by Stella Bagwell
The Cowboy SEAL by Laura Marie Altom
Montana Sheriff by Marie Ferrarella
A Ranch to Keep by Claire McEwen
A Cowboy's Pride by Pamela Britton
Cowboy Under Siege by Gail Barrett

SHIPMENT 7

Reuniting with the Rancher by Rachel Lee
Rodeo Dreams by Sarah M. Anderson
Beau: Cowboy Protector by Marin Thomas
Texas Stakeout by Virna DePaul
Big City Cowboy by Julie Benson
Remember Me, Cowboy by C.J. Carmichael

SHIPMENT 8

Roping the Rancher by Julie Benson
In a Cowboy's Arms by Rebecca Winters
How to Lasso a Cowboy by Christine Wenger
Betting on the Cowboy by Kathleen O'Brien
Her Cowboy's Christmas Wish by Cathy McDavid
A Kiss on Crimson Ranch by Michelle Major

HOME *on the* RANCH

WILD FOR THE SHERIFF

KATHLEEN O'BRIEN

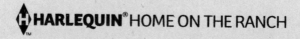

HARLEQUIN® HOME ON THE RANCH

Recycling programs
for this product may
not exist in your area.

ISBN-13: 978-1-335-45314-3

Wild for the Sheriff

Printed in U.S.A.

Kathleen O'Brien was a feature writer and TV critic before marrying a fellow journalist. Motherhood, which followed soon after, was so marvelous she turned to writing novels, which meant she could work at home. Though she's a lifelong city gal, she has a special place in her heart for tiny towns like Silverdell, where you may not enjoy a lot of privacy... but you never really face your troubles alone, either.

To Jane.
Those were the days, my friend.

Chapter One

Rowena Wright hadn't set foot on Bell River Ranch land for fifteen years. And apparently she still didn't want to. Though she'd driven a thousand miles to get here, she'd been sitting in her car for half an hour, staring at the brown-fingered weeds that crawled up the peeling paint of the back wall.

She had no idea what she was waiting for. It wasn't as if anyone was likely to appear on the sagging kitchen porch to welcome her in. The place was shut up as tight as a church on Monday, and the afternoon was waning. She ought to hurry, before the long aspen shadows turned the two-story, badly repaired timber-

and-brick structure into a death trap of rotted boards and unfamiliar furniture.

She ought to, but…

But if she shut her eyes she could almost hear Penny and Bree squealing on the tire swing, over by the stables. If she sat very still, she could feel the thrumming of horses' hooves as the cowboys cantered in through the two twisted bristlecone pines that flanked the front gate. If she inhaled hard, she could even smell her mother's Sunday-morning bacon floating on the air.

And oh, the air. Spring-fresh sunshine and buttercups. The perfume slipped its way through a chink in her armor she hadn't known existed. And the thought arose before she could stop it.

Home. The air here in Western Colorado smelled like *home*.

"Oh, for Pete's sake." She opened her eyes and yanked the key out of the ignition. "There's enough sap in those words, girl, for a whole boatload of syrup."

That was her father's expression, and her voice even sounded a little like his—gruff and contemptuous. Well, at least she'd inherited something useful from him, if only the ability to recognize mawkish nonsense when she heard it.

She got out and slammed the door.

"Home, my ass," she said, loud enough for his ghost to hear. Daring him to slap her, like he did in the old days. Weird, to feel profanity on her tongue again. Though she had spent a lifetime running, rebelling and defying authority, she had never cussed anywhere but here, on Bell River land. And never unless her dad was within earshot.

So profanity now must mean that, in some illogical, subconscious way, she didn't really believe he was gone. That was ridiculous, of course. Johnny Wright had been exiled from Bell River Ranch just as long as she had— longer, because the police had carted him away that first night, and it took a few days for the authorities to decide what to do with the three terrified, motherless daughters he'd left behind.

"Bastard." She glared at the house. She'd get her suitcases later. Right now she just needed to push past the invisible barrier that seemed to be blocking her entry. Whether it was Johnny Wright's ghost or her own inner child, that barrier was going down. *Now.*

She took one step, then halted as she caught

something out of the corner of her eye. Movement…maybe…in one of the second-floor Dutch gable windows. An almost imperceptible ripple in the dingy white curtains, as if a breath of wind had whispered through a warped frame.

Except that there was no wind. The skin at the back of her neck tingled as she scanned the meadow. The day was as still as a picture postcard. White clouds dotted the blue-domed sky, as immobile as paint smudges. By the gate, the sentinel pines stood in eerie silence. Even the harebells and candytufts might have been drawn onto the grass with crayons.

She took a deep breath and straightened her shoulders. She was imagining things. No one was in there. When she'd picked up the key from the rental agent, the woman had mournfully informed her that the most recent tenants had skated out at least two weeks ago, without paying April's rent.

So it was simply nerves. She'd expected a little of those, of course. The only answer was to face them down.

She climbed the back stairs, noting that a couple of them creaked ominously under her weight and would need to be fixed. The porch swing had collapsed, and its rusted chains lay in undulating curves beside it, like sloughed-off snake skins.

The key turned smoothly, thank goodness, and she moved through the musty laundry room and entered the large, bright kitchen. She noted that her breaths were quick and shallow, so she slowed them down, taking care to draw from her abdomen.

The kitchen. Her mother's sanctum.

She relaxed with a strange relief as the scent of the room hit her. It certainly didn't smell like Moira Wright in here. Fifteen tenants in fifteen years had left their own odor— bad cooking and neglect. A crusty pan still sat unwashed in the sink, half-full, a watering hole for mayflies. A blue-white scum had begun to form on the surface.

Awful. But not as awful as it might have been to inhale the rich, industrious mix of lemon cleansers, brass polish, cinnamon and cloves that her mother had always filled the house with.

Okay. One room down. Only ten more to go.

And the staircase.

Her heart thumped, but she forced herself to move forward. The large breakfast nook to her right held no table, no daffodils, no laughing little girls. She ran her fingers lightly across the bar as she passed, noting the dust that had mingled with the sticky rings of sloppy beer mugs. That was okay, too. Her father hadn't been a drinker. He didn't even have that excuse.

Then the pass-through counter that led into the great room—definitely no problem here. The tacky Barcaloungers and fake leather couches were so different...all the years of burly, burping men watching football had smothered the more delicate memories of Scrabble and sing-alongs, and her mother's sad eyes as she watched the snow through the picture window. Penny and Bree, who loved snow days, hadn't ever understood why the bad weather made their mother sad. But Rowena knew. Snow meant Moira couldn't get away, not even for an hour or two.

Rowena put her fingertips against the wall to steady herself as she approached the turn toward the front foyer. Remember, deep breaths. It was okay. She was okay. Just round this corner, and she'd see the stairs. But they would be only stairs. Nothing more.

Left foot in front of right. Breathe from the belly. Resist the urge to squeeze eyes shut.

It was only a foyer. No one would be there. No one would be lying there, broken, bloody, dying....

She turned.

And before her eyes could adjust to the new, colored shadows of the foyer, someone... something...screamed.

Dear God...

The sound broke the air like shattered glass. Shrill, piercing, terrible.

Rowena had to grab the wall to keep from sinking to her knees. Maybe five or six stairs up, a small dark shadow twisted, scuttled, lost its footing and thumped, still screaming, down to the foyer floor.

She stared, heart pounding, at the writhing heap on the floor, legs still churning. Incredulous, she saw that it was a boy, dressed in typical miniature cowboy denim and flannel. Maybe eight or nine. Towheaded and bug-eyed, at least right now. A dozen small objects scattered in a semicircle around him, obviously dropped from his hands or his pockets as he fell.

His screaming had stopped, but he seemed to be choking on the tangled stampede strings of his cowboy hat.

She bent over and put out a hand.

"Don't touch me!" The boy's shoes scuffed frantically against the hardwood floor as he propelled himself away from her. He hit the bottom stair, and could go no farther, so he clambered to his knees, his wide eyes shooting defiant fire. "There's no such thing as ghosts. Don't touch me!"

She fought the urge to laugh, if only from relief. Far from being an apparition, this panicked kid believed *he* was being attacked by a phantom.

"Relax," Rowena said matter-of-factly. "I'm not a ghost."

The boy stopped moving and squinted at her, clearly unconvinced. The light wasn't great here in the foyer. The windows all had decorative colored glass—a lovely aesthetic effect, but not very practical. She straightened, stepped over to the front wall and flicked the chandelier's switch. The dim blue, green and red shadows disappeared in a blaze of crystal brilliance.

"See?" She tapped her forearm with her palm. "Real flesh and bones."

The boy frowned. "Yeah, but… You look… You look just like the lady who…"

He didn't finish. He didn't have to. It wasn't hard to figure out who he thought she was.

Now that she was almost as old as her mother had been when she died, she looked exactly like her. Sometimes her own reflection in a mirror stopped her heartbeat.

The only curious part was how the boy knew what Moira Wright had looked like—considering he hadn't been born until at least five or six years after the...

The murder.

"I'm Rowena Wright. The lady who died here was my mother. That's why I look like her."

The boy squinted again, as if deciding whether to believe her. Something about his angry belligerence made her want to smile. He'd been squealing like a stuck pig less than a minute ago. He was still on his haunches on the floor, with his hands twitching on his knees. His chin was covered in dust, from where he'd done a face-plant at the foot of the stairs, yet it still thrust up and out an extra combative inch.

Pure bravado—a cocky, undaunted attitude at the moment he felt most vulnerable. She knew that technique all too well. In spite of herself, she felt a tug of affection for the little interloper.

"Your mom. Okay, I guess that makes

sense," he said, with the gravity of a judge handing down a verdict. "So… I guess this is your house?"

"Yep." She didn't say anything else, didn't ask the obvious question. In the better light, she saw that the objects scattered around him were candy. Tootsie Roll candies. Lots of them. He might be a trespasser, and he might have a pretty effective badass facade, but nothing proclaimed youth and innocence like a pocketful of Tootsie Roll candy.

He must have seen her looking at them, because for the first time he flushed, and quickly started gathering up the candy. He straightened onto his kneecaps, making room in his pockets, jamming the little twisted wrappers in with a rough, manly shove.

"Okay, well." He finally clambered to his feet. He ran his hand through his mass of wheat-colored hair and stuffed the tail of his shirt back down into his jeans. "I guess I'll get out of your way, then."

"Just like that?" She smiled wryly. "You're not even going to tell me your name?"

"I'd rather not." He dusted the knees of his jeans. "Wouldn't mean anything to you anyhow. And truth is, I'm not supposed to be here."

She raised one eyebrow. "No kidding."

He obviously recognized the sarcasm. He narrowed his lids and flattened his lips angrily, which made him look about ten years older. It also gave her a quick glimpse of what a handsome man he'd be someday, with that healthy, unruly thatch of blond hair and those thick-lashed, marble-blue eyes.

"I wasn't doing anything wrong, you know. I don't like, set fires or rip stuff up. Or smoke."

Tootsie Roll candy and cigarettes. What a thought. "Okay. That's good, I guess."

Her mild tone seemed to take the edge off his defensive belligerence. He relaxed his mouth and shifted his sneakers on the dusty floor.

"I like it here, you know? I like to be by myself. And it's a good house, no matter what people say." He flicked a glance up at her, clearly realizing how rude that sounded. "Sorry. But…you know how stupid people are."

She kept a straight face somehow. "Yeah, actually, I do."

He nodded, as if they finally understood each other. "My dad's the stupidest of them all. He knows Bell River isn't really haunted, but he like *hates* it when I come here. He said if I came again he'd kick my ass." He shrugged. "Sorry, but that's what he said."

A weird protective heat flared in her breast. "Your father beats you?"

"Naw." The boy rolled his eyes. "He talks tough, but he thinks self-control is like…the most important thing in the world. He'll just ground me for the rest of my life. He's like a control *freak*."

The man sounded delightful. No wonder the boy wanted to get away and be by himself.

"Okay, then, you don't have to tell me—"

"Alec?"

A grown man's voice, maybe five yards away. Even muffled by the walls, the anger in the word was evident. "Damn it. *Alec!*"

The boy's eyes widened. "Dad," he whispered, though Rowena wasn't sure whether he spoke to her or to himself.

His fear was contagious, and she almost suggested he dart out the back. The man's voice sounded furious, and she instinctively wanted to help the kid escape.

But her adult conscience stopped her. She didn't have the right to judge the situation. She had no idea what was really going on with this kid. At the very least, he was too young to have free rein of open country. These Gunnison Forest foothills were gorgeous, but full of dangerous wildlife, slippery rocks, treacherous white water and a thousand other natural hazards. The boy's father had the right to set whatever limits he thought were necessary.

"I'm sorry," she began, when the man's voice came again, this time clearly from right outside the front door.

"Alec Quinton Garwood. If you're in there, you'd damn well better open up this instant."

Rowena stared at the door, her blood draining down to her toenails.

"Garwood?" Though she spoke to the boy, she kept her gaze trained on the door, as if a wild animal were about to burst through. "Your name is Garwood?"

From the corner of her eye, she saw him nod miserably. "Yeah."

"And your dad… His name wouldn't be Dallas, would it?"

The kid made a surprised sound. "How did you know?"

Garwood. Oh, lord, of course. Suddenly the blond hair, the blue eyes, the genetic promise that he would be handsome beyond belief… they all made sense.

"Rowena?" The boy… Alec…used her name for the first time. "How did you know?"

"Lucky guess."

"No way." He moved closer. "You must… You know my dad?"

"Yeah. At least I used to, a long, long time ago."

She turned around, caught his anxious blue gaze and smiled as bracingly as she could. "Hold on to your Tootsie Rolls, Alec Garwood. Things are about to get a little bumpy round here."

Dallas had always known it would happen. Sooner or later, he'd open a door, turn a corner, look up from his desk and see Rowena Wright standing there.

It wasn't logical. It was simply an unshakable certainty that she wasn't gone for good. Even as the years accumulated, as tenants passed through Bell River Ranch, and people departed Silverdell, some in a casket, like his father, and others in a limo, like his ex-wife, he never doubted Rowena would return.

Not to see him, of course. He didn't kid himself that their brief interlude had been important in her life. But she'd be back for Bell River. From their earliest days as children, he'd known she was different. She wasn't just "at home" in the Colorado foothills ranch. She seemed, rather, a part of the landscape, some kind of mountain fairy who came truly alive only when outdoors, among the aspens and the creeks. She danced across fallen logs, scampered up rocks, sparkled through the water like a sunfish, and held court with eagle and deer.

Even when she grew into her teens, she'd never really changed. She didn't go to movies, or the mall. She'd been alternately torpid and difficult during school inside the classrooms, the way a trapped animal could flash from depressed defeat to violence. Rowena needed freedom and fresh air.

Yes. He had known she'd be back. How could a spirit like that live in exile forever? But he hadn't thought that day would be today.

Or that she would look so gaunt. Her beauty was still there, but buried beneath some kind of haggard exhaustion, like a cancer of the spirit. Her wild green eyes were circled with shadows, and her white shirt and jeans hung on her bones as if she'd blindly fished them out of a charity barrel.

Something squeezed in his chest, stealing

his words. He hadn't in a million years expected to feel pity for Rowena Wright.

And so he had nothing clever to offer. He could only breathe the stupidly obvious.

"Rowena."

Her tired eyes still knew how to look sardonic, apparently. She took him in, and he suddenly saw himself as she saw him, from the white-lightning scar that divided his right eyebrow to the shiny gold star pinned at his breast. From the neatly parted hair that wasn't quite as blond as it used to be, all the way down to the crisp crease Mrs. Biggars ironed into his pants and the polished loafers on his feet.

Three-tenths of a second. That was all it took to make him feel boring and overdressed, as if his uniform were as much a costume as Alec's cowboy hat.

"*Sheriff* Dallas Garwood." The crooked smile on her red lips was cryptic. "I should have known. Truly, I should have known."

"Hi, Rowena," he said, wishing he didn't sound so stiff. He hadn't ever looked up the statute of limitations on being a teenage jackass, but surely after fifteen years he was off the hook. "I didn't realize you'd come home."

"Come *back*," she corrected him with another crooked smile. "After all these years, it might be a bit of a stretch to call Bell River *home*."

"Okay," he said. "*Back*. Still, I didn't know. I had heard about the tenants skipping out, but I assumed the agent would handle it."

"Yeah. Well. Now that my father—" Her eyes flickered, and she started over. "Now that we've inherited it, we decided one of us should eyeball the old eyesore personally and decide what needs fixing before we rent again. We drew straws. Obviously, I lost."

"I see." He didn't, really, but so what? He'd been her lover, once, but never her friend. He didn't have a clue how to talk to her, or what it would be acceptable to ask.

Besides, he had come here for a reason— Alec.

He couldn't find a graceful segue, so he barged ahead. "Actually, I was looking for my son. He's got a bad habit of coming up here, though he knows he's not allowed. I'm sorry. I've tried to explain to him that it's trespassing, but he can't seem to stay away."

She tilted her head. "You have children?"

"I do. Alec. He'll be nine next month."

"Lovely. I assume that means you have a wife, too?"

He couldn't quite read her tone. She might be playing with him, or she might be honestly curious. It always had been difficult to read what Rowena was thinking. She hid so much so well.

"It means I *did* have a wife. She resigned from the job a couple of years ago." He let his glance slide over Rowena's slim shoulder, into the shadowy foyer behind. "So, any chance you've seen him? I don't mean to be abrupt, but if he's not here, I'll have to start looking—"

"Oh, right. Sorry." She smiled and backed away from the door.

"He was here," she said, holding out her hand to display the entryway behind her. Colored stripes from the stained glass painted the floor, but it was clear to see the foyer was empty. "But I'm pretty sure I heard someone go out the back door about the time I opened this one. I'd be willing to bet he'll beat you home, unless you hurry."

Chapter Two

Rowena's plan was to tire herself out by cleaning as long as she could, so that when she finally went to bed she wouldn't have trouble sleeping.

But something—maybe the unexpected appearance of Alec, or maybe the equally unnerving encounter with his father—left her so edgy she could hardly think straight. Every creak of the old house startled her, and when the wind picked up, she had the strangest feeling she could hear Penny crying.

She kept the windows open while she worked, just to air the place out. Gradually the cooped-up, mildewed odor began to fade, washed clean by the crisp May air. In the past fifteen years, Rowena had lived in a dozen places, some exotic, like Switzerland, and some simple, like small-town Kansas, but she'd never been anywhere that smelled as good as spring in Silverdell, Colorado.

The tiny town of about one thousand residents lay in the western foothills of the Rockies, an hour or so west of Gunnison. In early May, Silverdell hills were still flocked with late snow, and spring was only flirting with the greening flatland. The season wouldn't be ready to settle down and commit for another week, at least.

And that meant that, as soon as the sun began to fall, and the mountains threw long, eerie shadows on the flatlands, the temperature dropped like a stone. Rowena shut the windows and, wherever she could, pulled the drapes tightly over them.

She stood in the foyer, trying not to see shapes in the shadows, and wondered whether she might have overestimated her ability to put the past behind her. Clearly, it was going to be a long night.

But then, as if the Fates had answered her unspoken request, the doorbell rang.

She opened it eagerly, ready to welcome

almost anyone—the rental agent, a long-forgotten neighbor, even her favorite runaway, Alec. Even Alec's father, if it meant some living, breathing human being to talk to.

But her visitor wasn't any of those. It was a pretty young woman, maybe eighteen or twenty. A stranger to Rowena. She had pale skin, and long, loose hair the color of a bruised apple. When the door swung open, the newcomer dropped a heavy backpack on the porch, as if grateful for the chance to set it down.

"Hi," Rowena said, putting a question into the syllable—but no annoyance. A stranger, maybe, but still living, breathing company on a cold, half-haunted night.

"Ms. Wright?" The young woman had on jeans, a well-worn jacket and boots, which meant she could be absolutely anyone. It was the Silverdell uniform.

"Yes."

The woman put out her hand. "I'm Bonita O'Mara. I'm sorry to bother you when you just got here, but I heard in town that you might be looking for some help cleaning up the ranch. I'd like to apply for that job."

Rowena laughed. She had forgotten how efficient the Silverdell rumor mill was. If you so much as jotted a secret into your diary around here, the darn thing would climb down from your dresser and hop over to the feed store so that everyone in town could read it.

But she hadn't told anyone she was looking for help. She *wasn't* looking for help. Up until about an hour ago, she'd been confident she could handle the job herself.

"Really. Where did you hear that?"

"Sheriff Garwood told me," Bonita said. "I was checking at his office, to see if they might be hiring, but they aren't. He is a very kind man, though. He suggested I might talk to you."

The look on the girl's face, battered pride and tentative hope, was so familiar to Rowena it pinched something deep inside. Rowena had hitchhiked enough miles and slept in enough hostels to know an exhausted, essentially homeless girl when she saw one. She made a snap judgment and decided she trusted this soft-spoken waif.

"Well, the sheriff was right. I was just realizing that I'm in way over my head here. The cleanup will probably last a week or two, but I'll be leaving as soon as we find a tenant. Does a short-term job like that still interest you?"

Relief was like a sun wash over the girl's tired features. "Yes. Oh, yes, absolutely." She bent toward her backpack and began rummaging in the outside pocket. "I have a reference from Mr. Castro, over in Crawford, if you want to—"

"It's okay." Rowena smiled, staying Bonita's hand. "If you're willing to take a chance on me, I'm willing to take a chance on you."

Bonita smiled, but her eyes suddenly watered and sparkled in the light from the hall chandelier. "Thank you," she said.

Darn if Rowena didn't feel stinging in her own eyes. She blinked it away, feeling foolish. "You're at least eighteen, right?"

Bonita nodded.

"And I take it you're looking for live-in work?"

The girl nodded once again, humbly.

"Well, there are four bedrooms here in the main house, but if you prefer more privacy, we've got a manager's apartment over the barn, too. Though... I haven't been out there yet, so I don't really know what condition it's in."

Bonita hesitated. "It's— It's in fine condition."

When Rowena raised her eyebrows, Bonita flushed. "I have to tell you… I slept in there the past couple of nights. I'm sorry. I know I shouldn't have. But I was running out of money, and it was so cold. Too cold to sleep in my car."

Rowena almost laughed. First Alec, now Bonita, using this godforsaken ranch for refuge. Was Bell River ground zero on some secret map of runaway havens?

Apparently taking Rowena's silence for disapproval, Bonita brought her hands together in a gesture that seemed to be part wringing guilt, part prayer. "I'm really sorry. I'll work a couple of days for no salary, to make up for it."

Rowena smiled. They hadn't even mentioned a salary yet. She could probably offer the girl minimum wage, and she wouldn't bat an eyelash.

Maybe all this ingenuous hyperhonesty and naïveté was simply a good act, but somehow Rowena didn't think so. In fact, Rowena would be willing to bet that, for the first eighteen years of her life, Bonita had been well brought up, well educated, well cared for, with a dentist and a dermatologist, tennis lessons, piano lessons and parents who provided good role models for voice, posture and grammar.

But she was running from something.

And didn't Rowena know all too well about that? Didn't she know how, sometimes, even a temporary refuge could be a lifesaver?

"Don't be silly," she said, with a smile. "I plan to keep the whole security deposit from the lousy renters who stiffed us on April's payment. So let's just say they paid for your lodging."

Bonita looked unconvinced, but the comfort of confession seemed to have restored a little color to her cheeks.

"One thing, though." Rowena almost hated to mention it, but as long as they were being hyperhonest… "You do know about the house, right? Dallas probably told you about my mother?"

"Dallas. Is that Sheriff Garwood's first name?"

"Yes."

Bonita smiled, and Rowena rolled her eyes inwardly. She heard that special *something* in Bonita's voice—the same kind of fascinated awe that had always dripped from young female voices after they'd met golden-haired Dallas Garwood. That instinctive hero worship was one of the reasons Rowena had felt the need to topple him from his pedestal.

"Bonita, what did the sheriff tell you about Bell River Ranch?"

"Please. Call me Bonnie. Well…he told me your mother died here a long time ago, and your father went to prison for it. He said your father died in jail, quite recently."

Rowena took a breath. That was about it, in a nutshell. An ugly, rotting nutshell. All she could do was nod.

Bonnie touched her wrist. "I'm very sorry for your loss. Both of them."

The simple gesture was strangely touching. Ashamed to be so emotionally raw, Rowena cleared her throat.

"Thanks. But anyhow, because of what happened, some folks like to imagine the place is haunted. We've had trouble renting it, occasionally, because people get spooked. Does that kind of stuff bother you?"

Bonnie shook her head. "I'm afraid of plenty of things. Like not having a job. Like not having a place to sleep. Like having to go home again, because I couldn't make it on my own. But I'm definitely not afraid of ghosts."

* * *

We can't move them before the funeral.

It was the night after her mother's death. Bree and Penny had fallen asleep in Bree's room, twisted together in her single bed, which was way too small for the two of them, much less the three stuffed bunnies Penny wouldn't let go of.

Rowena sat alone in the upstairs playroom, in the nook created by the front Dutch gable. She liked it here, her rump flat on the floor, and her knees drawn up to her chest. You could see the night sky without a single tree limb to interrupt. You could count the silver stars that swam like fish in a clear black lake.

We can't move them before the funeral.

Her great-aunt Ruth had flown in from San Francisco and was downstairs in the living room now, talking to Nancy, her mom's best friend from Boston. And a really irritating social worker, who had practically moved in. They talked softly, but sound carried up that cathedral ceiling with ease.

The funeral is crucial. Seeing their mother's casket, attending the service, will give them closure. They'll understand she's really gone.

Rowena felt like snorting her disdain. As if

they didn't already understand their mother was *really gone*.

They had been the ones to find her. She lay at the foot of the stairs, one leg under her back, the other splayed to the side. Her yellow dress had caught crookedly beneath her, exposing her white underwear.

The position was so startlingly indecent that Rowena had known, in that instant, that her mother was dead.

Of course, there were other clues. Her head was bent impossibly parallel to her collarbone. Her black hair, already unbound for bedtime, spread out in a circle of sticky blood. Her empty green eyes stared right past Rowena, past Bree, even past her adored youngest, Penny.

Penny, who had just celebrated her eleventh birthday at a big shindig that afternoon, still wore her lacy blue party dress. But she had knelt straight in the blood, utterly oblivious to it, putting her hands on her mother's cheeks and trying to shake her awake.

Mom, Mom, Mom...

Penny had insisted on wearing that same dress to the funeral, even though they hadn't been able to get the bloodstains out of the hemline. Aunt Ruth had tried to talk her into wearing something more sensible— *You don't want to disgrace your mother's memory, do you?* But Penny became so agitated the stupid doctor shot her up with a sedative.

Brilliant. Rowena had read the man the riot act, until he threatened to sedate her, too.

And then, in an illogical scene cut, Rowena wasn't in the window anymore. She was at the funeral, with Penny clinging to her waist, dull-eyed and listless, almost too tired to weep, her flouncy blue dress trimmed in blood. Rowena could only imagine how nightmarish the funeral must seem, viewed through an eleven-year-old's drugged haze.

Mom, Mom, Mom...

The casket shivered. The lid slowly opened. Penny began to scream.

And then, somehow, it was Rowena who was screaming. She sat straight up in bed, with fists full of white sheets, and damp hair plastered to her cheeks.

A dream. Only a dream.

She drank noisily from the water glass she had put on the nightstand. Then she sat in bed, in Penny's old room, willing her heart to stop trying to climb up her throat. She stared out the window toward the barn, where a small, steady yellow light gleamed in the other bedroom window.

Her guest was awake, as well. Perhaps Bonnie, too, had been wakened by bad dreams. Perhaps all over Colorado, all over the whole world, people were fighting this same midnight battle.

Trying to forget, and not having very much luck.

It should have been a depressing thought, but, oddly, it wasn't. Rowena was sorry other people had to hurt, but she was selfishly glad, very glad, that she wasn't locked in this nightmare alone.

Three o'clock was the most terrible time of the day. No matter how slowly Alec walked home from school, or how many detours he took to delay arriving back at Otter Creek Trail, he didn't dare show up any later than three.

At 3:01 Mrs. Biggars would come stand out on the front porch, with a big kitchen spoon in her hand. She'd tap the thing into her palm, like the evil foreman with a whip in cowboy movies. And if any of his friends were walking with him, they'd start making "ooh" and "uh-oh" noises, and saying things like, "Alec's gonna get a licking."

Alec *hated* Mrs. Biggars. At school, when he and his friends made jokes about her, they called her Mrs. Bigg-Ass. But the closer he got to home, the less funny it sounded. She was huge, and really old, and meaner than a rattlesnake.

He wasn't late today, and she was out there anyhow, with that Lord-of-the-Rings-ugly-Orc face of hers scowling down the street, watching for him.

His stomach turned, simply looking at her. When he finally managed to find Dad a new girlfriend, the very last thing he'd do before he got on the plane to France is tell Mrs. Biggars how much he hated her.

"Take your shoes off out here," she commanded as he climbed the porch stairs. "I know you stamp around in every muddy puddle you pass between here and school."

He didn't even give her a dirty look—because that would have meant looking at her in the first place. He called her names in his heart while he scraped his sneakers off, using the stone pillar for a shoehorn. One of them rattled back down the steps, and he ignored it.

But Bigg-Ass didn't allow even that kind of

indirect sass. She quietly positioned herself in front of the door, so that he couldn't get in. He stared at her shirt buttons for ten seconds. Fifteen. But there was no outlasting Bigg-Ass. Clicking his tongue against the roof of his mouth in disgust, he turned, retrieved the sneaker and settled for arranging them with exaggerated prissiness by the door.

Then she moved. Mean old battle-ax.

The interior of the house was shadowy—"going green," she called it, but everyone knew bats loved dark caves. She closed the front door behind him, and the last rectangle of light and life blinked out like a candle.

Alec hated being indoors as it was, unless he was sleeping, but coming into this dark, silent house after having been cooped up in class all day…it was pure torture. He'd tried to tell his dad he needed a couple of hours to play. Just a couple of hours before he checked himself into this prison.

"Mrs. B. knows you too well," his dad had said, shaking his head with a smile. "She knows if you go out before you finish your homework, it'll never get done. Get it over with, and then you can play."

Yeah. Sure. Didn't his dad understand *anything?* How could you do math and maps and junk like that when you were going nuts? When all the muscles in your arms and legs were itching and twitching, needing to move? When your tailbone was already bruised from sitting, sitting and more sitting?

Sometimes he was so depressed that he simply sat at the kitchen table for hours, creating a maze out of pencils for an ant to figure out. Or finding faces in the wood grain of the table. He never got his homework done. Never. You'd think that would tell his dad *something*.

But Mrs. B. had been the babysitter who looked after dad and Uncle Mitch when they were kids, and Dad thought she was like Mary Poppins or something. And who knows? Maybe she used to be nice. But that was about a hundred years ago, and she was more like the witch in *The Little Mermaid* now.

If his mom were here, she'd never let Mrs. B. set one foot into this house.

That reminded him...

"Hey, did I get any mail today?"

Mrs. B. didn't turn around. She was stirring something that smelled supernasty on the stove. Great. Not even a good dinner to look forward to.

"Of course not," she said, chuckling. "You expecting some heavy bills this month?"

"Ha ha." He stuck the tip of his pencil in a small depression in the table. The lead broke off in there, so he started trying to gouge it out with his fingernail. But then his fingernail broke. He stuck the splintered-off bit in his pocket, so that Mrs. B. wouldn't start yammering about how he needed to drink more milk.

He sensed a sudden quiet by the stove and realized that Mrs. B. had stopped stirring. He ducked his head over his English book, to look like he was really concentrating and shouldn't be expected to make small talk.

"Oh," she said, in that fakey sad voice she put on when she wanted to sound sweet. "Oh, you were hoping for a letter from your mother, weren't you?"

"No." But he said the word too loud, and anyone could tell he really meant yes.

It was true. Last time they talked, he had asked his mother to send some books about French horses, so that he could pick out what kind he'd get when he came to live with her. On the internet, he'd found one called the Camargue that looked cool. She'd said she'd send a book as soon as she could.

That was almost ten days ago now.

"No," he repeated more calmly. "I sent away for an Xbox magazine, and I wondered if it came."

Mrs. B.'s silence called him a liar.

"You know," she purred, as if he hadn't spoken, "a mommy with a new baby is very, very busy. And your mommy doesn't have just one baby—she has twins! Imagine how much work that is! All the diapers, all the feedings, all the sleepless nights and—"

"Yeah, well, maybe she should have thought of that before she had them," he said, and he didn't even care how angry he sounded. He hated when Mrs. B. talked to him like a baby.

"But anyhow, I told you, I wasn't looking for a letter from her. She doesn't send letters, because no one sends letters anymore, except old people. She emails. And she calls. She calls me *all the time*."

That was such a whopper he felt his cheeks begin to burn. Mrs. B. was clearly about to yell at him for being fresh when the sound of Uncle Mitch's motorcycle in the back driveway saved him. He leaped up from the kitchen table and opened the door.

"Uncle Mitch!" The perfect person. Everyone knew Uncle Mitch wasn't as handsome or important as Dad, but he was what Dad called "a professional apple-polisher." That meant he could be silly and tease people, and they always liked it. Even Mrs. B.

"Hey, Smart-Alec." Uncle Mitch came into the kitchen, his helmet under his elbow. He high-fived Alec, dropped the helmet on the counter, then scooped Mrs. B. into a big bear hug.

"Hey, there, Mrs. B." He took a deep sniff of the boiling stew. "Mmm, smells delicious!"

Alec could hardly keep from rolling his eyes. Apparently he wasn't the only one who told whoppers. The stew smelled like a cross between dead fish and lizard guts.

"You'd better be on time for dinner, then." Mrs. B. tried to sound cross, but she had a hard time being mad at Uncle Mitch. Everyone did, except Dad. Dad was eight years older and acted like he was Uncle Mitch's father instead of his brother. Maybe that was what made Uncle Mitch and Alec such good friends. They knew what it was like to be bossed around all the time.

"Aw, I'm sorry, Mrs. B. I can't. I've got an interview that might run late. They're hiring over at the Triple R."

Mrs. B.'s face wrinkled even more. "You're

not supposed to be looking for jobs. You know your brother wants you back in school next term."

"And what Lola wants, Lola gets?" Uncle Mitch's grin deepened, and Mrs. B. smacked him playfully across the arm. Alec didn't quite understand the joke.

"Speaking of which," Uncle Mitch went on, "the rumor mill's buzzing. Word is that naughty Rowena Wright is back in town. You know if it's true?"

"It's true," Alec interrupted. "But she's not naughty. I think she's pretty nice."

Uncle Mitch and Mrs. B. swiveled like a cartoon double take. "What?"

One corner of Uncle Mitch's mouth twisted up. "How would you know?"

"I've met her. I went up to Bell River yesterday, and she was there."

Mrs. B. began blustering immediately, of course. "Alec Garwood, you know you're not allowed to—"

But Uncle Mitch wasn't the type to get distracted by dumb stuff like curfew and playtime parameters. "And you met her?"

"Yeah. She's nice. We were having a good conversation, until Dad showed up."

Uncle Mitch and Mrs. B. exchanged a look. "Your dad showed up at Bell River?"

He nodded. He wasn't sure why this was so shocking, but it was kind of fun being the one who had all the important information, for once.

"And he saw Rowena?"

Alec nodded again.

"Did *she* see *him?*"

Alec wrinkled his nose and eyebrows. "What kind of a dumb question is that? Dad's not like invisible or anything."

"Yeah, but…" Uncle Mitch seemed twitchy, as if this was really good gossip. "Tell you what, how about if I take you out for ice cream, and you tell me all about it?"

"Mrs. B. says I have to do my homework before—"

"She'll make an exception this time." And, amazingly, Mrs. B. simply nodded. Alec began to wonder exactly what kind of information he possessed. Though he didn't remember anything very exciting happening at Bell River, the fact that Rowena and his dad had both been there seemed to be an electric piece of news.

"Okay." He decided to push his luck while he actually had some. Before they found out he hadn't really heard much, because he'd been too busy running out the back door. "I want a double scoop, though. And don't try to buy me off with any yogurt crud."

Uncle Mitch laughed. "As long as you're spilling the details, Smart-Alec, I'll buy you ice cream till you puke."

Chapter Three

"I'd be willing to bet," Rowena said as she and Bonnie strolled down Silverdell's main commercial stretch that afternoon, "that, in any store on this street, you could find somebody who could quote my entire childhood rap sheet, word for word."

Bonnie cut a sideways glance at Rowena. Looking back, Rowena observed that, in the daylight, with the spring sunshine sparkling against that strange red-black hair, her mysterious new housecleaner was even more beautiful. "Were you really that bad?"

"Awful." Rowena smiled. "Well, at least by Silverdell standards. When I finally got out into the broader world, I learned there were a lot of things worse than swapping headstones in the cemetery, or sneaking a skunk into Sunday school."

"Into *Sunday school?*" Bonnie laughed. "You're right. We *are* going to have trouble getting anyone to post this help-wanted sign. You were a regular juvenile delinquent!"

Rowena shrugged. She had certainly tried to be. From the time she was ten or eleven, she'd chosen to run with the wild crowd, which had infuriated her father, who wanted desperately to be thought of as refined and socially important.

The old hypocrite! How refined, exactly, was murdering your wife?

Infuriating him had been the whole point, of course. And she'd been willing to pay the price, which was that nice families didn't want their daughters hanging out with her, or their sons taking her on dates.

Especially nice families like the Garwoods. Dallas's father had been the local fire-and-brimstone preacher, and Dallas was the town's golden-haired darling son. The original Dudley Do-Right, Boy Scout, Mr. Perfect, Too-Good-To-Be-True. He would have been the most boring male in town…if he hadn't been so outrageously good-looking.

And now Dallas had graduated from Boy Scout to Sheriff, still lording his purity over everyone less virtuous. Rowena smiled to herself wryly. Things really didn't change around here, did they?

"We'll find somebody. Surely someone has dementia and has forgotten the past. Or maybe there's a newcomer to town who hasn't ever heard the stories."

But she wasn't sure she was right about that. Predictably, the downtown area hadn't changed much, either. Little towns like Silverdell didn't have time for frivolous facelifts. They spent all their energy fighting to keep their big employers, like the lumber mill, the sandstone quarry, the brickyard and the liquor wholesaler. If they lost that foundation, their younger generation would have to hop on planes to find jobs elsewhere.

Even the mom-and-pop stores, the gift shop, the café, the bakery, were about the same as they had been fifteen years ago. Silverdell wasn't like Aspen or even Crested Butte, with a well-established public relations machine feeding it tourists year-round. The commerce base consisted mostly of the locals,

and Dellians, as they called themselves, liked
the tried and true.

As Rowena and Bonnie passed the news-
paper-and bookstore, the owner, Fanny Bronson, was standing in the window arranging
bestsellers. Rowena returned Fanny's wave
but ignored her openly curious stare. Rowena
and Fanny had gone to high school together,
and everyone knew Fanny had once had de-
signs on Dallas.

But then, who in that high school *hadn't?*
Every good girl had wanted to marry him,
and every bad girl had wanted to ruin him.

Only Rowena, though, had succeeded.
That's what they all found impossible to forgive. She'd destroyed his spotless reputation
just as surely as her father's shotgun had destroyed his perfect face.

The day after her mother died, Rowena had
overheard a couple of the town biddies gos-
siping as they dropped off a "sympathy" cas-
serole. "That oldest one takes after Johnny,
sad to say. Rowena, you know. The one who
tried to seduce the Garwood boy. Guess the
apple never falls far from the tree."

Her first instinct had been to crumple in a
heap and cry. She always hated being compared to her father—she didn't think they had

a single trait in common. But on that day the fury was even stronger than usual, because Mrs. Fillmore's comment proved that no one truly cared what had happened to her mother. No one. All they cared about was gossip and nastiness, and passing judgment on others for the pure pleasure of feeling superior.

But Rowena never allowed herself to cry. So instead, she'd leaned out the gable window and scoffed at the old ladies.

"*Tried* to seduce Dallas Garwood?" Fake laughter. "Mrs. Fillmore, you're such a fool."

She'd be willing to bet Mrs. Fillmore hadn't forgotten that one. Just as Mayor Simpson probably still believed she owed the city fifty dollars for shinnying up the light poles and unscrewing every streetlight on Elk Avenue.

In fact, this little street was one bad memory after another. Staring down its length of flower-filled barrels and brightly colored awnings, she wondered if their mission was hopeless. Would anyone here agree to put up her Handyman Wanted notice? Would she have the courage to ask them for even that small a favor?

Maybe she should explain that the sooner she got some help fixing up the ranch, the sooner she'd get the heck out of Dodge. That ought to please them.

"How about the hardware store?" Bonnie pointed to Miller's, a large 1880s Italianate building across the street. "Everyone goes there, especially handyman types."

Hmm… The Millers had testified at the sentencing phase of her father's trial. They'd talked about Johnny Wright's belief that Perry Miller had been having an affair with Moira. They testified that Johnny had refused to pay his outstanding bill, saying the debt should be forgiven as payment for Moira's "prostitution services."

The defense was trying to prove insanity, and maybe the Millers had thought they were helping Johnny avoid the death penalty, but the airing of all that dirty laundry had been deeply humiliating to Rowena, even long-distance.

Especially because, as it turned out, Moira had been in the very earliest stages of pregnancy…and the child did not belong to her husband. Or to Perry Miller, for that matter. Paternity never could be established, but enough rumors swirled to sink Moira Wright's reputation forever.

"No. Not the hardware store." Rowena

swiveled, searching for an alternative. Hadn't a single new store arrived in fifteen years? Wasn't there anyone in this town who didn't know about the scandal?

"Hey! Rowena!"

It was a child's voice. She looked toward the sound. It seemed to be coming from Sweethearts, the ice-cream store. Well, that store, at least, was new.

Alec Garwood was leaning on the door frame, and when she smiled at him, he ambled out, a triple-decker chocolate cone in his hand. He licked assiduously, but the sun burned brightly today, and the brown cream already oozed over his long, not entirely clean fingers.

"Hey," she said. She wondered who had driven him here. She figured he was still grounded for yesterday, so he couldn't have come alone. But she didn't let herself peer into the tinted windows. She didn't want to be seen giving a damn.

"How're things at Bell River?" Alec licked some more, adding a swipe or two to his fingers. "I didn't mention it yesterday, but a stray had kittens in your pole barn, and you probably need to put out some milk or something."

"Already did that." Bonnie smiled. "I'm

Bonnie. I'm sleeping in the apartment over the manager's barn right next to the pole barn, so I heard them last night. Noisy little critters."

"Yeah." He looked over his shoulder. "So... Dad's in there," he said. "He's blistering Uncle Mitch's hide."

Bonnie smothered a laugh, but Rowena instinctively felt sorry for Mitch. Dallas's little brother must be completely grown-up now. He'd been only about ten when the craziness with Rowena and Dallas exploded.

She glanced at the ice-cream store. She couldn't hear an argument, but she didn't expect the restrained Dallas Garwood to be raising his voice in public. His tongue-lashing would be more subtle than that.

"What's he mad at Mitch for?"

"For bringing me out to get ice cream when I'm grounded, and I'm not supposed to eat sugar anyhow. Oh, and for refusing to go back to college." Alec grinned. "For being a slacker and a jackass and a sorry excuse for an uncle."

"Oh." Rowena's chest tightened. That was harsh.

"It's okay," Alec assured her. "Uncle Mitch doesn't take it hard. He's like me." He extended his tongue to alarming lengths to clean a dab of chocolate off the edge of his upturned nose. "We don't really let that stuff bother us. That's partly what makes Dad go crazy."

Rowena wondered whether that much indifference could be genuine, but, before she could ask, two males came stalking out of the ice-cream shop. She would have recognized Mitch anywhere. He was just a grown-up version of his childhood self—all carroty hair and freckles, and an adorable twinkle in his light brown eyes.

He did indeed seem fairly unfazed by the thrashing he'd just received.

But then she got a look at Dallas, who was squinting in the sudden sunlight. His sheriff's badge seemed to be made of golden fire. His blue eyes looked about as friendly as gunmetal, and his strong jaw seemed to have been carved in an iron fury.

"Damn it, Alec," he said, taking his son by the shoulder, "this is your fault, too. You knew you were grounded. You can't just go off whenever you want, wherever you want, ignoring all the rules. When I say you stay home, you don't set one foot out of that house, do you understand?"

"Okay," Alec said, and Rowena heard a quiver in his voice. But he recovered nicely and twitched his head toward the women. "Don't you want to say hi to Rowena and Bonnie?"

Ugh. *Awkward...*

Rowena folded her help-wanted ad in her palm, which suddenly felt overwarm and damp. Dallas shot a glance her way, but he appeared to be too angry, still, to indulge in casual amenities.

Mitch, on the other hand, put out his hand, beaming.

"Rowena? Oh, my God. I can't believe it's you! Remember me? I was the bratty little brother. Still am, if you ask Dallas!"

"Of course I remember you," she said, smiling back. It was pleasant to get such a warm welcome from anyone, even the bratty little brother. "It's good to see you again, Mitch."

Bonnie had met Dallas yesterday, of course, so all that remained was for her to be introduced to Mitch. Rowena noticed that Mitch's twinkle intensified when he shook Bonnie's hand. Dallas was polite to everyone, but still stony.

"So, I was just hearing all about how you and Alec met." Mitch ruffled his nephew's hair and winked at Rowena. "Sorry about how he made himself at home at your place. He's hard to corral, this one. Ever had a horse you couldn't keep in the pen?"

She had, actually. Her favorite horse. She'd named him Smokey, because, like smoke, he could slip through the smallest chink in the paddock. He could even untie a knot with his mouth. She'd adored him for that wild streak, that determination to find a way to be free. He'd felt like a kindred spirit.

But then, on one of his illicit adventures, he'd gotten caught in some barbed wire. They'd put him down on the spot, rather than torture him by trying to cut him loose.

Her father had tried to make a moral out of the tragic ending. But Rowena refused to be cowed. She was pretty sure that she, too, would have risked death for a chance to be free.

Mitch didn't seem to notice she was a long time answering. He turned to Bonnie and widened his eyes, as if the most brilliant idea in the world had come to him. "I know! How about some ice cream for the ladies?"

Before either Rowena or Dallas could protest, Alec and Bonnie called "Yes!" in an enthusiastic chorus.

"Do you mind?" Bonnie turned to Rowena. "I know we still have to put up that ad, but—"

"It's fine," Rowena interrupted, hoping she could prevent the other woman from revealing too much about their mission. "None for me, but you enjoy."

Mitch apparently knew he should move quickly when he got a go-ahead signal, so he shepherded Bonnie and Alec back into the dim little shop, leaving Dallas and Rowena standing alone on the sidewalk.

Dallas still seemed to be working on his temper. He stared a few seconds into the middle distance, down the length of Elk Avenue, and then, with a slow intake of breath, he transferred his gaze to Rowena.

"Sorry about that," he said tautly. "Sometimes I feel like I have two kids, and neither one of them is exactly the obedient type."

"Of course not." She raised one eyebrow. "Stands to reason that, after they made you, the Garwood family was probably flat out of good-boy genes."

His lips tightened, but he didn't offer a comeback. More of that famous restraint. Or maybe, after all this time, he didn't even hate her enough to rise to her bait.

And why should he? Though the moment

her father showed up with his rifle had been terrifying, bloody and surreal, Dallas had obviously recovered a hundred percent. *Thank God*.

That first night, word raced through town that Dallas might end up blind. Or that the bullet might have entered his brain. Rowena had thought she'd lose her mind. While the police interrogated her father, she'd hitched a ride to the hospital, where she begged Preacher Garwood for news. But the man had turned her away with a blistering set of epithets she'd never before heard on the lips of a man of the cloth.

She'd always meant to find a way to apologize to Dallas. But twenty-six hours later, her mother had been killed, and nothing else on this earth seemed real.

Anyhow, obviously Dallas was too lucky to meet disaster as a result of his first and only sin. He wasn't going to die in the back of a flatbed truck with the town bad girl. Even bullets bounced off saints like Dallas.

Turned out her dad had merely grazed his temple. The only remnant was that thin white scar that bisected his right eyebrow.

She saw now that, if anything, the flaw only made him sexier. No doubt all the ladies yearned to hear about the crazy teenage sexploit that almost got gorgeous Dallas Garwood killed.

"I see you decided to hire Bonnie," he said after a few seconds of silence. "I thought you might be needing someone to help get Bell River in order. Those last tenants were bad news. I had to go out there more than once to settle things down."

"Yes. Thanks." She pushed a sweaty curl away from her cheek, trying to shove it back into her ponytail. She glanced at the ice-cream store, hoping Bonnie would hurry.

She wasn't very good at small talk. She was good at sarcasm. She was good at cool distance or hot war. She'd learned those games from her father.

But she didn't know how to pretend she and Dallas were just two normal people chatting on a spring afternoon on Elk Avenue. The skin on her back crawled, as she felt unseen eyes staring at her, mean women watching and speculating, and pointing Rowena out to their sons, the way they might caution about a rare but venomous spider spinning a web on the kitchen wall.

"Speaking of which, I should get going."

She took a step toward the store. "I'll just tell Bonnie we need to head back to Bell River."

Dallas nodded. "Sure," he said. "Although dragging her away from Mitch may not be easy. I recognized that look in his eyes when they shook hands. He's quite the flirt, and fairly determined once his interest is piqued."

He tilted his head and regarded her with a direct, disconcerting scrutiny. "A lot like a certain restless, green-eyed cowgirl I used to know."

A restless, green-eyed cowgirl. He made her sound like something out of a children's story.

She tried to laugh, but only a tense huff of air emerged. To her dismay, she didn't have a rejoinder ready.

He didn't lower his gaze. He didn't even blink.

"Don't worry, Sheriff," she said finally, lifting one shoulder. "You won't get any more trouble from her. That girl's been gone a long, long time."

"You know, I wouldn't be surprised if she is *on* something," Esther Fillmore said with a knowing squint of her rheumy left eye. She raised one thin finger and pointed it at Dallas, to emphasize her point. For a second he felt ten again, getting that finger for talking too loudly in the library.

Back then, he'd been terrified of having been caught misbehaving. All he could do was pray, *don't tell Dad, don't tell Dad...*

"Well, Mrs. Fillmore, even if Rowena is—"

"That's nonsense, and you know it," her husband piped up from behind her, where he was stirring the logs with the brass poker.

"It is not. Have you seen her? She's all skin and bones, and dark circles under her eyes. That's what they look like when they're on something."

Her husband laughed. "How on earth would you know that? You've never seen anyone *on something* in your entire life. You're a librarian, Esther. For heaven's sake, simmer down and leave the poor girl alone."

Dallas managed not to smile. But honestly, every time he got called out to the Fillmore house he wondered whether Alton Fillmore had finally reached the end of his rope, and Dallas would find Esther on the floor, with that same fireplace poker through her heart.

So far, the problem had always been some neighbor or Silverdell resident that had put a burr under Esther's saddle. Loud music, a car with expired plates, the single lady down the street entertaining "strange men at all hours."

But never Esther herself on the floor. No doubt about it—Alton Fillmore was a saint.

"Will you at least go by there, Sheriff? I'd feel better if you kept a close eye on the place. You know she always was a wild one. And the gene pool in that family..."

Esther shuddered, to show that true ladies couldn't quite bear to contemplate such filthy DNA.

"Sure, Mrs. Fillmore. I'll drive by. Or at least send a deputy." He tipped his hat to Alton and moved quickly back down the steps to his car. It was the department car assigned to him so that he could respond to calls at all hours—which he had to do often, since Mrs. Fillmore lived only two blocks from his house. In a quiet community like Silverdell, most of an officer's job was what they called "NNB," or "nosy neighbor bullcrap."

He sat for a second in the car, phone in hand, trying to decide which deputy to send out to Bell River. He was tired, and he needed to get home. Mrs. Biggars was accustomed to staying till either Mitch or Dallas arrived, but he didn't like to push it. Babysitting Alec couldn't be easy. The boy had developed an irrational hatred of the old lady and probably gave her hell all day.

Still…he couldn't quite bring himself to ask a deputy to go check on Rowena when he knew darn well she wasn't doing anything illegal or even mildly sketchy. Why cross-pollinate the slander, planting that dirty idea in anyone else's mind?

He tilted his watch and checked the gleaming blue hands. Only five minutes to midnight…he had thought it was later. And the ranch was not *so* far out, only twenty minutes away.

He turned the key and felt the engine come to life under his feet. He'd do it himself. The night was clear, starry and cold. A rime of frost would be forming on the rocks by Bell River. It would be a pleasant drive.

He wouldn't even have to see Rowena.

When he arrived at the Bell River gate, he saw that it stood open, which wasn't in itself dramatically odd. The weathered wood could use a coat of paint. Strips of it gleamed almost white under the moonlight. Through the years, tenants had found its warped boards an annoying obstacle and had left it unlatched more often than not.

The knotty bristlecone pines on either

side of the gate needed pruning, too, their branches growing across the entrance as if determined to bar interlopers, in spite of the open gate. Here in the moonlight, their shaggy arms were downright creepy.

But more troubling was the lack of light at the main house. Bell River's ranch house had been built very close to the entry—all the open land for cattle and sheep and crops stretched out behind the buildings. So it was easy to see that the whole place brooded in complete darkness.

Rowena hadn't ever been the type to turn in early. Maybe she wasn't here. But at midnight in Silverdell, there wasn't much to do… so where could she be? He felt an uncomfortable twist in his gut, and he pulled in a few more yards. House, dark. Stables, dark. Big barn, dark.

Old, unused pole barn, dark…or was it? As he watched, a small beam of light danced between the boards…blinking off and on like a distant signal. It was white, tinged with yellow—not the milky blue of moonlight, or the crystalline flash of metal.

It was probably a small flashlight with half-dead batteries. Not exactly the tool of choice for professional thugs. So no need to call for backup.

He pulled his own stronger torch from the console, killed the engine and walked carefully to the barn, avoiding rocks and large divots that could trip him up.

The light in the barn jiggled, swung up and down wildly, then disappeared. Yes, someone was definitely moving around in there, and they seemed to be moving just as quietly as he was.

He kept to the shadows so that he could get closer without being spotted. Once he reached the barn itself, it was easy to hug the wall. He edged as far as the window, where he could look in without effort.

At first all he could make out through the dusty, smudged glass was a huddle of shadows, with the flashlight lying beside it on the dirt floor, shining aimlessly toward the far wall. But then, a few seconds later, one shadow disentangled itself from the others and stood up straight.

It was a female, and she twisted backward with a groan. She was stretching as if her muscles hurt from stooping, her hands pressed against the small of her spine, but the effect was strangely sensual.

His body responded. He'd already been alert and flexed, ready to react, but this was different. In all the wrong places—speaking as a law enforcement officer—his body tightened and warmed, as if it knew exactly who stood there before his brain could possibly be sure.

Then, with a soft sigh, the woman picked up the flashlight, and its beam coursed over her face.

Of course, it was Rowena.

He suddenly felt ridiculous. Like some kind of Peeping Tom.

As if she sensed someone watching her, she swiveled, aiming her flashlight's weak beam toward the dirty window. "Bonnie?"

The pane must have been too dusty, creating a mirror effect, because she obviously didn't see him. She took a couple of steps closer, swinging the light across the glass.

"Is someone out there?"

He came around the corner to the door as quickly as he could, so that she wouldn't have time to feel truly frightened.

"I'm sorry," he said. "It's only me."

"Dallas?"

"I'm sorry," he said again. "I didn't mean to scare you."

Her eyes were wide, and now that he was closer he saw that they were red-rimmed and puffy, as if she might recently have been crying. One hand had risen to touch her throat. From her other, limp hand, the flashlight beam shimmered on the dirt, as if perhaps her fingers trembled.

But she squared her chin defiantly and lifted it.

"I'm not scared," she said. Then she frowned. "Were you watching me through the window?"

"No. I mean... I was just checking. I saw the flashlight moving around in the barn, and I wanted to be sure everything was okay."

"You saw my flashlight?" Her eyes narrowed. "From where? From the courthouse complex? From your living room window? You must have X-ray vision, Sheriff."

He wasted two seconds sorting through the possible rationalizations he could offer. He could say he was looking for Alec. He could say he'd been in the habit of checking Bell River while it was unoccupied. He could say...

But he hadn't ever been very good at lying. So he settled for a limited version of the truth. "We got a call, at the department. Somebody reported seeing…something irregular. They wanted us to check the place out, make sure everything was okay."

She stared at him a full minute. Then she gave him a derisive smile. "That's baloney."

Her tone stung. She'd always had a way of communicating what a fool and a bore he was.

"No, ma'am. I assure you, it isn't."

Ma'am? God, he sounded like John Wayne all of a sudden. Why did she still have this effect on him? He was a grown man now, not a teenage geek who just happened to be good enough at calculus to be offered the job of tutoring Rowena—and poor enough to need to accept it.

He was thirty-two years old. He was the sheriff. He was a father, a home owner, a damn good provider.

And yet…one contemptuous scowl from Rowena Wright, and he degenerated into a swaggering cartoon Yosemite Sam, his badge protruding from his puffed-out, self-important chest.

"Sorry, Sheriff. But it is most definitely baloney."

"No."

She stepped closer to him. "Oh, I don't

doubt that you got a call. I'll bet your phone's been ringing off the hook, while the good people of Silverdell try to find a way to run me out of town on a rail. I wouldn't have expected anything less. But that's not why you came out here."

"Of course it is." Wait…no…that wasn't what he meant. "I mean, the phone's not ringing off the hook, but I did come in response to a call. One of the residents is afraid there might be something illegal going on, or—"

"Or at least immoral?" She smiled, and he thought he'd never seen a more bitter turn of such sensual lips. "Unsavory? Wicked and wanton, as the Wright family is known to be? You should know. You remember how we are, don't you?"

"Rowena, don't be silly. I—"

But she shook her head, cutting off his protest. She moved even closer, until he could smell the lily-vanilla scent of her bath soap.

"Who was it? Mrs. Cheatwood? Or Mrs. Fillmore?"

He must have made an involuntary motion, because Rowena's smile broadened, now looking both evil and sexy as hell. He ought to stop this. Rowena was just hurt—though he wasn't sure exactly how, or by what—and she was playing a nasty game to hurt him back.

He ought to stop her right now. Before one of them did get hurt. The way they had before.

And yet, almost as if he were eighteen again, he couldn't force himself to speak a word, or lift a finger to put an end to it. He was like a cobra mesmerized by the deep, throaty voice and the hot honey of Rowena's breath.

"Of course," she said. "I should have known. Mrs. Fillmore has such a surprisingly fertile mind. And repressed good guys like you always go for the filthy stories, don't you? Did you come out here to see if you could get a look at these wicked goings-on, or maybe even get a piece of the action?"

Her voice dipped lower, and she reached out to trace his sheriff's star with the tip of her index finger. She followed the seven sharp points and valleys slowly. His body responded, twitching and rising as if controlled by invisible marionette strings.

"Rowena, stop this. You know you're talking nonsense."

"Am I?" Her eyes glittered in a sudden flash of moonlight that found its way between the roof boards. "Want to see what I've been doing, Dallas? Out here in the barn, in the dark, all by myself? Want to see it with your own eyes…and touch it with your own fingers?"

"No," he said thickly. *Garwood, wake up,* he commanded himself. *This is now…not fifteen years ago. Stop acting like such a stupid puppet. You know what a mistake it is to let her manipulate you.…*

She took his hand, ignoring his rejection, and tugged him toward the shadowed corner.

"It's all right," she whispered as she led him. "I won't tell anyone you looked."

Five, ten feet, and then suddenly she stopped. She flicked on her flashlight and aimed it toward the corner. On the floor, in a small nest of hay and blankets, lay a big amber cat, stretched out to allow its seven tiny, blind, silently wriggling kittens to suckle.

The cat blinked up at the light, still purring but tensing slightly, as if to warn them to stay away.

Rowena laughed quietly. "There you go, Sheriff. There's my midnight debauchery. Feel free to report the details to Mrs. Fillmore. Tell her it's true—Rowena Wright has a barn full of illegitimate babies, birthed in secret, in the unhallowed dead of night."

He shook his head. "Rowena—" Oh, hell, was that the only word he knew?

"Tell her she can even adopt one, if she'd like. We've got four reds, two calicos and one tiger." Another strange glitter from her narrowed eyes. "Tell her the tiger takes after her mother."

He tried again. "Rowena, I'm sorry—"

But her bitterness was like an impregnable shield, and she'd already wrapped herself away inside it. She flicked off her flashlight and moved toward the front of the barn.

When she reached the door, she hesitated. She didn't turn around and face him. All he could see was her rigid silhouette in the moonlight.

"One more thing, Sheriff. In case you'd like to investigate a *real* crime, you might want to check out the other side of the barn as you leave."

And so he did. Though Rowena was long gone before he found his feet and shook the last trailing mists of her trance out of his brain, he walked around to the north face of the barn. He swept his torchlight over it.

The letters were about a foot high, with

the unmistakable spattered outlines of spray paint. Red spray paint, glowing like a bloody threat in the beam of his flashlight.

Dirty bitch, the letters said.

And then, two simple, dagger words.

Go home.

Chapter Four

On Monday it snowed, making liars of the weathermen and the calendar, which all had predicted an easy slide toward spring. Not a very impressive snowfall, only a foot or so, but enough to turn the granite rocks to marshmallows and frost every aspen branch in sparkling white.

Then, in an abrupt about-face, it rained for five days straight. The river frothed and over-flowed its banks. The aspens dripped silver rivulets from every leaf. The front drive lead-ing to Bell River Ranch dissolved to mud.

On day two, Rowena pulled a coat over her head and dashed out to check on the kittens, but the mom had already relocated her family to the bare, dry hayloft. So all that remained was to move the milk and cat food up, as well.

Mostly, Rowena and Bonnie stayed indoors, cleaning and dusting and sweeping and polishing. Ordinarily, Rowena went stir-crazy when she was stuck inside, but the days passed with surprising speed.

As a child, Rowena had hated housekeeping chores. She'd always volunteered to muck the stables, while Bree and Penny helped their mom inside. Even Rowena's temp jobs through the years had all been outdoors, either with animals or children. She often said she'd rather be a pooper-scooper in the circus than clean rooms at the swankiest hotel.

Consequently, she was a total failure at polishing silver and feather-dusting chandeliers. But Bonnie got such a kick out of watching Rowena struggle and fume and tangle herself in curtains that goofing up became almost a game.

Rowena had noticed how quiet Bonnie was most of the time—too quiet, as if someone had scolded her too often for making noise. The first time Bonnie laughed out loud at one of Rowena's displays of cranky incompetence, Rowena counted it a personal victory.

After that, Rowena hammed it up shamelessly. By the fourth day of rain, Bonnie had relaxed enough to start singing as she worked. Her voice was beautiful. Rowena hated to make any sound that would overpower the soft soprano. She'd stand there, transfixed, with the floor buffer unplugged and useless, or the dishes dry in the sink, until Bonnie finally came in to see what was wrong.

Then they'd laugh some more. Funny, Rowena thought, how a sweet old folk song and innocent laughter could make a house feel more like...like home.

And then, on the fifth day, as she worked the buffer on the hardwood floors of Penny's old room, something plopped on her head. It felt like the finger flick "howdy" their horse trainer, Gentle Ben, used to give her as he passed by.

She touched her hair, confused. Her fingers felt something chilly and came away damp. Then another drop fell, followed quickly by another, and another. She tilted her face to the ceiling just in time to catch a dousing. Water poured through a crooked-circle hole even now opening in the plaster. Through it, Rowena could glimpse low, gunmetal clouds.

"Oh, rats," she said, softly, but heartfelt.

First, she yanked the cord and killed the power to the buffer. Then she glanced around for anything to use as a pail.

The only trash can in the room was small and made of wicker, but she'd inserted a new plastic liner. She jerked it over and positioned it under the unwelcome waterfall. The rain pummeled into the container so violently it splashed against the sides, leaping up and spattering her chin.

Rowena frowned. It wasn't raining *that* hard. There must have been a lot of water collecting in the ceiling for days, creating more and more pressure until finally the plaster simply couldn't hold.

Which meant the roof was…rotten.

"Bonnie!" She raised her voice. The hole in the ceiling seemed to be growing every minute, showing more and more turbulent silver sky behind—like some membrane that held two alternate realities apart in a horror movie. "Bonnie! Bring a bucket!"

At that same moment, Rowena's cell phone rang. On the other end, Bonnie's voice was breathless. "Rowena, come quick. I'm in the basement."

"I can't." Rowena shifted to try to catch

the newest current of water. "I need you to come up here."

"No, really." Bonnie's voice was tight. "You have to come here right now. It's really bad. The rain...it's completely flooded the basement."

Crimewise, Silverdell was a quiet town, but Dallas knew all too well that, if they had too many straight days of snow or rain, crazy came crawling out of the woodwork.

This week had been one of the worst. A bar fight with injuries, a hit-and-run out on the old bypass, two domestic disputes, and a suspicious fire in the priceless library of the Harper mansion. And this was in addition to the usual drunk-and-disorderly calls from over at the Happy Horseshoe Saloon.

Compared to that, a splash of nasty graffiti on the side of Bell River's pole barn didn't seem like a big deal. Still, when Saturday rolled around, and Dallas got a few hours off, he headed straight for Miller's Hardware.

Technically, he was picking up some paint. But his real agenda was to ask Farley Miller a few questions. Though Dallas didn't have a stick of proof, his gut told him Farley was behind the vandalism. Lots of people in town believed the Wright family was bad news, but only Farley had a serious, personal grudge and the antisocial temperament to act on it.

The hardware store was packed, of course, and stinking of wet leather, clammy denim and muddy cowboys. You could practically see the steam rising from flannel shirts as the heated store began to dry people out.

"Hey, Dallas," Perry Miller called from over by the fencing section. He greeted all his customers by name, no matter how busy he was. "I'll be with you in a minute, soon as I get Sally taken care of."

Sally Bruckson, the toughest seventy-five-year-old rancher Dallas had ever met, grinned at him from under wet, steel-gray curls. "Damn rain," she growled. "Lost twelve foot of wire in a mudslide. All my posts are tilting like drunkards. Luckily those fool cows are too dumb to notice."

Dallas laughed. "They're not dumb. Why should they wander off? They know they've got the sweetest deal in Colorado right where they are."

Sally grinned, but she knew it was true. She pampered those cows as if they were her children. Right up to the minute she sold them for steaks.

"No rush, Perry," Dallas said, turning to the owner. He scanned the store, keeping his voice neutral. "Is Farley around?"

Instantly Perry's face tightened. Through the years, the sheriff must have come around asking that question far too many times. Though Farley was twenty-five now, he still lived at home and worked for the family business. Hard to imagine anyone else—wife or employer—putting up with his lousy attitude.

Farley had been in minor skirmishes with the law since he was ten—the year his mother died. Her death had been a heart attack, pure and simple, but ten-year-olds didn't always think logically. For Farley, the fact that his mom died only three months after Johnny Wright dragged their name through court was evidence enough. No gun, no knife, not even a push from the top of a staircase, but Johnny Wright had killed her.

Problem was, Farley wasn't ten anymore, and he still blamed the Wrights for everything that had gone wrong with his life.

"He's in the back, I think," Perry said warily. His eyes darted across the teeming space, obviously hoping that was true. "Truck came in this morning, needed to be inventoried. But I can help you. I won't be a minute."

"Sure," Dallas said neutrally, not wanting to spook Perry, who was a nice man and deserved better in a son than that borderline sociopath. He took off his damp jacket and tossed it over his arm, then strolled down toward the paint aisle casually, though his gaze was alert for any sign of Farley.

He found him over by the barbecue grills and outdoor furniture, the one place no one would be shopping during this weather. He had slipped his small, wiry frame into a cushioned wicker armchair and was almost invisible. He was texting on his cell phone and yawning.

"Hey, Farley," Dallas said, coming around in front of the big chair and putting his foot on a wrought-iron table. The gesture looked chatty and relaxed, but it effectively cut off Farley's exit path. "I was looking for you."

The younger man's birdlike face hardened, but he couldn't escape without climbing over the armchair, and that would attract a lot of attention. Plus, Dallas had about eight inches and twenty pounds on him.

So Farley settled for an elaborate display of indifference. He flicked his odd blue eyes—too small and too pale to look quite normal—up to Dallas once, then yawned again. He finished his text, pocketed his phone and leaned back, getting comfortable.

"Yeah? What for?" He grinned, displaying the unfortunate results of being too stubborn to wear his retainers as a teenager. "You interested in a grill?"

"No. I'm interested in what you know about some vandalism up at Bell River Ranch."

"Well, let's see." One side of Farley's thin lips rose. "I know some trash moved in a week or two ago. If that's what you mean."

The snide little bastard... Out of nowhere, Dallas felt the urge to knock the wicker chair onto its side, and the smirking Farley with it. Who the hell did this overage delinquent think he was, calling other people *trash?*

He controlled the anger. It was a personal reaction, not a professional one, and even though he wasn't officially on duty...well, he wasn't ever really off duty, either. Not that far off duty, anyhow.

"No, it's not. I think you know what I *do* mean, Farley. Are you the one who—"

Perry suddenly appeared beside them, his broad, ruddy face anxious, and his hands balled up inside the pockets of his work apron. "Everything okay, Dallas?"

"Everything's great, Dad," Farley answered

before Dallas could speak. "The sheriff just wanted to know who put the graffiti up over at Bell River Ranch. I guess he thought I might have heard something. But I was telling him I don't know anything about it."

Dallas smiled coldly. "You know it was graffiti."

Farley was lazy and mean, but he wasn't stupid. His tiny marble eyes registered his mistake, and the yawn with which he tried to cover it wasn't entirely successful.

"How did you know that, Farley?" Dallas tilted his head. "I never said *graffiti*. I said *vandalism*."

"Yeah?" Farley cleared his throat, a phlegmy sound of a much older, pack-a-day man. "I must have misheard you. I thought you said *graffiti*. But whatever. I still don't know anything about it. I'm here at the store every day, and I'm home with Dad every night." He glanced at his father. "Isn't that right, Dad?"

Poor Perry. He nodded, but even that tiny movement looked painful, as if it practically broke his neck to do it. "What is it, Dallas? Is somebody upset about Rowena coming back? I thought it was temporary. You know, until they find a new tenant."

Dallas shrugged. "I don't know. That's what I heard, too, but the grapevine's been wrong too often for me to trust it. All I know is, somebody spray-painted an ugly message on the pole barn, and I'd like to know who it was."

"It wasn't Farley." Perry's hand settled protectively on his son's shoulder. "Why do you people always think of him first? I know he had some scrapes in the past, but that was years ago."

Years ago? More like eighteen months. That was when he'd smashed his dad's pickup into a pine tree at 2:00 a.m. and left it there—probably so that no one could measure his blood alcohol until the morning.

"Perry, if Farley is still feeling that much hostility toward the Wrights, maybe he should—"

"He's not." Perry's hand tightened on his son's shoulder. "He blamed them for a while… we all know that, but he outgrew it. Be fair, Dallas. You know how it is. Nobody's perfect. Shouldn't a person be allowed to live down the dumb things he did when he was a kid?"

The message was clear. Dallas's past wasn't spotless, either, and no one had forgotten. His "dumb thing" had been Rowena.

"I'm not talking about the past," Dallas said carefully. "I'm talking about something that happened a week ago."

"A prank. Some kids, probably—"

"Maybe. But I'm taking it seriously, Perry, and you should, too."

He glanced at the smirking man in the chair, surprised at how much he hated the mental picture of Farley out there in the darkness, marking the barn with his foulness— while mere yards away Rowena slept alone in the creaky old ranch house. "Whoever spray-painted that wall is sitting on a lot of anger. Rage like that can get out of control in a hurry."

Farley shrugged. His chiseled features, which had looked dainty and sweet on his mother, had a touch of feral cunning. "Any emotion can, Sheriff. Like…for instance… lust? I wonder. Are you one of those men with a taste for trash? Is that why you've suddenly gone all mad dog about protecting Bell River?"

"Farley." Perry's expression was embarrassed, maybe a little sad that his son was such a weasel. He didn't look shocked, though, which meant Farley must have made similar comments before.

But suddenly Dallas didn't give a damn what Farley said. The little bastard didn't understand Rowena Wright at all. Yes, she was capital-*T* Trouble, and God help any man who tried to tame her, but she wasn't trash.

"Talk all you want, Farley. That's what people like you do. Just stay the hell away from that ranch."

Chapter Five

The roofer and the flooding specialist arrived at the same time. They each said they needed about an hour to complete their inspections, which meant that Rowena had to find something to do to keep from going crazy while she awaited their verdicts.

She couldn't sit still inside, so she went out the back door, down the kitchen stairs and into the garden. The fickle weather had changed again, and the sky was now a cloudless blue umbrella. Though the earth was pockmarked from the rain and brown from the freeze, the sun felt good on her skin.

She strolled all the way to the end of the

cultivated area of the backyard, over near the barns, and found the small plot of land that used to be her mother's vegetable garden.

It was in ruins, of course—but its perimeters were not entirely erased. That must mean that some tenant along the way had tried to keep it going. Her mother had enjoyed only mediocre success herself, partly because of the unpredictable Colorado frosts, and partly because her efforts had been hit and miss. Like everything else in Moira Wright's life, the poor carrots, beets and kale were at the mercy of her moods.

As Rowena stared at the muddy ground, she pictured her mother kneeling there, the summer wind blowing through her long black hair, and her green eyes sparkling in the sunlight. In this memory, her mother's cheeks were full and rosy, and she wore one of her prettiest flowered dresses. Her happy clothes, Rowena used to call them privately. When her mother was depressed, she didn't eat much, and those full-skirted dresses grew too big for her to wear.

Rowena's shirt ruffled in the cold wind, and she folded her arms across her chest, aware that this was a trait she'd inherited.

Whenever she was stressed, she could barely stomach food.

Right now, everything she owned swam on her, and she knew she looked awful. Her hair had no shine, and the face she saw in the mirror was too bony, with too many shadowed hollows.

She might as well wear a neon sign that proclaimed her dissatisfaction with her life. Which was annoying, since this footloose, no-roots life was the one she'd chosen for herself.

The life she'd fought for. Run away for. Forfeited everything for.

She pulled away a strand of hair that tickled her mouth, then gave up as the wind gusted and sent the rest of it flying over her face like a black veil. In spite of herself, she felt her spirits lift a little. The fresh, crisp air smelled wonderful, especially after all the rain, and merely being outside was heaven.

That's all that was wrong with her—too much *indoors.* Her last job had been doing the books at a ranch over in Sheridan, and she'd been cooped up till she thought she'd go mad. Maybe next month, when she started her new job training horses at a stable outside Austin, she'd be a little happier.

From the corner of her eye, she caught a glimpse of movement by the barn. Was her graffiti artist back, now that the rain had stopped? Her temper flared, a primitive reaction.

But then she remembered. Earlier today, while she stood knee-deep in the flooded basement, with planks of lumber, rubber galoshes, soggy cardboard and fishing poles floating around her like a bad dream, the phone had rung. Bonnie answered it and relayed the message. Apparently good-hearted Perry Miller from the hardware store had heard about the graffiti and wanted to send someone over to paint the barn wall for her.

It was the kind of charitable gesture she probably would have rejected at any other time. She would have preferred to prove that she could handle her own problems. But at that moment, when it felt as if the house was collapsing around her, she hadn't cared much about false pride. She'd be glad of the help, and she'd sent that message to Perry via Bonnie. She thanked him, promised to pay him for the paint and labor and then promptly forgot all about it.

When Rowena rounded the edge of the barn and saw a wiry young man standing there, bent over an array of painting supplies—brush, pole, tray and can of barn-brown paint—she suddenly wished she'd said no.

Because…ugh. Perry had sent his son. She had only vague memories of Farley Miller from childhood, but she remembered that he'd always given her the creeps. He'd been quite a few years younger, forever trying to insinuate himself into the older crowd, and failing. Mildly nasty. The kind of kid she always thought of as a bug-torturer.

She wondered what bribe his dad had offered to make him do such a neighborly favor.

When he saw her coming, he straightened to his full height, maybe five-six including his elevated boots. He didn't speak, just stood there, hip cocked, paintbrush dangling beside his leg like a six-gun.

When she was only a yard away, he put up one finger to tip back the brim of his baseball cap and smiled.

"Hey, there, Rowena," he said, with an insolent undertone, as if they knew each other well, which was ridiculous. "My dad said you needed some help up here."

To illustrate, he gave the side of the barn wall an unnecessarily long, slow study. The large red letters were only half-hidden by the smears of thin white paint she'd slapped on minutes before the rain began.

"Yes, he called. That was very nice of him." The simple words didn't quite come naturally now that she was looking into Farley's small, rabbity eyes.

He wore so much aftershave that the minty smell stung her nostrils. She had to force herself not to back up a few steps, just to get away from the olfactory assault. Did he actually think that was an attractive scent?

"And it's very nice of you, of course, to do it. I appreciate it. I've got my hands full with...other problems up at the house."

"So I gathered." He tilted his head in the direction of the roofer's van. "*Big* problems, from the look of it."

Something in his voice savored the prospect, and she felt her shoulders tighten. "Well, I guess we'll see. I haven't been given the estimates yet."

Suddenly, his glance darted over her shoulder, a twitchy, high-alert movement that made him look even more like a small animal.

What was he looking at? Was the roofer headed out here now, astronomical estimate in hand? She sensed that, for some private reason, Farley would get a kick out of that. But when she turned, she saw what he'd seen—a truck pulling up the back driveway

It was a late-model flatbed Dodge, sleek and pearly blue and well cared for. She didn't recognize it, and it didn't have a repairman's logo painted on the side.

But apparently Farley knew the vehicle well. He started nodding, as if in answer to some internal comment, and his eyes narrowed even further.

"Son of a bitch," he said under his breath.

Rowena darted a glance his way. Not because she was shocked by the language—working on ranches, you got used to cussing—but because the intensity seemed out of proportion.

They both watched as the truck angled neatly beside the rails of the horse paddock. An instant before the driver's-side door opened, a beam of sunlight glinted off golden hair, and the involuntary clenching of Rowena's midsection told her who it was.

Dallas.

Her curiosity deepened. Why should the sight of Dallas Garwood's truck fill Farley with that kind of bile? Was Dallas here officially? Was Farley in some kind of trouble with the law?

But when she looked back at Farley, he had already turned away. Ignoring the arrival of the sheriff, he was bent over the paint can again, absorbed in prying the lid off with one of those little silver openers.

How strange. She noted, almost subconsciously, that his exaggerated display of indifference didn't match the sudden angry rigidity in his body.

And, then, as if her brain had finally decided to start working, she understood.

Perry Miller hadn't sent his son here to be neighborly. He had sent Farley here because the young man had painted this graffiti in the first place, and his father knew it.

Rowena's stomach swooped uncomfortably. Suddenly she needed to get away from the wiry young man, who stank of aftershave and aggression.

Dallas had emerged from his truck, so she headed down the path toward him. She wasn't eager to face him again—he always made her feel slightly edgy and on the verge of doing something stupid. But, compared to Farley, Dallas suddenly seemed safe.

After squinting briefly up at the unclouded

sky, Dallas reached through the open window and extracted a black ball cap, which bore the department logo front and center.

Funny, it was still so weird to think of him as the sheriff. He carried the position so much more casually than old Sheriff Granton used to do. The old man had always worn what he called his Class A uniform, complete with hat and stars, tie and medals.

Dallas obviously wore his authority with less pomp. Instead of Granton's long-sleeved hunter-green shirt, tie, crisp pants and tan hat, he dressed in soft khakis, black polo shirt and that black cap, which contrasted so dramatically with his hair.

She was struck anew by how preposterously good-looking he was. His golden hair sparkled with sunshine, and his blue eyes glittered inside that thick fringe of black lashes. With his lean, muscular arms, his broad shoulders and the mountains at his back, he could have been an ad for the healthy outdoors life.

"Afternoon, Sheriff," she said, her usual sardonic tone tamed a little—if only because she was grateful for any company other than Farley's. "What brings you here?"

"Just keeping an eye on things. I heard

Farley's father volunteered him to paint the wall, and I thought I'd make sure the project...didn't run into any problems."

"Why would it?"

"Farley's projects sometimes do."

"I see." So she wasn't the only one who suspected Farley had been her vandal. "You think he did it, don't you?"

He hesitated a minute before answering. "Yeah. Probably. But I can't prove it, so..."

He let that drift off, and the two of them spent a few seconds in silence, watching Farley, whose every stilted motion proclaimed that he knew he had an audience.

Finally, she turned back to Dallas. "Kind of a coincidence that his father would send him up here, though, isn't it? I mean, is it possible that Perry knows?"

Dallas put one foot on the lower rail of the paddock, then leaned his elbows against the highest rail, getting comfortable, obviously prepared to stay until Farley was done.

"Probably," he said again, thoughtfully. "I think, in some misguided way, he might be trying to make amends. He's a good guy, and he probably regrets giving Farley an alibi he didn't deserve."

"An alibi? Does that mean you actually

questioned him?" She was shocked to discover Dallas had pursued the matter at all. Graffiti was hardly a big-deal crime, and after the attitude she'd taken with him the past couple of meetings, she wouldn't have expected him to go out of his way to help her with anything.

He shrugged. "I didn't question him, exactly." Dallas glanced her way, his eyes amused. "I simply went up to Miller's and rattled the cage a bit."

Great image, given that Farley looked like a… She studied him. Maybe more of a ferret. "And now you're here to make sure you haven't stirred up the animals?"

He grinned. "Exactly. People like Farley are usually pretty meek in broad daylight, but I want him to remember I'm watching."

She started to say "thank you," but at the last minute it felt wrong, as if it would imply he was cautioning Farley as a personal favor to her. Dallas probably would have done exactly the same thing if a tenant had been living here, or if Bell River were abandoned.

He was the sheriff, and he wouldn't turn a blind eye to vandalism on his watch. He was simply doing his job, in that superdiligent way Dallas Garwood did everything.

So she didn't thank him. But that felt wrong, too. Buying time, she bent over to pluck a snowdrop from an isolated tuft that had sprung up beside the paddock. Her timidity annoyed her. She couldn't remember ever being so tongue-tied around him. Once, as the bad girl leading the good boy astray, she'd been able to play him like a puppet.

Now…she was the one who felt confused and powerless. And she had no idea why.

Luckily, he didn't seem to notice her silence. He twisted his left wrist, the motion defining those corded muscles, and glanced at his watch. "In fact, I sent Mitch up to the house to let you know I'd be here. A ridiculously long time ago. I wonder where he got to?"

"He probably just got as far as Bonnie." She remembered the twinkle in Mitch's eye as he talked Bonnie into ice cream. Bonnie had found at least a dozen ways to bring up his name in the days since then.

"Great." Dallas shook his head, but he didn't seem exactly annoyed. "Guess that means I won't be seeing him anytime soon."

"I'll go see if he's around." She dropped the snowdrop blossom onto the dirt, eager for the chance to remove herself from this conversation she didn't know how to handle.

"No, that's all right. I was hoping he'd pick up Alec for me, that's all. There's still time."

"You should go," she said quickly. "Really. It's…it's nice of you to offer to stay, but I can handle Farley. He's a creep, but I'm sure he's not danger—"

"Don't worry about it. It's no big deal."

She opened her mouth to protest, but he had already turned back toward the barn, his profile rimmed in sunlight. He made the whole thing seem so trivial.

So why did she want to stop him? Why was she so reluctant to look as if she needed his help?

As if he sensed her frustration, he glanced up, a question in his vivid, sunlit blue eyes. His hair had fallen over his forehead, and one golden wave tickled at his lashes. He might be fifteen years older, but he wasn't one inch less attractive.

"Rowena," he said, resting his elbow on his knee and dangling the little silver key casually. "Relax. It's my job. And even if it weren't…it would just be one neighbor helping another. No obligation. No strings."

She felt her cheeks redden. "I know. It's just that I really can handle it—"

"No one is questioning whether you *can*," he said. His glance cut toward the house. "But it does look as if you're pretty busy today."

She followed his gaze to the front drive, where the contractors' trucks were still parked. The flooding guy had come outside now, and he was squatting by the western wall. *Great.* That probably meant the water wasn't from anything as simple as a busted pipe. He was worried about the foundation.

The roofer was no longer in sight, which meant *he* was probably sitting on the front porch, writing up his estimate. She felt a shiver ripple through her, thinking of how high the numbers might go.

"Big problems?"

She wondered if her dread showed on her face. "I'm not sure yet," she said. "But yeah. Maybe." She bit her lip. "Big enough, anyhow."

Bigger than the sisters' repair fund, which had been steadily dwindling as the ranch aged and problems crept up more frequently.

"Are you planning to rent the place out again?"

She nodded. "Of course."

He tilted his head, gazing not at her, but at the ranch house. "Why 'of course'? The house needs work, but it's basically sound, right? People have been wondering whether maybe you and your sisters might put it up for sale."

She felt her shoulders tighten. "No."

Her vehemence obviously surprised him—and, to tell the truth, it surprised her a little, too. In actuality, she was the only one of the three Wright sisters who did *not* want to sell. In their emails through the years, Bree and Penny had suggested unloading the place several times, but selling hadn't been an option, not as long as their father lived.

His death three months ago, of a brain tumor that had been diagnosed while he was in prison, had changed everything. Bree's very first email had suggested that it might be time to consider letting the white elephant go. In a careful return email Rowena had reminded her that the timing was still awful. Land prices were depressed, and a so-called murder house was always tough to move.

The others had seen the truth of that, naturally. So she'd bought some time. Because she was between jobs, she'd volunteered to be the one who spent a few weeks here sizing up the situation.

But her sisters were expecting a report any day. What was she going to say? Until the roof started leaking yesterday, she'd hoped that she could persuade them that renting was still the most advantageous option. She'd even planned to use her own small savings to take care of any minor repairs that might tip the balance.

But her savings wouldn't stretch to cover a new roof. The shiver inside her started again as she considered the thousands it would cost. Not to mention shoring up the foundation, if that had started to crack...

"Why?"

She turned to face Dallas, who was no longer looking at Bell River. Instead, he seemed to be studying her face, as if he'd never really seen her before. His eyes held a strange expression, something unfamiliar that made her uncomfortable.

She frowned. It wasn't her most likable trait, covering vulnerability with harshness, but it worked.

"Why *what?*"

"Why are you so dead set against selling Bell River? Surely none of you would ever want to live here again."

Damn it, that expression on his face was

pity. She swallowed a hot rock that suddenly appeared in her throat. She didn't allow people to feel sorry for her.

"Why wouldn't we?"

"The memories, I guess. It can't be easy to—"

"The *memories?*" Suddenly her voice was gruff. "You mean the ghosts, don't you?"

His brows rose. "The gh—"

"Oh, don't worry. I've heard the stories from the Realtor. She had to explain why she can't charge normal rent for the house. Apparently the whole town thinks my mother's spirit goes shrieking through the house every night. They think she tumbles down the staircase every midnight on the dot, like some cheesy horror show."

"Rowena."

He put out a hand. She knew what that hand would feel like. He had calluses on the pads of his fingers, from working hard, from playing the guitar, from being the perfect manly man. "No one thinks—"

"Yes. *Everyone* does." She blinked, furious to discover that her eyes were filling with tears.

His hand closed around her upper arm. She could feel the strong fingers through her sleeve, and, in spite of her struggle to contain it, one hot tear escaped, sliding down her cheek.

No. She wouldn't. In all these years, she had never cried about this—not even at the very first, when she was alone, sitting at the top of that staircase, trying to imagine if her mother had been terrified as she fell.

She wouldn't... But why, suddenly, did his chest seem irresistibly strong, capable of absorbing even fifteen years' worth of tears? She felt herself leaning forward, one inch, two...as if drawn by a magnet. Was it the star embroidered on that soft black shirt? Under all that crusty independence, was it possible she was only a lost little girl, ready to cling to the first nice policeman she met?

He tightened his fingers. "Seriously, Rowena. Even if some incredibly stupid people do think—"

"It's not *if,* Dallas. They do. But they're wrong. Death doesn't work that way." She pulled her arm free. "Believe me, I wish it did. I wish I could see her again, just once. Alive *or* dead."

Chapter Six

Homework time was never exactly a party at Alec's house. But math homework time was pure hell.

Tonight, after an hour of sitting at the kitchen table with his dad, tussling over a whole page of word problems, Alec had decided he could no longer take it. He'd just entered Phase One of the stomachache routine—absentminded belly rubbing, as if you didn't know you were really doing it—when Uncle Mitch came home unexpectedly.

Saved by the bell. Uncle Mitch hated homework, too, and he always created enough chaos that Dad would give up. His dad shot

Uncle Mitch a "go away" look, but of course Mitch ignored it and pulled up a chair.

"God, not word problems," he groaned. "You'll be in here all night. It's too bad. I thought we could hit some balls down at the park."

"He can't go out," his dad said curtly. "Miss Darren sent home a note today, asking for a conference. Apparently genius here hasn't done his math homework for nearly a month."

"Yeah. Well. Homework." Mitch wiggled his eyebrows at Alec, who tried hard not to laugh. "The devil's invention."

Of course, Alec did laugh. He was a sucker for his uncle's dumb jokes. They exchanged a complicated thumbs-up/high-five hand thing. They were kindred spirits about school. They hated it worse than fire.

"It's not true about the homework, any-how," Alec said. His words were distorted because he had his mechanical pencil between his teeth—he liked to make little indentations in the plastic with his molars. "She just wants to see Dad. She's got a crush on him."

His dad groaned. "For God's sake, Alec—"

"For real?" Mitch's eyes lit up. He turned to his brother. "Veronica Darren is smoking hot, you know. Blond hair, blue eyes, big…"

He glanced at Alec. "Big brain. Full of math stuff. A little young for you, though."

"Mitch—" Alec's dad put a warning in his voice, which was silly. As if Alec didn't know already that his teacher had a big chest. His dad still thought he was like…five or something. By the time you were eight, you already had spent hours talking about boobs.

Mitch simply smiled innocently "Seriously, Dallas, I'll meet with her if you don't want to."

"No." Alec frowned and put down the pencil. "Dad has to go."

His dad glanced at him, his face tight with sudden suspicion. Alec screwed up his mouth, mad at himself. He shouldn't have blurted it like that.

His dad raised one eyebrow.

"I'm just saying." Alec shrugged, trying to seem offhand. "You know. She's nice. You might like her."

"Like her?"

"Yeah. You know. You might take her out or something, and then maybe she would cut me some slack."

To his surprise, his dad laughed.

"Why is that funny?" Alec scowled. "Because you're divorced? She knows, and she doesn't care. Jackie Brenton's father has a girlfriend, and he only got divorced at Christmas."

Alec decided not to point out that Mr. Brenton's girlfriend had caused his divorce. Maybe Dad didn't know that. Alec only knew because he used to sleep over at Jackie's house, and they put empty water glasses up to the walls so that they could hear the fights better.

"Why is it funny?" He kept his brows furrowed, and he was pretty sure he looked just as angry as his dad sometimes did.

"It's funny because I'm not going to ask a woman out on a date to get you out of doing your math homework." His dad shoved the math paper an inch closer to Alec's elbow. "So stop avoiding and do it."

Alec rolled his eyes, but he picked up the pencil again. He wasn't worried. He knew Uncle Mitch wouldn't let the last of the sunlight fall into a black hole of word problems.

"Wait…wait." Uncle Mitch held out a hand. "This is interesting. Why do you think she likes your dad?"

Alec frowned, concentrating on the question harder than he had on a single math problem all afternoon. "It's hard to explain. She is always asking if he can come in. Like for career day, or for drug awareness day or whatever."

"That might be just because he's the sheriff." Mitch looked unconvinced.

"That's not all. Sometimes she'll say stuff like, 'Your father's a fine man, Alec. He'd be so disappointed in you.'"

"Well, he *is* disappointed in you," his dad interjected, though he no longer sounded as if he believed he could get this homework handout finished tonight.

"Yeah, but she has this look in her face. Not a teacher look. More like…in the movies. And she says *your father* all whispery, like she's in church or something."

"Ah. The whisper." Mitch leaned back in his chair, grinning. "Oh, yeah, she's got it bad."

"Right?" Alec smiled at his uncle, vindicated. "So you should do it, Dad. You should ask her out. She already knows you're the sheriff, and not a rich guy like Jackie Brenton's dad. She likes you anyway. It's not like she'd say no or anything."

"Yeah, Dallas." Mitch chuckled. "I say jump at it. She already knows you're poor and boring. And divorced. Amazingly, that doesn't seem to bother her. You never know when you'll get this lucky again."

"Hey." Alec's cheeks flushed. "That's not what I meant."

To Alec's surprise, Uncle Mitch's joke made him a little angry. He resented the mocking tone. Though Alec was glad to have a partner in crime, he wasn't going to allow anyone to insult his dad. Besides, what he'd said was ridiculous. They might not be rich, but they weren't poor, and Dad wasn't boring.

Well, not *always.*

And even if all that had been true, which it wasn't, it wouldn't have mattered, because Alec's dad was really handsome. Movie-star handsome.

"*Lots* of women like Dad."

Mitch raised his eyebrows in silent skepticism.

"They do! Miss Blankner at the library flirts with him all the time. And Dr. Sally, and the drugstore lady. Even Darlene's mother flirts with him, but that doesn't count because she's married."

Alec's dad groaned again. "Alec, those women are just friends. They don't—"

"Dad." Alec gave his father his best long-suffering look. "You know it's true. One time

I even heard Mrs. Biggars ask you whether it hurt to be devoured by Miss Blankner's giant cougar eyes."

His father tried to look stern, but he couldn't pull it off. He shook his head, rubbed his eyebrows hard and then finally started to laugh.

"Okay, maybe some of the ladies do flirt, but look…" He took a deep breath. "Some women are like that. They flirt with everyone. Besides, Silverdell is a very small town, and it isn't exactly running over with unmarried men, especially ones with steady jobs."

Uncle Mitch nodded, grinning. "It's called being a big fish in a little pond. All the cougars want to eat you for dinner."

His dad laughed again. "Remind me not to let you teach him about metaphors." He was still smiling when he turned back to Alec, but his eyes had darkened and gone serious. Alec could read his dad's eyes better than a book.

"But the truth is, Alec, I really don't notice, because for the past couple of years I've been focused on you. On us. On making sure everything is good here."

Good here without Mom, that's what he meant. Like that was possible.

Alec thought hard. "What about Bonnie?"

His dad frowned. "Bonnie? You mean Rowena's friend?"

"Yeah. She's really pretty. Maybe you would like to date her, instead of Ms. Darren. I mean, if you think it's wrong to act like you're bribing my teacher."

"Hey. Smart-Alec." Uncle Mitch waved his hand in a "no way" gesture. "Now you're talking crazy. Bonnie O'Mara is mine. Or will be, if I have anything to say about it. You sic your dad on someone else."

"But who? If he doesn't like Ms. Darren, or Dr. Sally or—" He broke off, delighted. "I know! How about Rowena? I mean, she's not exactly pretty, but she's kind of…you know, dramatic, like ladies in the movies who stand on the edge of the cliff, with their hair flying out behind them—"

"That's an interesting idea," Uncle Mitch broke in, his voice all innocence. "Rowena's not as sweet as Bonnie, but she has pretty big—"

"That's enough!" Alec's dad threw his pencil onto the table and stood, his chair making a loud scraping noise on the tile. "You two monkeys get out of here. When Alec flunks out of third grade, maybe you guys can earn a living as stand-up comedians. Right now, though, I've got reports to write."

Uncle Mitch winked at Alec, as if to say, *see? That little homework problem just disappeared.*

Alec didn't wait to be told twice. He leaped from the chair, grabbed his baseball mitt from the counter and joined Uncle Mitch at the kitchen door. He could almost feel the wind in his ears already, and his legs burned, itching to run.

At the last minute, though, he turned to say goodbye to his dad, and he was surprised to see him standing at the sink, staring out the window at the maple tree in the front yard, which was just starting to bud some spring leaves. The heels of his hands were on the edge of the sink, spread wide, as if he needed to prop himself up.

And for the first time, Alec felt a pang of… something…for his father. Something different from the usual annoyance, or even the love and respect that never quite went away, no matter how mad he was at him.

This felt weird, and sad…kind of like pity. Was he actually feeling *sorry* for his dad? His dad, who knew everything, could tell everybody what to do and was stronger than anyone? Even stronger than Uncle Mitch, because remember that time the rabid fox came into the backyard and Uncle Mitch's hands shook too much to shoot it?

The realization took his breath away for a minute, like getting hit in the chest by one of Uncle Mitch's wild pitches. Instinctively, he looked up at his uncle, unsure what to think.

Uncle Mitch was also watching his dad, and his face looked weird, too. But only for a second. He quickly put back on his normal laughing expression, and ruffled Alec's hair.

"Come on, then. We can take the phone book with us. We'll start with pretty Ginger Abbott and go right through to ugly old Mrs. Zinman, if we have to. I promise you, kiddo. We won't stop until we find a girlfriend for your dad."

Rowena's laptop, which she'd set up on the tall counter between the great room and the kitchen, was new, but it wasn't exactly top-of-the-line. It took forever to whir to life. So while it burbled through its routine, she got comfortable on the bar stool, shut her eyes and breathed in the sweet, complicated smell of the burgundy mushrooms Bonnie had been slow-cooking all afternoon.

Without opening her eyes, she smiled. "How much wine did you put in those things? I feel tipsy just from smelling them."

Bonnie laughed. "Nearly a whole bottle. So if this Skype call is important, I suggest you finish it before you start eating."

Important. Rowena opened her eyes and stared at the still-booting computer. Was that the right word for this conversation?

Surely not. It was simply a call to her sisters, Bree and Penny, to tell them what had happened with the roof and basement. They'd had at least a dozen three-way phone calls over the past few years—though this was the first with Skype, and the visual connection did add a layer of discomfort, at least for Rowena. Bree, the extrovert, had insisted.

Maybe Bree had a premonition that the news was bad, and wanted to be able to read Rowena's body language to judge *how* bad. But it wasn't as if Rowena planned to lie—or even sugarcoat. She couldn't afford to. The final verdict was grim. Bell River's roof was rotten from stem to stern, and the foundation was, as she'd feared, giving way. Added together, the repairs would total five figures…a million miles above Rowena's pitiful savings.

Still. What was the worst that could happen? Rowena already knew what they'd say. Bree would immediately bark, "Sell, for God's sake. Sell." Penny, who was the gentle, pensive kind, would suggest they sleep on it.

And what would Rowena say? Irritably, she tapped at the space bar, as if that would make the computer go faster. She had no idea what her response would be—and yet she was strangely impatient to get the call over with.

Luckily, Bree never arrived late for anything. When she said she'd call at eight, she meant it. Not eight-oh-one. Eight on the dot.

So Rowena's computer had better hurry up. It was seven-fifty-five right now.

Sighing, she gazed out over the great room. It was so badly decorated it almost hurt to look at it.

"You know what I used to dream of doing with this ranch?" She cast a glance over her shoulder toward Bonnie. "You'll laugh, it's so preposterous. I used to imagine opening it up as a dude ranch."

Bonnie didn't laugh, of course. She simply said, "Really?" in an interested tone and continued to stir the mushrooms.

"Yeah. Ever since I was a kid, maybe ten or eleven. I must have seen a dude ranch on a travel show or something, and I got the idea we should do that with Bell River."

She remembered the bubbling excitement that had sped through her veins as she considered her plan. She had tried to imagine all the details. Which outbuildings they'd turn into cabins. How many employees they'd have to hire. She'd be a trail guide, of course, and the horse trainer, but who else would they need? A cook, probably, and someone to make the beds. She wasn't going to do any of that.

She'd spent hours deciding what they would name the guest rooms. Famous horse names? Famous cowboys? Indian tribes? Wildflowers? At the time, she'd been partial to the old syndicated Western TV shows, so she finally settled on calling the biggest room Bonanza, and the others would be High Chaparral, Big Valley and Little House.

"I loved the thought of the ranch filled with people. It seemed so—" She hesitated, unsure what adjective to use. Why *had* the idea appealed to her so intensely?

It seemed so...

And then she realized what word she was seeking.

Safe. A dude ranch had felt safe. All those smiling tourists fishing in the river and tossing horseshoes, and then padding out of their rooms at night to get warm milk. Wizened, kindly old cooks, and plump, smiling housekeepers who always had time to listen to upset little girls. Brave trail guides who looked like Little Joe and Adam Cartwright and weren't afraid of anything.

Yes, safe. Much safer to have a hundred strangers' eyes watching, day and night, than to live on here alone, with no one to witness what her father might do.

"It felt alive," she settled for saying. "I would have loved showing the guests the prettiest bends in the river, and teaching them how to handle the trickiest horses."

Bonnie smiled. "I bet it would have been a huge success. Did you ever mention your idea to anyone?"

"I told my dad." Even Rowena could hear the heaviness that fell over her voice when she said his name. And then she repeated quietly, almost under her breath, "I told my dad."

For a piercing moment, her heart ached as if she were ten again, halfway up one of the bristlecone pines beside the front gate, fighting tears, her fists balled in her lap, whispering over and over, "He's not my real dad, he's not my real dad. I *hate* him. He *can't* be my real dad."

She stared at the tacky red-and-brown "Indian" rug someone had hung on the west wall, only half seeing it. It probably had come from Teepees "R" Us, and if she were to live here permanently, it would be the first thing to go.

In fact, would she keep anything? Maybe those framed Colorado landscape sketches, which were lovely. And perhaps that pottery bowl over on the end table.

That was it. The rest of this "renter" junk would have to go.

"So what did he say?" Bonnie had come over to the counter, as if she really cared about Rowena's answer. "Your dad didn't like the idea, I assume?"

Rowena forced a smile, then bent toward the computer, which was finally up and running. "He thought I was insane."

"Oh. That's a shame."

Rowena laughed as she opened her Skype account. "A shame" was an understatement. In fact, it was a surprise to discover how much the memory still hurt. He'd been so mocking, grilling her on all the business angles she, of course, hadn't considered.

It had been so easy to intimidate her. He

was a handsome, educated man, with chiseled features, wavy salt-and-pepper hair, a long, lean, powerful body. He had tossed out every piece of jargon in the arsenal. What about zoning codes? Insurance? Health care? Taxes? Intangible assets? Permits? Licenses? Health inspections?

And then, when her idea had been thoroughly trampled, he'd sent her outside to cut a cord of firewood. No, he didn't give a damn whether her hands were still blistered from mucking stalls the day before. *Since apparently she had enough free time to dream up idiot schemes...*

Rowena took a breath. Bonnie was such a good listener. If Rowena wasn't careful, she might find herself wallowing in these old sob stories.

"Oh, well," she said matter-of-factly. "It was just a kid's fantasy."

"But why? Why was he so negative about it?"

Rowena shook her head. "I don't know. We never knew where his temper came from. He was very...unpredictable."

"Well, I don't think a dude ranch is a bad idea at all." Bonnie stirred the pot again, releasing a curling cloud of steam that smelled heavenly.

"Why does it have to be a fantasy?" She spoke over her shoulder. "Have you ever considered making that dream come true? Now that the place is yours?"

"No, of course not." Rowena looked around, wondering if that was true. Wasn't some small part of that ten-year-old dreamer still left inside her?

"For starters, Bell River isn't mine. It belongs to all three of us. And, besides, where would I get that kind of mon—"

But the clock had struck eight, and the call buzzed through right on time. She stopped midsyllable and looked down at the computer. Bonnie had turned around and was staring at it, too. You'd have thought the darn thing was a time bomb.

"Would you rather I went in the other room?" Bonnie's voice was so soft Rowena could barely hear her, and her eyes looked worried.

"No, of course not." Rowena smiled wryly. "My sisters and I don't know each other well enough to have any secrets."

Chapter Seven

Taking a deep breath, Rowena moved the microphone closer, then hit the key that answered the call. Almost immediately, a window appeared on her screen, and she saw Bree. She looked different, but in a good way.

She had last seen Bree three months ago, at their father's funeral. She was one year younger than Rowena, but on that strange day Bree had looked five years older—serious, silent, subdued. She'd walked slowly in her sedate brown coat suit, and her yellow hair had been pulled back into an elegant Grace Kelly chignon.

Today, she seemed to have recovered her

innate vitality. She wore one of the vibrant florals that had been her hallmark since she was a child, and her long, shining curls tumbled free around her shoulders. She looked happy—pink-cheeked and healthy, blue eyes bright.

Bree had always been the sunbeam of the family, the friend-maker. She loved everyone, and everyone loved her.

The only person on the planet she didn't much like was Rowena.

"Rowena?" Bree bent forward, as if she could peer into Bell River's great room. "Is your webcam on? I'm not getting anything."

Rowena looked down, and sure enough the little red light was glowing, indicating that her camera was off. She set it correctly, then looked up.

"Can you see me now?"

But she knew Bree could, because a transparent look of dismay had moved over her sister's face. Rowena fought the temptation to put her hand up and smooth her hair, or reach into her purse and dig out a lipstick. So much for hoping she didn't really look as bad as she feared.

Bree frowned. "Ro, are you eating?"

"Of course I'm eating." Rowena shifted on

the bar stool, which was suddenly uncomfortable. "Where's Penny? You told her it was at eight, right?"

Bree laughed. "You know Penny. She's probably writing a sonnet, or communing with a lark. I'll text her."

But at that moment, another window appeared on the screen, and suddenly Penny was with them.

"Hi, Rowena! Aw, Ro, aren't you eating? You promised me you'd eat."

Rowena rolled her eyes, but she didn't really mind when her baby sister scolded her. Penny's goodness had always inoculated her against Rowena's temper—and even, most of the time, against their father's temper, too.

"I'm sorry to be late, Bree," Penny went on. Rowena noticed that her little sister was out of breath, and her hair was dark and dripping wet. "I would have been here at eight, but you should *see* the amazing rainstorm we're having!"

Bree laughed indulgently. It wouldn't have occurred to her to be annoyed, either.

Maybe because the sisters had been separated when they were so young, and never had the chance to watch each other grow and change, the dynamic among them had been set fifteen years ago. They were, in a way, like a painting of three sisters, frozen at one pivotal moment. Rowena would forever be the rebellious, stormy big sister who served more as a warning than a role model. Bree would always be the one who was eager to please the adults with her smiles and enthusiasm. And Penny would always be the fairy child.

Rowena's heart pinched, remembering how warm Penny had been as a baby. Rowena, five years older, had been just old enough to help with bathing and dressing. What a miracle her soft skin and tiny fingers had seemed!

Little Penny, with her honey-brown Alice in Wonderland hair and her liquid Bambi eyes. Pea, they called her. And sometimes Sweetpea.

They were all so different. Sometimes the superficial extremes—Rowena's black hair vs. Bree's yellow-gold, for instance—had led people to tease that they all must be from different fathers. Rowena had often fantasized about that, dreaming that some exotic prince, or gypsy, or itinerant horse whisperer was her real father—which would account for Johnny Wright's lack of love for his changeling first daughter.

Later in prison, during the rages that came

over him in the late stages of his disease, he had insisted that *none* of the girls was his flesh and blood. During those fits, he'd refused to see even Penny, the only one who ever visited, and, ironically, the only daughter whose paternity was clearly stamped on her features.

"Okay, then," Rowena interrupted, her voice tight. "Here's the bad news." She began reading off the figures. When she finally looked up, she saw dismay plastered across her sisters' faces.

"I'm having other estimates done, of course. But these contractors have been around Silverdell forever, and their reputations are gold. So I'm not expecting to hear smaller numbers from anyone else."

"God." Bree massaged her temple. "We have *got* to unload this relic."

Rowena leaned back in her chair. "How? Who is going to buy it unless we make the repairs? Heck, who is going to buy it even if we do?"

"Let's find out." Bree frowned. "Let's get the ranch on the market and see what happens."

"You know what will happen. Nothing. Not at the price we'll have to ask."

Bree's sigh acknowledged the truth of that. The mortgages on the ranch were enormous. Their father had taken out a second loan to pay for his trial, and then a third to finance his appeal. Then the real estate market had gone bust, and until now the ranch had been hopelessly upside down.

"So what choices do we have?" Bree ran her hands through her hair. "Are you saying we should let the bank foreclose? I have a business, Ro. I can't afford to let my credit go—"

"Oh, no," Penny interjected woefully. "Not foreclosure. Surely there's another answer."

"Maybe there is," Rowena said.

Rowena felt a flare of panic when she heard herself speak. She hadn't intended to bring this up. They would think she was crazy. Good grief…she *was* crazy.

"Really?" Penny opened her eyes wide. "What?"

But Bree's gaze sharpened. "What do you mean, Ro?"

"I mean…" Rowena's lips felt stiff. "Maybe we could find a way to get the ranch to pay for itself."

"I think we've tried that." Bree didn't snap,

exactly, but her words were crisp. "Isn't that what a rental property is supposed to do?"

"That's not what she means," Penny said. She might be a dreamer, but she was profoundly intuitive, and she obviously heard something new in Rowena's voice. "You've got a real plan, don't you, Ro?"

"I wouldn't call it a plan. It's just…just a thought."

"Well?" Bree was probably tapping her fingers on her desk. Unless, of course, she'd broken that habit. Rowena always had to remind herself about the fifteen years of blank pages between them.

"I wondered whether…well, you know how some ranches have been renovated and changed into…like vacation spots? Where people come when they want to live the Western lifestyle for a week or two?"

Bree and Penny both looked mystified, and Rowena felt like kicking herself. She was making a mess of this. She'd done a better job of describing the idea back when she was ten.

"I guess so." Penny smiled encouragingly. "You mean like…a dude ranch?"

"Yes. We've got so much land here, and that's one thing you can say for Bell River. It's got beautiful views."

"It also has only four bedrooms." Bree held up four fingers. "I don't see how a dude ranch could possibly pay for itself with only four guests at a time."

"The rooms are huge, though." Rowena wasn't sure why she was arguing this. She didn't really want to pursue the idea.

Did she?

"They could be divided, making eight rooms in the main house. And we could also renovate the outbuildings. The barns, the old manager's quarters, the garage—we could turn them into separate cottages."

"With what?" Bree lifted her eyebrows. "Monopoly money?"

"We'd have to get a business loan, obviously. And we'd have to start small, probably adding rooms and activities and things in phases, but I don't see why it wouldn't work—"

"Who would handle it? You keep saying 'we,' but I have a business here in Boston, and Penny has to take care of Ruth in San Francisco. We can't take on a project like this."

"No. Of course not. I know that."

"Then who exactly would oversee the planning, the financing, the construction and, eventually, the day-to-day running of a full-service dude ranch? Surely we couldn't afford to pay someone to do all that."

Rowena opened her mouth, but no words came out.

Who, indeed?

Suddenly the enterprise seemed absurd. A pipe dream, too grandiose and at the same time too stupid even for a ten-year-old to consider. It would take months, maybe years, to get a dude ranch up and running. It would take...

Commitment.

"Maybe Rowena could!" Penny had leaned forward, her eagerness lighting her face.

"What do you think, Ro? I know you have a job in Texas next month, but this would suit you so much better, don't you think?" Penny smiled. "You're amazing with horses. And nobody knows Bell River like you do."

"Being good with horses isn't the same thing as being good at launching a business," Bree cut in. "I don't think Rowena has the right experience, the right skill set or, frankly, the right temperament for an undertaking like this."

Rowena lifted her chin. The fact that Bree was correct didn't make hearing the truth any easier. She hadn't even gone to college—

much less majored in business, as Bree had. She didn't have any domestic talents, or any desire to acquire them. All she had was a hot temper, a town full of enemies and a reputation for running away.

"Bree." Penny's soft voice chastised her sister gently. "If Rowena were committed to doing this, she's perfectly capable of—"

"But that's exactly it," Bree broke in again. "Is she capable of commitment? I've never seen any signs of it."

In the hush that followed, Rowena was acutely aware of every minute sound in the room. The bubbling of the pot on the stove, the delicate electric hum of her laptop, the creak of wind against the large arched windows.

"That's not fair, Bree," Penny said, her gentle voice now threaded with something tougher. "We don't really know what Rowena's commitments have been all these years—"

"Penny, take off your rose-colored glasses for once. Have you ever sent her a letter to the same address twice? Europe, Canada, Los Angeles, Florida? Horse trainer, au pair, French tutor, telemarketing—and God knows what else."

"She just hasn't found the right career."

Poor Penny—it was sweet of her to defend Rowena, but Bree's antagonism had nothing to do with the multiple jobs, or shifting addresses. Truth was, Bree had never forgiven Rowena for the first move she'd ever made— the day she ran away from her great-aunt Ruth's house, where she and Penny had been taken after her mother's death.

Ruth had been in her early seventies then, and she had professed herself unequal to the task of raising three girls. Bree had other options—two of their mother's closest friends had been desperate to take her—and so Ruth had agreed to take Rowena and Penny with her to San Francisco, while Bree had been carted off to Boston.

No one seemed to think it was wrong to break the sisters up. In fact, they'd regularly been instructed to remember how lucky they were not to have ended up in strangers' homes. And maybe they were. Rowena had been too angry, too bewildered and bereft, to see it that way.

Eleven-year-old Penny had been as simple to handle as a sick lamb. She had clung to any shred of love she could get, and had obeyed Ruth's every command. No music in the house. No running in the house. No friends in the house. No, no, no...

But Rowena had been too headstrong, too defiant. She and Ruth had fought. Daily. Bitterly. And then, after about six months, Rowena had run away.

Leaving Penny behind. And Bree had never forgiven her for that.

Bree's fake laugh now was brittle. "What was it, Ro? Fifteen jobs in fifteen years?"

"Eighteen, actually." Rowena forced a smile onto her lips. "The au pair horror lasted only three months. And I was a terrible French tutor."

"Okay. So." Bree shook her head. "It certainly sounds like commitment issues to me. But tell me I'm wrong, Ro. Tell me that, if we launched this crazy scheme, you'd stick it out, and wouldn't leave us in the lurch."

"Bree." Penny again, imploring.

"No." Bree was steady, but intractable, still shaking her head. "Tell me, Ro. Tell me you wouldn't get itchy feet, or cabin fever or whatever comes over you, and I'll apologize."

A thousand images flashed through Rowena's mind. First Bell River itself—the lacy waterfalls, the polished rocks, the granite outcroppings and the wildflower rainbows.

Then her mother, crumpled at the foot of the stairs. Her horse, Smokey, lacerated by a web of barbed wire, and still fighting to be free. Dallas, slumped over the edge of his flatbed truck, blood pouring from his forehead.

"Sorry, Bree," she said, the words tinkling like pieces of broken glass. "I'm afraid that's a promise I can't make."

Bree's face didn't move. She didn't even show her triumph.

"All right, then," she said matter-of-factly. "Let's decide how to pay for these repairs, and then let's get the house on the market before the damn thing sinks us all."

Each third Saturday of the month, Dallas took Alec to the Silverdell horse auction, a regional event that brought in ranchers from every little town south of Aspen and east of Crawford.

Of course, out here in the wilds of Western Colorado, that didn't mean a whole lot of people. But the auction brought in some decent horses—especially these days, since the bad economy had forced cutbacks everywhere. Many a Thoroughbred Dallas would love to own had sold here in the past few years, for prices he actually could afford, if only he had the time to take care of a horse.

Predictably, Alec didn't see why time should be an impediment. The boy longed for a horse of his own. He thought it was outrageous that he had to wait until he was ten, and, according to Dallas, more likely to accept responsibility for feeding, grooming, exercising the poor beast.

Somehow, Dallas stuck to his guns, though it wasn't easy in the face of his son's feverish campaign. Many an auction had ended with an icy drive home, Alec's arms folded tightly over his chest, his jaw set in mulish resentment.

Lately, though, Alec had inexplicably turned down the heat. He still watched each horse with hungry intensity, and he still deposited half his allowance into his horse bank, but he'd quit badgering Dallas to let him buy one right this minute.

Dallas was relieved, of course. But he was also a little suspicious. It wasn't like Alec to give up—not when his heart was set. *Stubborn* was his son's middle name.

The change had happened about…maybe three, four weeks ago. So what had been going on for Alec then? What kind of secret agenda could the little devil have?

Dallas couldn't think of one, so he decided to relax and enjoy the outing. It was his first full day off in almost a month, and it felt good to toss on old jeans, a faded T-shirt and his oldest, most comfortable sneakers.

The auction had already begun by the time they arrived, so finding a seat wasn't easy. The bleachers were overflowing—no surprise there. The great weather had stuck around. Cornflower-blue sky, cotton-candy clouds and a light breeze balmy enough for him to leave his jacket at home. Whether they wanted horses or not, the Dellians had come out simply to feel the sun on their faces.

Alec stood on his toes, hunting for an empty spot. Suddenly he jerked, excited. "Look! There's Rowena!"

Without even a glance to see if Dallas approved, Alec bolted toward the people who stood at the southern edge of the show ring. If Rowena really was among them, Dallas couldn't see her, but he followed anyhow.

He wouldn't mind seeing Rowena today. He would like to see how she was doing. He hadn't run into her since the barn-painting day, and the word in town was that Bell River was practically collapsing in on itself, and it would cost her a pretty penny to shore the place up.

Sure enough, Alec was right. Rowena stood against the railing of the show ring, her back to them, but he easily recognized her by the long, shimmering hair, falling free against her green T-shirt in a black cascade. The breeze teased at the curling ends, twirling them softly against her shoulders and arms.

Alec bounded up to her and tugged her hand, as uninhibited as ever. She smiled, said something Dallas couldn't hear, and then she glanced over at him. After a delay so subtle he might have imagined it, she smiled at him, too.

And instantly his pulse sped up. She might be fifteen years older, exhausted and ten pounds too thin, but she hadn't lost the lithe animal grace that had always got to him. He swallowed his heart back where it belonged and moved forward.

"Ladies and gentlemen." The auctioneer's microphone was about twice as loud as it needed to be for a crowd this size, so that effectively stopped conversation before it even started. "Our next horse is Finnian's Flash-dancer, a beautiful paint mare, an elegantly made little filly. Sired by Blue Spot Run, out of Dame Edna—you all remember her. Lots of spirit in this one."

Rowena leaned forward, as if the paint mare interested her. That surprised Dallas. The horse was pretty, no doubt, a golden-brown with white markings on her back, looking almost like a saddle. And four crisp white shanks, from knee to fetlock, as if she wore leg warmers. He chuckled as he belatedly made the connection. Leg warmers. Flashdancer.

Okay, pretty to look at, yes. But she wouldn't keep her head down as she circled the ring, and her lively prance boiled with too much repressed energy. Even Dallas, who was hardly a horse expert, could see that, in spite of the impressive bloodline, this horse was a handful.

When the auctioneer finally finished extolling the mare's virtues and launched into his rapid-fire request for bids, Rowena raised her hand.

Alec immediately stood on tiptoe again. "You're going to buy her?"

Rowena smiled. "We'll see. It depends on how high she goes."

Now Dallas really was curious. "Does this mean you've decided to stay at the ranch?"

She shook her head. "No. I'm heading to Texas in a few weeks. I'll train for a rancher in Austin. There's room for me to stable a horse of my own, so..."

She let the rest of the sentence drop, her attention focused on the filly, who was still clearly out of sorts. Dallas bent his head, so that he could be heard without screaming. "You sure this is the one you want? She looks as if she might have a temper."

Rowena swiveled slightly, bringing their faces within inches of each other, and gave him a Cheshire smile. "You say that like it's a bad thing."

"Well...in a horse it is. Isn't it?"

"Depends," she said. "Born-in nastiness is a problem, but Flashdancer has a legitimate reason for being bad-tempered. I watched her owners unload her this morning. They shouldn't ever have been allowed to own an animal. They're little more than animals themselves."

Though she still smiled, he heard the undercurrent of anger in her voice, and so did Alec, whose brows drove toward his nose, hard.

"Jerks," the boy said gruffly. "There are a

lot of people who would really love to have a horse like that. And would treat her nice."

Rowena nodded. "That's right. That's why I'm going to buy her, if I can."

"Yeah?" Alec's frown lightened. "You think you can fix her?"

"She's not broken. She just needs to be shown the right way to behave. But, yeah, I can fix her."

She raised her hand again, showing that she'd been listening to the auctioneer with one ear all along. Dallas glanced around the crowd and saw that the bidding was winding down. If Rowena wasn't overestimating her skill with horses, she was about to get a hell of a deal.

"Sold. Three hundred sixty-five, to the lady in green."

"You got her!" Alec's eyes were bright in the noonday sun as he tracked the horse's every movement. Flashdancer was still threatening to buck even as they led her back to the stall. "You got a horse like that for three hundred and sixty-five dollars?"

"Don't get any ideas." Dallas knew what his son was thinking. Alec already had two hundred and sixteen dollars in his horse bank. He'd been assuming a good animal would cost him a thousand, at least. "Rowena's buying her for a bargain because most people are afraid to buy a skittish horse. If she can't retrain her, she'll be stuck with a horse she can't use."

Rowena's black-wing eyebrows lifted, and the left corner of her mouth tucked in, creating a dimple. His heart did the stupid dance again. Fifteen years ago, the need to kiss that dimple had driven him straight out of his mind.

"Don't bet against me, Sheriff," she said, her voice low and throaty. "I can make that filly eat out of my hand before nightfall."

"Yeah." He shook his head slowly, and smiled in spite of himself. "Yeah, I guess there's not much doubt about that."

Chapter Eight

At that point, Rowena had intended to walk away. She'd been sociable, she'd made nice, she'd accepted the olive branch Dallas was obviously offering her. Generous of him, when you thought about it. He had every reason to dislike her, every reason in the world to be sorry she'd returned to town.

She hadn't been sure he still lived here— that was how carefully she'd avoided talking or reading about Silverdell through the years. But, if he were here, she'd expected him to be frigidly polite, at best. She figured he'd cross the street to avoid having to do more than tip his hat. And, at worst, she'd been braced for open hostility.

But apparently that wasn't Dallas Garwood's way. He hadn't been petty as a teenager, and he still wasn't. And…as long as she was admitting his good points…he had a very cute, very gutsy son.

Still, it was time for her to get back to the ranch and prepare things for the new horse. Bringing civilized closure to an ugly chapter in their lives was great. But enough was enough. A powerful chemistry had smoldered between them all those years ago—the chemistry that had allowed the Bad Girl to coax the golden halo right off the Saint's head and dance all over it. That chemistry hadn't disappeared. If she wanted to, she could probably mess him up all over again.

But she didn't want to. She'd learned that lesson, even if she hadn't learned anything else in her life. You couldn't mess with other people's hearts without messing yourself up, too.

Just as she was choosing the perfect exit line, Alec piped up again. "Can we come with you to see Flashdancer? Maybe we can help you get her ready. Do you have a trailer? Do you think she'll like it in a trailer? Do you have a stall ready for her at the ranch? They sell saddles, over at the pavilion. Some of them are friggin' outrageous, with silver and all that stuff, but some of them are pretty cheap."

"Alec." Dallas's voice was stern.

"What? Because I said *friggin'?*" The boy scowled at the perceived injustice. "*You* say *friggin'.*"

"No. Because you're annoying Rowena. Back off. Let her go meet her new horse in peace."

The air whooshed out of the little boy, as if he were a punctured balloon, which made Rowena cringe. She hated to disappoint him, but she had to agree with Dallas. Flashdancer would be a wonderful horse, but not until Rowena got the kinks ironed out. Right now, the filly was about nine hundred pounds of edgy beast with a lot of pent-up anger to toss around.

"You're not annoying me," she said quickly. "But I'm not sure it's safe to—"

A sudden commotion behind them stopped her in the middle of the sentence. A man cried out, "Hey, he needs help!" and, amid the noise of people scuffling and a horse neighing furiously, several others gasped.

By the time Rowena could turn around, Dallas had already started walking. He seemed to have identified the source of the trouble instantly, and he swung himself over the show ring's paddock and onto the sawdust in one muscular arc.

"Dad!" Alec's voice sounded more bewildered than afraid. "Where are you going?"

"It's okay," she said, putting her arm around Alec's shoulders instinctively, protecting him from the shoving and pushing around them. But she hadn't found a decent vantage point yet, so the words were only empty noises, really.

"That's my little sister," a boy's voice cried out over the fray.

Rowena shepherded Alec forward, carving her way to the rails, so that she could see. As the neighing had warned her, the horse in the show ring was going nuts. A huge black stallion, at least fifteen hands, was rearing and bucking, pulling at his lead so hard the walker could barely hold on. A few feet to the side, another horse, who was waiting his turn for auction, was panicking, as well.

A couple of other men had run up to help the guy holding the lead, but they only made matters worse. They waved their hands and yelled at the horse with transparent fear and fury—both of which would increase the stallion's agitation.

Most alarming of all, right behind the horse lay a small child, a little girl in a bright red pinafore, and her small form remained utterly still no matter how close to her the frightened horse danced. Dallas was striding toward her, raising small storms of sawdust at his heels.

"Get that horse out of here." He spoke loudly, and firmly. But he was absolutely calm, and Rowena gave him an internal thumbs-up. You had to remain cool around a spooked horse. If he knew that, he must know, too, that he had to wait, wait for the men to pull the horse away....

But apparently he didn't care. He kept going. *Oh, no...*

Rowena turned to Alec. "I need you to stay right here. Don't go anywhere, and don't speak to anyone. Can you do that?"

He nodded, still wide-eyed.

Rowena touched his head, then climbed over the paddock and moved out toward the horse. Other people in the crowd had the same idea, but she spoke firmly, and pushed them aside.

"Get back. Get back," she commanded in level tones. "You'll only make it worse."

Within a few seconds, she reached the men straining at the stallion's lead. "Get back," she said one more time. The authority in her voice seemed to shock them at first, but then they surrendered the lead, and melted away like the cowards they were.

Forward motion would have halted the rearing immediately, if anyone had thought of it in the first few seconds, but now it was too late for that. The whites of the horse's eyes were visible all around, and he was rearing so steeply, and so recklessly, that he was in danger of falling over and breaking his legs.

Not to mention what he'd do to the limp body on the ground behind him.

She turned herself slightly to one side, so that she didn't adopt a predatory posture, and spoke in her most soothing tones.

"Good boy. It's all right," she said, over and over. The words didn't matter. Only the attitude mattered—confident, calm, unthreatening.

The minute a little slack in the lead told her the horse was descending, she released the pressure, to show her approval. He seemed calmer, though he was still breathing heavily, so she urged his head down and inched him forward, just to break the rhythm—and to put as much distance as possible between the stallion and the little girl.

And Dallas.

Out of the corner of her eye she watched him. He chose his moment well, and he moved with no abrupt gestures, no noise or panic. The horse didn't even seem aware of him, thank God, and Rowena wanted to keep it that way.

In her peripheral vision, she saw Dallas carry the child out of the ring, but she kept breathing and talking. She brought her face close to the horse's and breathed deeply. She was careful not to exhale hard enough to irritate his skin, and all the while she continued to murmur soothing sounds.

Finally, the ring was clear. Dallas and the child were safe. The threat was over. As she let her grip on the lead relax, Rowena's heart began to beat wildly, as if only now she could allow herself to register how dangerous the situation had been.

Finally, the stallion's owner came loping up—where the hell had he been? He apologized in broken, shamed sentences for his absence, but she could hardly listen. He thanked her, but she waved the words away. And so, saving face by barking orders to his employees, he took the lead and walked the sweaty, confused horse to the stables.

The whole episode hadn't taken more than a minute or two, probably, but Rowena felt a trembling in her arms and legs. It was as if, in those short minutes, she'd run a marathon, or dug a ditch to China.

While she worked with the horse, the world had narrowed down to only Rowena and the terrified animal. Now, all the sights, scents and sounds of reality came flooding back. The energetic burble of people talking, discussing the near tragedy. The laughter of children, already on to something else. The sweet smell of sawdust, and the musky scent of horse.

And then, strangest of all, people began to come up and smile at her, thanking her and telling her how amazing she was. People she didn't know and, surprisingly, a few she had known once and tried to forget.

Dallas had disappeared, of course. He had more important things to do than stand around here, patting her back for doing something that hadn't really been all that spectacular.

She numbly thanked everyone, until there was just one person left. She looked up, and recognized the grown-up version of Tina Blakeley, a plain, quiet woman she'd gone to high school with. Tina used to work at the feed store on weekends.

"Do you know how the little girl is doing?" Rowena decided to ask her, because Tina felt almost like a friend. They hadn't exactly been pals in high school, but, because they shared a love of horses, they were never quite enemies, either. "I couldn't tell if she was even conscious."

"It was Mable Madison. Jimmy Madison's daughter. You remember Jimmy?" Tina didn't wait for a reply. "I think she's fine. She was awake by the time Dallas got her to her parents—they'd left Mable with her brother, and she wandered off. An ambulance just arrived, but I don't think they're going to need it."

A cool wave of relief spread between Rowena's shoulder blades. The episode could have turned out very differently. She'd worked at a ranch in Texas a year or so ago, and one of their horses got spooked. He kicked holes into the skulls of two big, brawny cowboys.

"It probably was her red dress," Tina said, looking toward the now-empty ring. "Lots of horses don't like bright colors." Tina's cheeks flushed. "But of course you know that. You always knew ten times as much about horses as I did."

Rowena shook her head. "Anyone could have—"

"Maybe. But no one did. No one but you. That's what I wanted to ask you about. Are you doing any training while you're at Bell River?"

"No." Rowena responded instinctively, but it didn't take long for her to rethink her answer. Money was going out of Bell River with a giant whooshing sound, but nothing was coming in. Her Austin job had called yesterday, putting off her arrival another couple of weeks, which meant she'd probably be at Bell River almost a month.

Why shouldn't she make a few bucks?

The possibility hadn't occurred to her before, because she hadn't imagined that anyone in Silverdell would dream of hiring her.

"Well, I guess I could. But it would be only short-term. I won't be staying in town all that long."

"Oh, good!" Tina blushed again. "I mean, not good that you won't be here long, but good that you will do some training. I really could use some help with the mare I bought last year. May I call you, then?"

"Sure." Rowena gave her the cell number, then said an awkward but polite goodbye. She'd begun to wonder why Alec hadn't joined her.

Maybe he had kept his word, and stayed put....

But she knew what it was like to be a restless, independent child. She knew how difficult it was to subdue the urge to explore, especially when the breeze was warm, the trees were greening and excitement filled the air.

She went back to the spot where they'd parted. Nothing but strangers. *Darn it.* Where was he?

All of a sudden a small body plopped in front of her, whooping with glee. "Holy cripes, Rowena! You were awesome!"

To Alec's credit, he had been only a few feet from where she left him—except that it was a few feet directly up, in the branches of the nearby bristlecone pine. In his enthusiasm, he practically collided with her, and hit the brakes just short of knocking her down. He hesitated, as if he had intended to hug her, but decided at the last minute that hugs weren't cool.

Instead, he held up his hand for a high five. "You're like a horse whisperer!"

She laughed, and low-fived him back. "Hardly."

She started walking, and Alec fell in step, obviously delighted to be beside the hero of the moment. "Yeah, but you like hypnotized that horse! You put the whammy on it, like those guys in India or wherever, the ones who charm snakes."

"Not quite like that," she said, though something inside her was smiling. "With horses, it's all about keeping your cool. If you are panicked, the horse can tell, and he panics, too. But if you're completely calm—"

"Then bam! You put the whammy on him!" Alec finished the sentence with a jubilant shout.

His boisterous enthusiasm was cute, but she did wish he had a slightly deeper appreciation of the gravity of the situation. People could have been hurt, and badly. If that stallion had slipped from her grasp, and thundered his way around the ring…or if he had decided to kick back while Dallas knelt behind him, Alec Garwood might well have lost his father this sunny May morning.

"Ms. Wright?" A red-haired young man stepped in front of them, a diffident expression on his freckled face.

"Yes?"

"I'm Deputy Bartlett." He smiled. "Chad Bartlett. The sheriff is tied up at the moment, so he asked me to come get Alec."

Alec groaned. "Aw, really?"

Even Rowena felt a little drop of disappointment. She had expected Dallas to join them. Foolishly, she had even been looking forward to it. Why? Had she wanted him to flatter her, too, and tell her she was amazing?

Ridiculous. Her ego wasn't that needy. And he wasn't a gullible eight-year-old. He knew what she'd done, and how relatively easy it had been to do. He'd taken all the risks, really, not Rowena.

"Can you tell me how the Madison girl is doing?" Rowena didn't want to pry. She and Jimmy Madison had never been friends—he was one of the honor society, student council set. The kind who was friends with people like Dallas.

But she had to know. "Was she badly hurt?"

The deputy shook his head. "She hit her

head when she fell, and it knocked her out, so they took her to the emergency room. I think that's standard procedure, though, because she seemed okay to me." He tilted his hat back an inch and grinned. "Feisty little thing, if you know what I mean."

Rowena was glad to hear it. But if the little girl was fine, what was keeping Dallas?

As if he read her thoughts, the deputy answered her unspoken question. "Sheriff's talking to Connelly now. He's the owner of the stallion. I guess it's not against the law, bringing an animal like that out in public, but it ought to be." He shook his head. "Anyhow, I better be getting Alec back."

"Come on, Deputy Bartlett," Alec wheedled. "Tell him you couldn't find me!"

"Sorry, Alec. Sheriff said we can't ask Ms. Wright to babysit you."

"She doesn't mind!" Alec's assertion was robust, as if there could be no doubt. "We were talking about stuff."

"Sorry," the deputy said again, this time more firmly. "Sheriff's orders. I bring you back stat."

Apparently *stat* was shorthand for *end of discussion*. Alec still grumbled, but he accepted his fate with a decent amount of civility. He allowed himself one dramatic sigh, and then he tucked his shirttail back in and took his place alongside the deputy.

"See you later," he said cheerfully, smiling back at Rowena. In that instant, his blue eyes looked very much like his father's.

She laughed. But as she watched them walk away, a wave of emptiness swept through her, hollowing out her chest.

Emptiness? The word startled her into movement, and she began to walk in the other direction. Why should she feel empty? She was a born loner. She didn't need company, especially from a kid she hardly knew.

What she needed... She needed to be busy. She needed a project, a goal—and not desk stuff, like calling roofers for estimates, or looking up the going price of a sump pump. That was partly why she'd bought the horse, wasn't it? She needed to get outside, to work so hard in the sun and the wind that her body and mind were numb when she collapsed at the end of each day.

She would only be here a month, and she wasn't going to spend it mooning over Dallas Garwood. One month. That was all the time she had left at Bell River. Probably *ever*.

At the end of their phone call, Penny had

sided with Bree, making it two to one in favor of putting the property on the market. The dude ranch idea was a fantasy, Bree had said. Rowena hadn't done a lick of investigating, didn't have a clue how to run a business, didn't know the first thing about domestic duties of any kind. And if she wasn't willing to commit herself utterly to the task...

Point taken. In Bree's eyes, Rowena was a gypsy, claustrophobic about commitment, and would bolt from the project the minute she got bored.

Well, Bree wasn't far wrong about any of that. And Rowena refused to be manipulated into making promises to change. No way she was going to sign away her soul, simply to buy Bree's permission to explore her dude ranch idea.

So they each kicked in a third of the price of the biggest repairs. The minute they'd hung up, Rowena had called the roofer, the basement guy and the Realtor.

So that was that. Thirty days here, and then on to the trainer job in Austin. Rowena moved to the railing of the show ring, and leaned her elbows on it, sighing. Another trainer job. Another crummy apartment in a hot, flat town with no mountains, no snow. Another bunch of dusty, flirty cowboys she wouldn't date. Another revolving door of nameless horses it didn't make sense to love.

Thirty days. She drummed her fingers on the railing, her mind going a mile a minute. She'd be a fool to waste it feeling sorry for herself.

In fact, she realized with a sudden burst of determination, she'd be a fool to waste it doing anything except...

Checking out what it would take to turn Bell River into a dude ranch.

Chapter Nine

"Damn it! That hurt!" Bonnie, who stood on the highest rung of a stepladder, trying to nail wire into place above one of the stable's six stalls, pulled her fingers away and shook them hard. "I swear, I'm going to break every bone in my hand with this hammer."

Rowena, who was attaching new hinges so that she could rehang another stall's door, looked up and groaned sympathetically. "Sorry," she said. "There's not much light up there, I know."

It was true. Most of the stable's upper area was in shadows. But one shaft of sunlight streamed in just over Bonnie's head, picking out the red strands of hair that her black hair dye hadn't quite covered.

She would be stunning as a redhead, Rowena realized. Those blue eyes, and that pale, perfect skin... She was as delicate as a porcelain figurine.

But definitely not the outdoorsy type.

Funny, how people were different. Inside the house, where Rowena was hopeless, Bonnie was a magician. She could banish mildew, dust bunnies, cup rings and soap rings and rust. Under her loving strokes, windows sparkled and candlesticks gleamed.

Best of all, she could create heavenly ambrosia out of kitchen scraps. Her meals were so irresistible Rowena was sure she'd gained three pounds in the past week alone.

But out here, their roles were reversed. Out here, Rowena was the one with the magic wand. She could tame the animals, coax an extra foot out of the plants and make leaning walls stand straight.

And she could tack down that wire in half the time, without breaking a single bone.

"Why don't you call it a day?" She smiled up at Bonnie, who sucked gently on her wounded thumb. "You could go start dinner. I'm starving."

That earned a smile. Rowena knew Bonnie had made it her mission to put some flesh on Rowena's bones. And she certainly had the talent.

Hmm…wonder if that meant she had been a chef's daughter, or if her family had owned a bakery?

Rowena had turned guessing Bonnie's past into quite a diverting game. Bonnie was eerily quiet sometimes, and often she sat so still she might have been a statue. Did that mean she'd once been…a nun? A spy?

Rowena never asked, of course. She understood how desperate a person could be to shed her past as thoroughly as a snake sloughing off an old skin. She also knew, unfortunately, that it probably wouldn't work. It was as difficult to outrun your past as it was to outrun your shadow.

She did hope that one of these days, as Bonnie started to feel safer at Bell River, she might volunteer a detail or two. So far, though, nothing.

"I wanted to stay out here and help you." Bonnie frowned, looking through the open stable door at the broken paddock rails. "I'm fairly useless, but there's just too much work for one person."

That was definitely true. The contractors were already working on the foundation. They and the roofers were the only professionals the collective funds of the three sisters could afford. The rest had to be up to Rowena.

But if she labored alone, she would never have Bell River market-ready in thirty days. She might have to hire someone, at least part-time, in spite of the cost. But who? They hadn't received a single call in response to the help-wanted flyer.

She tapped the screwdriver into her palm, trying to quell the shimmer of guilt she felt about buying the new horse. The money was part of it—but right now time was the most valuable commodity in her life. Training Flashdancer would take valuable time away from the Bell River repairs.

She hadn't intended to buy anything yesterday. She had attended the auction purely on a whim.

But when she saw those ghastly men yanking the filly's head around, and whipping her merely to get her out of the trailer and arranged in a stall, something had snapped.

"I wonder where they are?" Bonnie glanced

at her watch. "Didn't he say he'd bring the horse at three? It's half past already."

But just as she spoke, sunlight flashed off the side of a shiny truck as it turned into Bell River from the main road. Behind the truck, a gleaming white trailer bumped along slowly, moving in and out of tree shadows.

"Here they are," Rowena said. She couldn't help smiling, the guilt completely banished by the excitement of possessing her new horse. Though the five other stalls were a wreck, Flashdancer's stall had been pristine and perfect for hours. Rowena had stayed up half the night putting on the finishing touches.

As the trailer pulled up, she saw that two men were inside. One, the driver, she recognized as Ethan Stills, the older man she'd hired at the auction. The other person...

The doors opened, and the two men stepped out, one from each side of the truck's cab.

The other one was Mitch.

"Hey, there, ladies!" He smiled as he strode toward them. "Ethan asked me to ride along and help."

When he reached the stable, he kissed each woman's cheek gallantly. "It's great to see you again, Bonnie! Rowena, your new filly is gorgeous!"

"She is, isn't she?" Rowena glanced toward the trailer, where Ethan was preparing to open the doors. "She's going to be a lot of work, though."

Mitch winked. "Beautiful females always are."

Rowena glanced at Bonnie, who was suddenly inspecting her wounded thumb intently, head bowed.

"But they're worth it," Mitch added, his voice full of implications.

God, what a flirt he was! But she had to smile. He was actually quite adorable, and he looked even more boyish today than ever.

"Let's get Flash out of that trailer," she said, deciding on the spur of the moment to shorten the name. She turned to Bonnie. "Come on... Don't you want to meet her?"

The four of them got the filly installed in no time. Flash didn't seem jangled by the ride in the trailer, and accepted her new quarters happily. Within ten minutes, she was contentedly munching on hay, studying the stable and nuzzling Rowena every time she put out her hand.

In fact, she acted like a different horse altogether, now that she was among friends. Something sweet, like warm honey, seemed to course through Rowena's veins every time she looked at the filly. It had been fifteen years since she'd owned a horse, and she'd almost forgotten how deeply comforting the bond could be.

Even if she had to go to Austin, she'd at least have Flash with her. She wouldn't feel so alone.

"I should go get dinner started," Bonnie said finally, when everyone had admired the horse for several minutes.

Rowena instinctively looked at Mitch. She wondered whether he'd concoct an excuse to go up to the house with Bonnie.

But to Rowena's surprise, he didn't even try. "I'll be riding back with Ethan," he said. "So I'll catch you later, okay?"

Bonnie nodded, gave Flash's muzzle a goodbye pat and left the stables. Ethan was checking the trailer hitch, so, for the moment, Mitch and Rowena were alone.

He gazed around him, obviously registering all the breaches in the sidewall, the loose boards, the peeling paint, drooping stall doors and rotten paddock rails. "You've got your hands full here," he said. "I understand you're putting the ranch on the market. How long have you got to pull things together?"

"About a month," she said, weary again, merely thinking of the work ahead of her. "My new job starts mid-June, so it's a fairly fixed target."

"You looking for help?"

"I've got a flyer up at the grocery store. Handyman Wanted." She picked up a board that had nails sticking out and slipped it into a safe spot on the tack room shelving. She couldn't risk letting Flash run into it. "No one has called yet, though."

Of course they hadn't. Short-term, part-time, sweaty chores at minimum wage weren't exactly anyone's dream job.

Mitch cleared his throat. "How about me?"

She looked up. "You...? You as a handyman?"

"Why not?" He tilted his head and grinned. "I have hands. I'm a man."

She raised her eyebrows. "And I'm not hiring a comedian."

His face sobered. "I know. I'm not trying to be a jerk. I'm just saying I can do the work. I know how to build things and fix things. I'm not bad with horses." His smile peeked out again. "I mean, I'm no Rowena Wright, but I do okay."

She had seen that, as they worked with

Flash. In fact, he'd handled her better than Ethan, whose truck proclaimed that he'd trained horses for thirty years. Some things you couldn't learn. With horses, instincts were as important as experience.

Still…if she was going to spend the money to get a helper, she would need one who could work fast and stay focused.

"This isn't about Bonnie, is it?" She didn't bother to sugarcoat it. "You aren't just a moth looking for an excuse to buzz around the flame?"

He laughed. "Well, I promise to do my buzzing off the clock. But I have to admit that getting to see Bonnie now and then is one of fringe benefits of the job."

It wasn't the conventional answer, but she had to appreciate the candor. She put her hand on Flash's neck and studied Mitch's face.

"What would your brother think about it?"

Mitch shrugged. "He'd hate it. And frankly, that's another one of the fringe benefits. It's time he learned he can't dictate how my life is going to go."

She bit her lower lip, trying to weigh the factors. She would love to use Mitch. He was fun, easygoing, smart and strong. Even better, he was a known quantity. She was confident he didn't secretly hate her, and he wouldn't be using his job to sabotage her or gather gossip for the local grapevine.

Or to spray-paint obscenities on the barn wall.

However, he might be using the job as a stage for romance, or as a knife to stick in his brother's back.

"Rowena, listen." He came closer, his hands in his pockets. "I need a job. I need *this kind* of job. Dallas is determined to send me back to college and make me be some kind of surgeon, or judge, or grand pooh-bah of the skyscraper set. But that's not me. I'm an outside kind of guy. I like to work with my hands. I like to get dirty, and I like to see what I've created, at the end of the day."

He lifted one corner of his wide, friendly mouth. "Somehow I think you understand that."

As Rowena hesitated, Flash turned her head and pushed her wet, cool nose against Rowena's cheek. She wasn't usually superstitious, but for a split second it seemed as if the horse was trying to nudge her into saying yes.

"Hey, you coming, or not?" Ethan's dour face, a mass of wrinkles beneath his wiry silver hair, appeared at the stable door. "I've got a schedule to keep."

Mitch hesitated a second, clearly hoping Rowena would give him an answer. Then, with an almost imperceptible slump of his broad shoulders, he turned to follow the older man to the truck.

Darn it. Rowena hadn't ever been able to resist that kind of sad puppy-dog face. She'd always crabbed about what pests her younger sisters were, but in truth they had been able to make her do almost anything.

"Mitch, wait."

He turned eagerly. "Yeah?"

"If I hired you, and Dallas..." She started over. "If it caused problems..."

She frowned. This was ridiculous. "What I mean is...how soon can you start?"

The next day the temperatures soared up into the mid-seventies again, and stayed hot for days. So much meltwater swept down from the mountains that Bell River, which bisected the ranch's five hundred acres into two distinct sections, had lifted at least two feet. By true summer, it would rise up to the high road, drowning the grasses and wildflowers that had dared to plant themselves along the banks during the dry months.

Rowena was delighted to have sunshine and a dry pen in which to work Flash, and Tina Blakeley's mare, Marybelle, who had arrived a couple of days ago for training. Rowena worked with Marybelle in the early morning, having discovered the horse was more cooperative before noon.

Then she could turn to her special pleasure—Flash. She'd been putting the paint through the basics for about half an hour when she saw Dallas's shiny blue Dodge turn in between the bristlecone pines.

She paused, watching the pine branches brush the windshield, then drag over the roof like a carwash. She'd have to get the trees trimmed soon, before they completely obscured the entrance. Nothing said haunted like an untended bristlecone pine. The fantastic, twisted trunks and grasping branches could look quite malevolent, a lot like the "witch trees" that grew up in the mountains.

What was he doing here? Instinctively, she cast a glance around the property, wondering if Alec might be hiding in the stables, or under the hay. He did seem to love it here. Why this ranch, she wondered, and not one of the more elegant ones upriver? Maybe it was just that Bell River was the closest to the town proper, and the easiest to reach on his bike. Two miles was a long ride, but a determined, healthy boy could do it.

Dallas parked near the house, but he'd obviously seen her in the pen, because he didn't bother knocking at the door. Instead, he headed straight back toward the paddocks.

As she waited, she stroked Flash's neck briskly. The filly loved the rubbing—most horses did—but also it gave Rowena something to do other than watch that six-foot hunk of supple, athletic virility stroll toward her.

Dallas was in uniform again today, if the casual black polo and soft khakis could be called a uniform. The balmy breeze ruffled his shirt against his long torso...which she noticed had gained a chiseled-marble set of decidedly adult abs over the years.

He'd left his cap in the car, but he'd donned a pair of dark-tinted sunglasses, a shield against the midday glare. Sunlight sparked off the lenses, creating fiery white stars that matched the radiance of his badge. She almost laughed at how even nature conspired to showcase his splendor.

"Hi, there," she said when he got close enough. She kept her voice and her face carefully neutral. Until she knew his mission, no sense showing her cards.

"Hey." He had reached the paddock, but he made no move to enter by the gate. He rested his hand on the nearest post, leaving the fence between them, and turned his profile toward Flash. "How's she doing?"

"She's fantastic." Rowena rubbed the filly's neck again, all the way to the crest. "I went back to the basics, just in case, but she's been perfect so far. No behavior problems at all. It's as if she understood from the start that things would be different here."

He smiled. "Excellent. She's a pretty horse, looks healthy. And if anyone can train her right, it's you."

Rowena turned her head into the filly's neck again, uncomfortable with that level of flattery. She kissed the satiny skin, and the horse blew air softly through her nostrils in response. They were connecting well and building trust already.

Which was more than she could say for her interactions with Dallas. She never had a clue what he was really thinking—his impeccable good manners could cover a million less pleasant emotions.

And as for her... Talk about erratic! She went from hot to cold and back again, until she felt dizzy. The night after the horse auction, she'd even had a rather unsettling dream about a man...and she didn't realize it was Dallas until she saw his hands were full of golden stars. When she woke, she lectured herself for an hour, laying out in harsh terms exactly how irrelevant Dallas Garwood was in her actual, current, everyday life.

Still. Simply remembering the dream made her fingers feel unsteady.

"So," she said, fiddling with the bridle, "what brings you here, Sheriff? If you're looking for Alec, I haven't seen him."

He laughed. "No. I know where he is, for once. He's at school. Or at least he darned well better be."

Rowena wouldn't put any money on it, but maybe she was projecting her own truant behavior onto the boy. She had to be careful about that. She realized she'd begun to identify with the boy to an unwarranted degree.

"Okay, then. What does bring you here?"

"A couple of things." Dallas took off his sunglasses, which didn't diminish his glow, because the sunbeams simply decided to sparkle against his blue eyes instead. "The first thing is a thank-you. I didn't get a chance to tell you then, but I really appreciated your help the other day. I'm quite sure that devil would have kicked in my brains if you hadn't charmed him the way you did."

She shrugged. "I doubt it. But if I helped, I'm glad. Is the little girl okay?"

"She's fine. They kept her in the hospital overnight, but I get the feeling they were thrilled to be able to discharge her first thing in the morning. Little Mable Madison is…" He squinted, and chewed on the side of his lip. "Did you ever see *The Exorcist?*"

She laughed. "You mean Jimmy Madison… our own Jimmy Madison, the president of the chess club, has a hellion for a daughter?"

"Yep. I guess ironies like that are Fate's way of getting the last laugh. I was a pretty placid kid, and look at *my* son. Harry Houdini and Huckleberry Finn in one wild and woolly package."

It was a fairly accurate description, at least from what Rowena had seen of Alec. And a fairly affectionate description, too, which surprised her. Maybe St. Dallas wasn't quite as judgmental as he used to be.

"Alec's got a lot of spunk," she said.

Dallas nodded. "Yeah. If by spunk you mean attitude, rebellion and sass."

"That's exactly what I mean."

They shared a smile, and their gazes held an instant longer than was strictly necessary. Then she looked away, down the front path, to where the pines guarded the Bell River gate.

The few seconds of silence that followed were oddly comfortable, and neither of them rushed to fill it with words. Dallas tucked his sunglasses into the placket of his shirtfront and put his foot up on the lower rail. The breeze played with his hair, tickling his eyelashes with the honey-gold strands.

But very soon Flash found this silence boring. She began to bump her nose against Rowena's shoulder restlessly. Unless Rowena wanted to let this afternoon's training go to waste, she should put Flash back in her stall.

She turned to Dallas. "You said a couple of things brought you here. What was the other one?"

His brow furrowed, as if the sun was too bright. Bringing his foot down, he slipped his sunglasses back on, and took a breath.

"Mitch."

"Mitch?"

But she was just buying time. She could easily guess why he wanted to talk about his brother. He must have heard that Mitch would be working at Bell River, and he didn't like it.

Why he didn't like it, she wasn't sure. Options abounded—take your pick. Mitch shouldn't spend that much time around Bonnie, who was a mystery, and might be Bad News. Mitch shouldn't spend that much time around Rowena, who was indisputably Bad News. Mitch's time was worth more than Rowena was paying. He was too good for a blue-collar job—he should get back into college.

Maybe, God help her, Dallas even feared that Mitch might fall victim to her wicked seductress ways—as Dallas had, all those years ago.

As her mind sped through the possibilities, the unspoken camaraderie that had hung in the air began wafting away like smoke.

"Yeah, Mitch. You see, he's… I wanted to let you know that…" Dallas reached up and massaged his shoulder. "I think it's likely that Mitch is going to apply for your handyman job. I'm hoping you won't hire him."

She raised her eyebrows. "Really."

All her infuriated pride was in those syllables, and Dallas was too smart to miss it.

"Yes," he said. "But let me explain. It's just that—"

"You don't need to," she broke in, gathering Flash's reins together so that she could lead the filly away without a snag. "Explaining would be awkward, and it would be a waste of time."

Dallas's expression was inscrutable, with his eyes hidden behind those starry black lenses. When he spoke, his voice was even, but oddly flat. "Why would it be awkward? I know you need a handyman. I promise I'll find you someone else, someone far better qualified than Mitch."

"It would be awkward because Mitch has already applied for the job." She lifted her chin slightly. "And I have already hired him."

Chapter Ten

The late-afternoon sun blazed into his windshield as Dallas swung his truck into the Silverdell Elementary School parking lot. His tires squealed, protesting the sharp turn, and from the backseat his son complained in a persecuted tone, "Gawd, Dad. Easy."

He glanced at his watch. Almost six. *Damn it.* He was inexcusably late for his appointment with Ms. Darren. All thanks to another NNB call from Mrs. Fillmore, who had temporarily transferred her paranoia from Rowena to her next-door neighbor, a single man who, she felt sure, was burying bodies in his backyard.

To make matters worse, Dallas had been forced to bring Alec with him, though Veronica Darren had specifically asked him not to. But he had no choice. Mrs. Biggars was sick, and Mitch, who had promised to babysit, had been a no-show. Ever since he'd begun working up at Bell River, Mitch had barely been at home long enough to sleep. Still, he'd sworn he would handle Alec during the meeting. Dallas was ticked off.

He took a deep breath as he turned the key to kill the ignition. Probably not helpful to walk into a difficult conference already in a lather. Going to teacher meetings was a lot like talking to a cop. Everything you said, or didn't say, could and would be held against you. A grouchy dad would be proof that Alec's problems began at home.

"Can I play on the jungle gym?"

Dallas looked in the rearview mirror, which reflected only Alec's eyes and hair. For a minute, it was like catching a glimpse of Dallas's younger self—hair sticking up everywhere, eyes intense and clearly plotting exploits.

He wondered if Alec would believe it if Dallas told him how wild he himself had been as a small child. Probably not. His preacher father had beaten obedience into

Dallas—literally—by the time he was ten. If any spark of the messy-haired adventurer remained inside him now, it was buried so deep that even he forgot about it most of the time.

"I'll be sensible." Alec leaned forward, begging. "Honest. I won't dream up anything bonkers."

Dallas knew better than to believe that. Alec never did anything completely normal, though each time he professed to be shocked that his dad thought his behavior was "bonkers."

However, that mildly nutty, irrepressible streak was what made Alec unique. So Dallas kept as light a hand as possible on the reins, trying to prevent truly dangerous behavior without squashing the spark of individuality. He had no intention of repeating his father's mistake.

He cast a glance down the side of the school, where the big playground equipment rose in complicated pipes and domes of red and yellow.

He was glad to see it was empty. Paradoxically, Alec was far less likely to get into trouble when he was alone. With the exception of Mrs. Biggars, most people provided Alec with inspiration, not supervision. Alec always somehow persuaded the others that his ridiculous schemes made sense.

"All right," Dallas conceded. "But no big ideas."

"Big ideas" was their code word for the times when Alec got inspired. Like deciding to see if his best friend's Doberman enjoyed catapulting off one end of the seesaw, or whether bees would eat store-bought honey if you placed it, bare-handed, in their hive.

Or if he could find his way to Bell River on his own.

"Dad," Alec said, frowning as if the very notion was unjust. "I'm not like...*five!*"

Smiling, Dallas stepped down out of the truck, but, just as he did, he saw two people coming through the main entrance to the school.

Alec hopped out, too. "There's Ms. Darren right now!"

Dallas looked, curious in spite of himself, after Mitch's extravagant praise. The woman was indeed pretty, and under her cute denim jumper with an apple embroidered on the front placket she was, as billed, nicely designed. Her blond hair lay straight and shiny on her slim shoulders. Her eyes were round and so blue he could see the color from ten yards away. Like robin's eggs in a nest of soft brown lashes.

The person with her was Bill Reeves, the security guard. Bill smiled a goodbye to Ms. Darren, then turned back and locked the door. Dallas noticed, as the teacher came toward them, that she carried her coat, purse and computer bag.

Going home. After forty-five minutes, she'd obviously given up on him.

At that moment, Ms. Darren spotted them. Her steps faltered briefly, and then, a polite teacher-smile on her face, she made her way to Dallas's truck.

"I'm sorry, Mr. Garwood." She tilted her watch, but didn't quite look at it. "I waited, but…"

"No, *I'm* sorry," Dallas said. "I got held up at work. And, as you see, I had to bring Alec. The babysitter is MIA."

"But I won't be in the way. I'm going to play on the jungle gym." Alec waved at them, then loped off toward the playground before Dallas could stop him.

Ms. Darren's smile hadn't changed, but her forehead furrowed. She was very young, Dallas realized. She'd taken over the fourth-grade class midyear, when Alec's regular teacher departed for maternity leave. He realized now she'd probably arrived with the ink still wet on her college diploma.

So…twenty-two or twenty-three? Not legally off-limits, but, given those doelike, worried blue eyes, emotionally still in the minor leagues.

What had Alec been thinking, imagining Dallas would want to date her? But he knew kids believed the world was divided into two categories, kid and grown-up. Anything over eighteen was grown-up, and fair game.

In many ways, he realized, Veronica Darren resembled his ex, Allyson. Same coloring, same innocent eyes and tremulous lips—except that Allyson had a core of steel under that face. The kind of steel that made it easy for her to walk away from her six-year-old son and never look back.

Maybe that's what Alec had hoped Ms. Darren's appeal might be. He missed his mother terribly and probably found the similarities comforting. He had no idea, of course, how little Dallas cared for that look now.

"I can't get back into the school tonight," she said. "Mr. Reeves has set the alarm. Maybe we can reschedule?"

"Sure." Inwardly, Dallas reviewed the upcoming days, but he didn't see any openings, at least not during her regular hours. Weekdays, nine to five, were pretty much on the clock for him. "How about a week from Thursday?"

She frowned, and he realized his mistake. School would be over very soon. If Alec really was failing math...

She glanced toward the playground. "There's a picnic table at the edge of the playground. We could sit there, and we'd still have some privacy. It's unorthodox, but—"

"That's great." Dallas felt guilty about keeping her so late. She'd drive home in the dark. Streaks of purple and gold had already begun to fill the western sky. But he hated the idea of trying to arrange a second meeting. Plus, her tone sounded genuinely troubled.

Just like all the other teachers.

Ever since Allyson and he divorced, he'd been to one meeting after another exactly like this. He knew, almost to the letter, how the script would go. She, Ms. Darren, was worried. Alec wasn't performing up to his academic potential. The Excel chart of his grades had too many empty slots where he hadn't turned something in.

And then the tentative toe dipped nervously

into the conversational deep end. She would say she understood Alec's mother had moved abroad, had a new family, rarely came back to Silverdell....

He sat on the picnic bench, the iron warm from the crazy summerlike weather, and faced the earnest young beauty with his friendliest expression. Maybe he could eliminate some of the preliminaries.

"Ms. Darren, I understand Alec's been slacking off, and isn't getting the grades he's capable of. You've probably noticed that he has trouble sitting still and focusing, but the doctor doesn't think it's ADHD. He concentrates fine when he's interested."

She nodded. "I've seen that. He does well in science, and of course in any learning with a kinetic component. But I'm concerned, because he seems—"

"The past couple of years have been tough for him." Might as well get this out in the open. Ms. Darren was so tentative that it might take her till dinner to find the courage to broach the domestic situation. "His mother and I divorced two years ago, and she moved to France with her new family. Alec misses her, of course, and it's going to take a long while for him to fully accept that his mother and I won't be getting back together again one day. I know he's unhappy—"

But Ms. Darren shook her head firmly. "No. That's the part that I wanted to talk about. I would have expected him to have some unresolved mother issues, but he doesn't seem unhappy. In fact, his friends tell me he's got big plans."

Dallas laughed. "Alec always has big plans."

"But these plans are very specific." She hesitated, touching her computer case with her fingertips, as if she hadn't decided whether to take out her paperwork, but wanted to be ready. "*Very* specific."

Over by the monkey bars, Alec was just a shadow swinging and a faint sound of make-believe war training, complete with exploding grenades. Typical Alec. No matter what the teachers told him, Dallas wasn't really worried about his son. Not in that deep, terrifying way he'd seen parents worry when he came to their houses late at night to tell them their sons were in jail, or in the hospital, or still missing.

Alec was angry and hurt, and he was still sorting things out. But he was essentially sound. He'd come through, in the end.

But Ms. Darren didn't know his son that

well yet. She couldn't be as certain that his core was solid. It was actually sweet of her to be so concerned about a boy she'd met only a month ago.

So he didn't brush off her anxiety. "Okay," he said. "Specific like what?"

"Well, he seems to think that he might be able…to…" She entwined her fingers. "To play matchmaker, I guess is the best way to put it. To find a…a girlfriend for you."

Oh, poor Veronica. She must be mortified. He'd like to throttle the kid for making his nonsense so obvious.

Dallas smiled. "Yeah, I've noticed. He's about as subtle as a bulldozer."

She drew another breath. "And, well, you see, I think maybe he—"

"I hope he hasn't been pestering you about it," he said, laughing as if it was all a good joke. "He's a nice kid, but he's an idiot. I think he's dreaming he'd get a more lenient report card from a teacher who was dating his dad. I told him that wasn't how teachers worked." He grinned. "Or dads."

She didn't respond, seeming to think that over. Finally her hands relaxed. "Oh." She chuckled. "Seems like a lot of effort. Most kids simply coax their dads into doing their math homework for them."

"Yeah, well, that's Alec. He never takes the easy way, if there's a more dramatic, more convoluted plan he could hatch instead."

She glanced toward the monkey bars, where Alec was hanging upside down, his knees hooked around the top rail. "He's... a classic. I really do like him a lot. But I'm going to have to talk to him about this."

Dallas smiled at her. Her concern for Alec was transparently genuine. "I'll talk to him, too."

"Thank you." She blushed slightly, unless it was the pink tones of the sunset suddenly highlighting her cheeks. "And please, call me Veronica."

"Veronica," he agreed, nodding. For a split second, he wished she was his type. It would be so simple to date a pleasant woman like this. She was traditional, soft-spoken and nurturing. It would be gentle and safe. It would be calm and predictable.

It would be dead-dog boring.

He pushed aside the sudden image of an untamed, green-eyed wild child flying her stallion across a bend in the roaring, spring-swollen Bell River, her hair streaming out behind her, as black as her horse's mane. "Chicken!" she'd shouted over her shoulder as his own horse had balked and refused to jump. "You'll never catch me now!"

Rowena Wright wasn't his type, either. She was complicated, rebellious, hot-tempered and dangerous.

There must be a woman who fell somewhere in between. Actually, he was hoping Fanny Bronson might be a good compromise. After Alec's nagging the other day, he'd invited Fanny out to dinner and a movie. She was sane and smart, and not bad to look at. So, though he wasn't exactly brimming with enthusiasm, she had seemed like a logical place to start.

"It's especially important that he understand, you see, because..." The hesitation was back in Veronica's voice.

Dallas forced himself to pay attention to the conversation. "Because...?"

"Well, I haven't told the students yet—I haven't really told anyone—but I've become engaged."

"Congratulations," he said. "That's terrific!"

And, for him, it really was. Surely even

Alec wouldn't continue to try to play cupid with a married woman.

Now, if only he could get Alec to lay off the *whole* idea. If only he could make him understand that a spark couldn't be concocted with a recipe, like an experiment in chemistry class. You couldn't simply say: take one hundred and five pounds of creamy skin, silky hair and dewy eyes. Add one lonely divorced guy. Mix until fire ignites and wedding bells ring.

That kind of fire had to come from within Dallas. And he just didn't feel it for pretty Miss Darren.

Or for anyone.

No. A cold trickle went down his spine. That last part was a lie.

The frustrating, self-destructive truth was that he did feel fire. So much fire it hurt like hell. But not for Veronica, with her sugary femininity. Nor for Fanny Bronson, with her active mind. And not for any of the other eligible females in Silverdell.

No, like a fool, he felt fire only for that unreliable, untamed wild child who had nearly killed him once.

Rowena.

He closed his eyes. God help him.

Rowena was the one woman who could never be more than a quick thrill and a long, slow regret for any man. The one woman who had no interest in roots, home or family. Perhaps it wasn't her fault. Maybe she'd just been hurt too often, damaged too much, to know how to love.

But whatever the reason, she was the one woman who would play with his heart—and, even worse, with Alec's—and then bolt in the night, without ever looking back.

Chapter Eleven

Alec sat on the window seat of the big bedroom at Bell River, chewing slowly on his last Tootsie Roll, trying to make it last. This was probably his best day ever.

First off, Uncle Mitch had brought him along when he went to Bell River to work, because Mrs. Biggars was still sick. Rowena hadn't minded a bit. She had found a bunch of chores for him to do, and she said she'd pay him, too.

For the first couple of hours, he'd filled water buckets and raked out a few stalls. Ranchers sure had a lot of work to do.

When he got a break, he played with the

newborn kittens in the barn, which was awesome. Then, for the past hour, he'd been upstairs in the old master bedroom, scraping crummy green-flowered wallpaper off the walls with a putty knife. That wasn't as much fun, because it was indoors and all alone, so he was taking a break.

The window seat looked out over the training circle, where Rowena had been training her awesome new horse. It was so cool, watching her drill Flash over and over, until the horse did exactly what she wanted. When Rowena let her run, and she cantered in and out of the tree shadows, her white legs moved up and down like magic—like the most beautiful horse on the most beautiful carousel ever.

He could sit here and watch forever. He swallowed his Tootsie Roll and felt a hum of happiness. Yep. The best day ever.

Actually, the good stuff had started this morning, when his dad announced that he had a date tonight. A real date. With a woman who didn't even work for him, and wasn't a cousin or anything.

"It's nothing serious," his father had said, turning a frown toward Alec when he accidentally did a fist pump of victory. "It's just dinner and a movie with an old friend. You remember Fanny Bronson?"

Alec's excitement had faded a little when he heard that. Fanny Bronson was not very *va-va-va-voom,* as Uncle Mitch put it. The way Alec put it was…well, she didn't have anything sparkly about her. Not her smile, or her hair or even the way she laughed. Plus, she always smelled musty like paper, because she owned the bookstore.

But maybe she was fun to talk to. If she'd read all those books, she might know interesting things. Or, heck, maybe Dad thought she looked good. You never knew what grownups liked.

The important thing was… Dad would be out on a real date! Step one of Alec's mission was in play. He put his arm up to his mouth, as if he wore a secret wristwatch walkie-talkie.

"Fort Base, this is Alpha Base. We've got a green light for Operation Freedom. Do you read me, Fort Base? That's a Go for Operation Freedom, at eighteen hundred hours."

"I read you, Alpha Base. Update, please, on Operation Wallpaper Purge?"

Alec glanced toward the doorway, where

Rowena had just appeared, her arm up to her mouth, too. He grinned. She was so darn cool.

He jumped down from the window seat and picked up his putty knife. "We've had a little problem with Operation Wallpaper Purge, Captain," he said, saluting. "It was necessary to take a short break due to..." He searched for something funny.

Rowena tilted her head. "Excessive boredom among the crew?"

"Sort of," he said, wondering if she'd be mad. He had finished only half of one wall. She might even refuse to pay him. Darn it. He had been counting on the money. He'd had to take a dollar out of his horse bank yesterday for his Tootsie Roll supply.

But she didn't seem mad. She had a glass of lemonade in her hand, and she offered it to him. It didn't go very well with a Tootsie Roll, but he took it anyway. It seemed pushy to ask for milk instead.

Then she sat on the edge of the big bed and arranged some colored pictures on the spread. They looked like pretty buildings and flowers and stuff, but he couldn't really tell.

"What do you think, Alec?" She stared at the pictures, her head tilted and her lower lip between her teeth. "Do you think this looks like a fun place to visit?"

He set his lemonade carefully on the footstool he'd been using and came closer so that he could see.

"Hey! That's Bell River Ranch! That's this house!" He looked at her, surprised. "I mean, it is, but it isn't, you know what I mean? There's more stuff in the picture, like that big sign, and cars, and lots of people. And the road is paved, see? It looks..." He didn't want to be rude, especially before he got his money. "It looks better."

"It sure does. And that's because our friend Bonnie turns out to be a fantastic artist." Rowena shook her head, as though the fact shocked her. "These are more than good. She has a very special talent." She moved the pictures around, studying them as if she had forgotten Alec was there. She murmured quietly, "What on earth is she doing *here?*"

Alec kept looking, too. He didn't like most pictures, but he liked these. He liked almost anything that was connected to Bell River. "Why did she draw them?"

"I asked her to. I'm thinking about making some changes at the ranch, and I wanted to see how they'd look."

Alec's stomach tightened. "Changes like what? Dad said you were going to sell it."

She leaned back against one of the carved wooden posters and folded her hands in her lap. "Well, probably I am." She glanced at the pictures again, and her eyes looked sad. "I'm really only dreaming."

He looked carefully at the big, pretty sign Bonnie had drawn by the front gates of her painting-ranch. Bell River Dude Ranch, it said.

"Oh, I get it," he said. "You're going to make Bell River a dude ranch. Like where people come to play cowboy and get away from their offices and wives and stuff."

"Yeah." Rowena smiled, as if he'd said something very funny.

Alec liked it when she smiled. It seemed to send out warm rays, like a stove. It made her look different...almost as pretty as Bonnie or Ms. Darren. And a heck of a lot prettier than Fanny Bronson.

He wondered if his dad had ever seen Rowena smile.

"Yeah, exactly like that," she said.

"That would be awesome!"

"It would." Her smile faded. "But it also would be expensive. I've been checking into some of the details, and everything I learn makes it seem crazier and crazier."

In just these few seconds, he had already begun to love the idea of Bell River as a dude ranch, and it made him mad to think it would never happen. He frowned, picturing his horse bank at home on his nightstand. He'd been so excited about putting new money in tonight. But suddenly that felt kind of selfish.

"I could work for nothing." He flushed, looking at the puny little rectangle of wall he'd finished so far. "I can do a lot better than this, really. I could have this whole room done in…" He looked at the high ceiling and considered. "Two days!"

"Don't be silly," she said. "If the ranch can't afford to pay for its workers, how would it stay in business?"

The logic of that didn't quite make sense, but he couldn't figure out how to argue without seeming fresh. Besides, another problem had just occurred to him.

"Yeah, but… I wonder if people would want to stay here anyhow," he said. "You know, because of all the stupid ghost stories and stuff. They might be scared."

She didn't deny it, and his heart felt very heavy. This was serious. She might be able to borrow money, but she couldn't do anything about the ghost problem.

"But wait!" He lifted his head, struck by a new idea. "Maybe you could make it a good thing instead! Some people might think it was exciting. They might come with their cameras and their cold-air detectors and pay you to lock them in here alone for the night!"

The minute he said it, he felt weird. Maybe it was rude to suggest using her dead mother to get customers.

But that was the good thing about Rowena. She never got mad about stupid stuff. She just chuckled.

"I don't think one guest per night would exactly pay the bills. But you're very nice to try to help, Alec. I appreciate it."

She looked back down at the pictures, but her index finger was tapping on the bedspread, as if her mind was a million miles away.

He went back to scraping wallpaper, working hard to remove every single ugly green flower. He wanted to make up for being lazy before. In his head, he pretended he was outside, digging up a garden of nasty green weeds. He concentrated so hard that he jerked a little when Rowena spoke again suddenly.

"Alec. How did you know what my mother looked like?"

He turned, feeling cold. "What?"

Her eyes were squinty, thinking it through. "That first day, when you thought I was her ghost. How did you know what she looked like? My father burned all the pictures of her before he went to jail. And you weren't even born when my mother died. So…how did you know?"

He lowered his putty knife and stalled a minute, using his fingernail to push off the gummy green paper attached to its straight edge.

Should he tell her about the box? Should he tell her about the pictures?

He didn't like to. He hadn't planned to ever tell anyone. In a way, the box and the pictures felt as if they belonged to him. He had decided that, if she ever really sold Bell River, he would come back in the night, pull the box out of its hiding place and take it home with him.

But when she said that thing about her father, he could hardly believe it. Her dad really burned all her mother's pictures? For a minute, he felt strangely adult, and he recognized how much that would hurt. Suppose his dad tried to erase all Alec's memories of his mom?

Suppose…suppose instead of getting a divorce, his dad had *killed* her?

He had a sudden surge of nausea, as if he might puke all over the hardwood floors. He clamped down real tight on his stomach and made the nausea go away. All that was left was a prickly new awareness that life could be a lot more horrible than anything he'd experienced yet.

And the certainty that the box and pictures did not belong to him. They belonged to Rowena.

"He didn't burn them all," he said quietly, staring down at his putty knife. "I found some, in a secret place."

She didn't freak out, but he sensed her whole body go stiff. She seemed to be waiting for him to explain, so he went ahead.

"Remember, I told you I used to come here when I was upset. Sometimes I'd hang out in the bedrooms. They're neat, and I would poke around." He stuck out his jaw. "I never broke anything, or made a mess. I only liked to look."

"That's okay," she said. "Just tell me about the pictures."

"Well, in the pink bedroom, there's a bookcase. You can't tell anything's strange when it's full of books, and you probably can't tell at all unless you're really exploring. But one of the pieces of wood behind the bookcase is loose. You can take it out, and there's a little secret space back there."

"And there were pictures of my mother in that secret space?"

He stood, feeling suddenly very important. "Not were. *Are*. You don't think I would move them, do you?" That felt like a lie, since he had planned to take them if she sold the ranch, so he frowned. "Not unless I had to, that is. So they're still there. Do you want to see them?"

She nodded, and stood, too. "You bet I do," she said. "Lead the way."

The pink bedroom still had a twin bed and some other furniture, but the bookcase was empty, so it was easy to pry the special board loose and pull out the little metal box. It fit in his hand perfectly, about as big as his pencil box at school. He figured it used to be silver, because you could see yourself in shiny spots here and there. But almost every inch of it was gray and black and ugly, as if something had grown on the metal.

He pulled it out carefully and offered it to Rowena, even though he would really have liked to open it himself and show it to her. But he wasn't sure she was even breathing, so he simply handed it over.

She plopped onto the little twin bed without looking, as if she weren't quite aware of her own movements. He stood close as she lifted the hinged lid and began to take out the items inside.

The first thing her fingers found was a gold chain, with a small gold medal hanging from it. Still as shiny as anything his mother owned. There were two of those chains in the box. He wondered if they might be superold and worth a lot of money. That would be awesome. Maybe Rowena could sell them to start the dude ranch.

But the way she looked at the medal, and wrapped her fist around it, and then put the fist against her shirt, as if something hurt... He didn't know what the medal was, but he was pretty darned sure she didn't intend to sell it.

He flushed when he spied an old Tootsie Roll wrapper, crunched up and stuck to the side of the box. It felt like an accusing finger, pointing right at him. But accusing him of what? He hadn't taken anything out of that box, except to look at it and imagine stories about it.

There were only four pictures, but every one of them had her mother in it. Her mother dressed in ski clothes, on the side of a mountain, smiling, her hair flying everywhere, as if she'd been dancing in the snow. And then her mother lying on her side by a fire, in a green, slippery-looking robe that was almost as pretty as the things his mom wore.

In the other two, her mother stood with a man. The man was tall and he wore ski clothes, too.

Rowena didn't say anything for a long time. He began to wonder whether she was disappointed that there were so few. Maybe she had been imagining hundreds. He scuffed at the floor with his sneaker, feeling as if he'd failed her. But that made him kind of cranky, because it wasn't his fault there were only four.

"Oh, my God." Rowena's voice was husky and rough, like a whisper that held back something intense. "Oh, my God."

He frowned at her. He had no idea what she was upset about. He wedged himself closer, between the foot of the bed and her knee, so that he could see.

But he couldn't see anything. Not anything upsetting, anyhow. She was holding the photo with the picture side down. Somebody had written a few words on the back, but the words weren't exciting or scary or anything. It didn't say like, "The treasure is buried beneath the barn" or "It was Miss Scarlet in the library with the wrench."

It just said, *Rowan, Bryce Canyon*, and then a date—*November third, 1982*. That was...well, it was a long, long time ago. He wasn't good enough at math to be sure *how* long ago, but at least twenty-five years. No... He tried to do the subtraction exactly, but he had to carry and borrow, and he was bad at that.

More than twenty-five, though, for sure. Ancient history. He'd never even heard of anybody named Rowan, anyhow.

"What's wrong?" He peered into Rowena's face, which had gone pale. "It's only a picture, and nothing bad is happening in it. They look nice, and really happy. Aren't you glad to find it?"

She took a breath, then rustled the pictures back into a stack and set them into the dirty box. "Yes. Of course I am. It's just..."

She shook her head, and rested the palm

of her hand over the box. "It's a little over-whelming. I think I'll look at them more later, when I'm not so busy."

Well, that was a big letdown. Alec tried not to feel disappointed, but he did. He had hoped she would be all excited and happy, and she'd tell him how smart he'd been to find them.

"Okay," he said, kind of huffy. Maybe the pictures were of *her* mom, and technically everything in here was *her* stuff, but she never would have found them without him.

She seemed to recognize that he was upset, but she didn't seem to know what to do about it. She kept running her hands through her hair, and taking deep breaths, and looking around the room as though she'd never seen it before.

"How about we quit for the day and..." Her eyes darted, as if looking for inspiration. "And go get some ice cream!"

Alec felt like saying no. He felt like sulking. He wasn't a baby who could be insulted, then bought off with ice cream.

However... He looked at the big grandfather clock that stood at the landing at the top of the stairs. It was 6:00 p.m. Right about now, his dad and Fanny Bronson would be sitting down at the Silverdell Grille. The Grille was the nicest restaurant in town, with tables in little bay windows that looked out onto Elk Avenue.

And it was right next door to the ice-cream store.

"Okay," he said, careful not to let his new big idea show. "Ice cream would be pretty nice."

Chapter Twelve

The heat wave must have created a craving for ice cream among the Dellians this week, because by the time Rowena found a parking space on the crowded downtown streets, Sweethearts was packed.

Alec insisted on sitting outside, on a sidewalk bench, instead of at the cute soda fountain or heart-shaped tables inside the ice-cream store. He said it was too loud in there to talk to each other, which was true.

But outside wasn't much better. The bench Alec chose perched almost directly in front of the Silverdell Grille, with its colored lights strung across the awnings. It, too, was booked to overflowing capacity tonight. Music and chatter billowed out of the restaurant like smoke, so Rowena and Alec mostly just sat quietly and worked on their cones.

Actually, silence suited Rowena fine. She didn't quite trust herself to make small talk. The minute she had looked at those photos, a weird tingling had begun inside her, and it hadn't gone away yet. Though she told herself to stop obsessing about the pictures until she had time alone to sort out what they meant, her brain kept cycling through the same unanswerable questions....

Why had her mother hidden the photographs? It must have been her mother, and obviously her father had never found them, or they'd have been charred to ashes with the rest of the photo albums.

And, most importantly, who was Rowan? Though his ski clothes and cap didn't reveal many details, he had looked lean, tall, athletic, dark-haired and handsome. How had her mother met him? Why had she never mentioned him? What was his last name?

Had he taken those two pictures of her mother? If so, he must have known her... intimately. The picture of Moira by the fire emanated an intense sensuality, as if the photographer had used the camera to caress her outstretched body. And she clearly had been in a happy phase, because her curves were graceful and feminine, with none of the angular tension of her half-starved depressions.

But the other picture, the one on the mountain, had been even more disturbing, somehow. In that photo, her mother's joy practically sizzled off the paper. She was vivacious, uninhibited, glowing. Even on her happiest days at Bell River, Moira Wright had never, ever looked like that.

If this mysterious Rowan had taken those pictures, he had been her mother's lover. Rowena knew it without doubt, just as she knew that today was Friday. And if they were lovers…the fact opened up a whole new, unsettling cluster of questions.

Rowan.

Rowena.

Only a child wouldn't notice the similarity—and she hoped that Alec was still young enough to have missed it. But what did it mean? Was it merely a coincidence? Or was it perhaps a nostalgic indulgence…a secret nod to a past lover that Johnny Wright had never suspected?

Or….

November third, 1982.

Rowena's birthday was July 11, 1983. She had never been pregnant, and she had no idea how to calculate the exact distance between conception and delivery, but she knew how to count to nine. And November to July was close enough to make her blood itch nervously in her veins.

"Rowena, you're letting it drip all down your hand!"

Alec's shocked voice brought her back to the present. She became once again aware of the restaurant's singer covering an old, sad Patsy Cline song, the balmy evening breeze tugging at her ponytail, and the butter pecan ice cream running in cool, sticky beige tracks from her fingers to her wrist.

"Drat." She swiped with her napkin, but that didn't help much. Oh, good grief, it was on her jeans, too. Groaning, she twisted her wrist toward her mouth and began licking furiously. "Can you go get us some extra napkins, Alec?"

"Sure." He jumped to his feet, but immediately froze in his tracks. "Wait. Look! It's my dad!"

No way. She scanned the crowded sidewalk, letting the ice cream do what it wanted. She could *not* be this unlucky.

Alec laughed. "Wow. What a surprise, huh?"

She glanced quickly over at him, alerted by the phoniness in his voice. The pretend shock on his face confirmed it. This wasn't a piece of bad luck. This was a staged encounter.

"Well played, Garwood," she muttered under her breath. But she lifted one corner of her mouth when she said it, because she wasn't really angry. Embarrassment had never killed anyone. Besides, it hardly qualified as a sin for a boy to want to see his father.

"Alec?" Dallas's expression of shock was the real thing. She wished she could turn to Alec and say, *see?* That's what you look like if you're *really* surprised.

"Dad! Hey! How was your dinner?" Alec was as innocent and eager as a puppy. "I didn't remember you'd be here. Rowena brought me to get some ice cream!"

Dallas's eyes narrowed, but he didn't scold—perhaps because, right behind him, Fanny Bronson came waltzing out of the restaurant, resting her hand on Dallas's back.

In the past fifteen years, Fanny had grown up, of course. She used to be a scrawny teenager, but she had all the curves she needed now. And a red silk dress so glam it probably didn't see much action here in Silverdell, the headquarters of jeans and flannel shirts.

"Hi, Dallas," Rowena said, waving her ice-cream-striped hand. She wasn't sure that he'd yet registered the fact that Alec was with *her,* not Mitch. Dallas looked nice, but nowhere nearly as decked out as Fanny. Of course, he didn't need to be. Fancy accoutrements would only distract from the main event, which was his face...or maybe his body....

Stop it. What was wrong with her? She was the one woman who *didn't* drool over Dallas, remember?

She turned toward the other woman. "Hi, Fanny."

"Rowena!" Fanny's face lit up, and she lunged over for a spontaneous hug. Rowena kept her hands out to the side, not wanting to smear butter pecan all over the red silk. But she was too shocked to react fast enough anyhow. "I was so happy to hear you were back in town!"

She was? Rowena wasn't sure how to respond to this. She was still a little foggy from the emotional jolt of seeing her mother's secret pictures.

"It's good to see you, too." Rowena smiled politely, but she wouldn't go any further than that white lie.

"Why are you with Rowena, Alec?" Dallas stood under a strand of colored lights. It cast a blue glow over his face and hair—and it made him look like a movie star.

Rowena's midsection pinched, and she removed her gaze. But wow. No wonder Fanny had wrapped her slim fingers around his jacket sleeve so tightly.

"Mitch brought Alec with him when he showed up for work," Rowena explained so that Alec wouldn't have to. "Then, when we decided we wanted ice cream, Mitch couldn't get free. When I left, he and Bonnie were waist deep in hay."

Dallas's left eyebrow went up. "Really. Is that as compromising as it sounds?"

Fanny laughed, a musical sound that was quite lovely, but somehow made Rowena feel hot and irritable inside. The comment wasn't *that* funny. Obviously he was just being snide, because he didn't approve of Mitch taking the job, and he didn't approve of Mitch's interest in Bonnie, either.

But too bad. Mitch was a grown man, and if he didn't want to go to college, his big brother couldn't exactly slap him in chains and drag him to class.

"No," she answered crisply. "It's not social hour. It's very hard work. We got a ton of hay delivered this afternoon, and they are trying to get it distributed and stored."

"A ton?" His gaze sharpened. "Surely not just for your new paint alone. Does that mean you're taking in other horses?"

She nodded, though she wished she didn't have to explain this in front of Fanny, who would undoubtedly share it with everyone who stopped into the bookstore tomorrow.

"I'll be doing some training while I'm here. Just a couple of horses, in addition to my own. Only short-term programs, of course."

"Of course." Fanny beamed. "We hear you're selling Bell River, as soon as the market improves."

"No, she's not!" Alec spoke with a mouth full of ice cream, but each outraged word was easily understood. "She's going to turn it into a dude ranch."

Oh, no.

Rowena groaned inside. She should have known better than to show Bonnie's drawings to anyone, least of all a kid like Alec.

He never stopped talking, and his imagination had a tendency to run away with him.

"No, I'm not," she said before Dallas and Fanny could give voice to the amazement already on their faces. "It's a silly idea I toyed with long ago." She turned to Dallas's son. "It wasn't serious, Alec. It's just…make-believe. I told you that."

He scowled hard, as if her words were a slap in the face, and she realized he'd let himself believe it could be real. In his imagination, he'd already seen the ranch remodeled, thriving, with all those happy guests unloading their suitcases from Bonnie's painted cars.

He probably had fantasized that he would work there, too. Maybe he thought he could be a trail guide. She'd certainly seen herself that way, when she was about his age. She had been sure she was perfect for the job. She knew every secret curve in the stream, every tree that attracted hawks, every cliff that overlooked a magical expanse of wildflowers and deer. She had loved the thought of showing those splendors to the guests.

She suddenly realized something else. Alec just might love Bell River as much as she did.

Poor kid.

He hadn't stopped frowning. "It's *not*

make-believe! You said you'd do it if you had enough money."

She hadn't said that, exactly, but close enough. Alec wasn't lying, and he wasn't trying to make her appear foolish. He was merely repeating what he had understood her to say.

"I don't think I explained the situation well enough," she said to Alec calmly. "We can talk about it later, though, okay? We don't want to interrupt your dad's time with Fanny."

He glanced at his father, then at Fanny, who bestowed an enormous smile on him, apparently acting on the theory that a single father would prefer deeply maternal women.

Alec didn't look impressed. After a brief hesitation, he offered Fanny an equally over-the-top smile in return. It was almost like a dare. *Call me on my phony smile, and I'll call you on yours.*

Rowena smothered a chuckle. Yep. She really liked this bratty kid.

Fanny wisely decided to ignore Alec. She lifted her face to Dallas and squeezed his arm playfully. "Dallas, we probably should get going. The movie…"

Dallas was staring at Rowena with a blank expression she found unnerving. What was he thinking behind those unrevealing eyes? Was he still angry about Mitch? Was he upset about Alec ending up at the ranch this afternoon?

The gaze lasted only a couple of seconds, but it felt longer. When he finally turned his attention to his date, Rowena felt her heart slow down, as if it had been released from a prolonged, painful captivity.

"You're right," he said to Fanny. "We'll be late." He gave Alec a hard look. "You get back to your uncle, and stop bothering Rowena."

"I'm not bothering—"

Some meaningful flicker must have passed across Dallas's face, because Alec didn't finish the sentence. He deflated, caught in a sickly yellow glow cast by the nearest overhead light. He suddenly seemed only about half the size he had been a minute ago.

"Okay, Dad."

They exchanged polite goodbyes, and then Dallas and Fanny left.

Against her better judgment, Rowena let herself watch them go. Were they headed to his truck? Or did he have a car he used for special occasions like this? Would Fanny nestle herself against him on soft leather bench seats? Would he put his arm around her silky shoulder?

Would they even make it to the movie? Fanny's house was probably on the way. She'd probably cleaned it up extra nice, just in case she could lure him in.

At the thought, Rowena's chest tightened, as if she were angry. Or hurt.

"I hope you guys have fun," Alec called. But when Dallas turned with a cryptic smile, Rowena knew she was hoping for something entirely different.

She wanted their evening to be a world-class bust. Boring. Disappointing. One they'd have no desire to repeat.

She frowned, hearing the ugly voice inside. That was mighty spiteful, even for her. Did she really hate Fanny that much? Of course not. She didn't give a darn anymore what kind of snob Fanny had been in high school. All that had happened a million moons ago.

So where was this childish nastiness coming from? Would she care if any other woman were walking by Dallas's side? Suppose it was Penny? Or Bonnie? Or his ex-wife?

Oh, hell. She shut her eyes in disbelief. Whoever it was, Rowena would feel exactly the same way. Petty, fussy, irrationally antagonistic.

There was a word for this feeling. And the word was…

Jealous.

Four hours later, shortly after eleven-thirty, Dallas pulled his truck through the open gates of Bell River. As he bumped up the moonlit dirt drive, he made a deal with himself. If he saw evidence that Rowena was still awake, he'd knock. If darkness and quiet loomed over the ranch, he'd turn around and go home.

Home—where his son and his brother were sleeping. *He hoped.* Home, where, if he were in his right mind, he would already be doing the same.

Instead, the minute he'd been able to politely deposit Fanny back at her house—only three blocks from his own—he'd made a U-turn and headed out onto the open highway.

He pulled around the back of the main house, guided by instinct mostly. The Wright women had never spent much time in the front rooms. The kitchen, with its adjoining breakfast nook and family room, were the heart of their activities.

It was at the table in that breakfast nook

where he'd given Rowena calculus lessons. He couldn't say he "taught" her...because she hadn't learned a lick of calculus, not in the whole three months.

Sure enough, when he reached the back drive, lights streamed through half the first-floor windows. Without allowing himself to overthink it, he killed the truck's engine and emerged into the night.

He took about three steps, and then a teasing drawl rose out of the shadows of the back porch. "Well, howdy, Sheriff. I didn't expect to see you again tonight."

He squinted, letting his eyes adjust to the bright windows so that he could find her. Gradually, the dimly lit veranda swam into focus, and he realized she was curled up on the porch swing.

He *had* come too late. She was clearly ready for bed. She wore a long flannel nightshirt, with a dark sweater over it, and some fuzzy kind of slippers. Her hair looked damp, as if she'd recently showered—a deduction confirmed by the hint of violet-scented shampoo that wafted toward him on the cool night breeze.

"Mitch just rehung the swing today," she

said, dropping her legs to make room beside her. "Want to come help me christen it?"

Under the studied playfulness, her words carried a challenge. Was he going to mention Mitch and the job?

But Dallas didn't argue lost causes. Her hiring Mitch was a done deal. Being surly about it wouldn't change anything. He would have to count on Mitch getting bored by real labor. Frankly, Dallas would put money on that happening sooner rather than later.

So he simply smiled. "Mitch hung the swing himself? Then not a chance."

"Oh, it's safe enough, I promise." She rocked the swing gently with her slippered foot, setting up a pleasant, rhythmic creaking. "Come on up and tell me what brings you out in the middle of the night. Is it Alec? Or has Esther Fillmore accused me of some new and titillating wickedness?"

He had approached as far as the bottom step, but he waited there. She was in a sardonic mood. He remembered those. They usually meant she was unhappy about something, and they almost always had led to some rebellious behavior—as they had the other night, when she showed him the kittens in the barn.

And as it had so many nights in their long-lost past.

"No," he said calmly. "It's not Esther. I'm here because I was hoping we could talk."

The creaking stilled, then resumed its regular pace. "Talk about what?"

"About us. About the things that happened fifteen years ago. You and me…your dad…"

"To what end?" She sounded more bored than flustered. "It was so long ago. And, given that I'll be here only a little while…"

"It's not as if we can just avoid each other, Rowena, even for a few weeks. Bell River acts like a magnet on Alec. And Bonnie seems to have the same effect on Mitch. It's a small town, and we'll run into each other. Maybe it would be easier if we talked it out. Tried to make some sense of it all."

Creak…creak… She kept swinging, but didn't speak for several seconds. When she finally did, her voice had abandoned some of its brittle affectations.

"All right," she said, pushing her wet hair behind her shoulders. "I doubt that it's possible to make *sense* of it, but I can see you might still have questions."

Oh, yeah. He had questions.

"Please, though. Come up here so we can

talk quietly." She touched the seat beside her. "I think Bonnie's asleep, but…"

He climbed the steps, most of which squeaked under his weight. Just one of a thousand repairs she'd have to make. He joined her on the swing, glancing up toward the hooks, calculating the odds that Mitch had, for once, done his work carefully.

For a minute or two, they sat without speaking—as if they each had to adjust to the sudden intimacy.

He didn't look at her. Instead, he took in the feel of Bell River. The night was clear and cool, with a fresh wind that picked up nearby scents and floated them across the porch in perfumed waves.

He inhaled deeply, the odors triggering memories of other early-summer nights here. He smelled the mountains, of course, and the riot of wildflowers, invisible in the darkness. Rowena's new hay still filled the air with grassy sweetness, and her stables gave off the sharp scent of new paint.

More subtly, he could smell the dark sugar of red roses. Moira Wright used to grow climbing roses all around the porch, and a blossom or two must have survived. And then…somewhere more distant, the distinctive orange scent of a patch of wild bergamot.

"Bell River really is a beautiful piece of land," he said. He wasn't trying to open a conversation about her plans. He was stating a fact.

"Yes. I hope that'll help sell it."

He tried to imagine Bell River Ranch belonging to other people. It would be good for Silverdell in general, he supposed. A deteriorating property going vacant half the time was an invitation for vagrants, vandals and hormone-crazed teens to come on in and brew some trouble.

But how would Rowena feel, when she could never return here? Would it hurt to realize she would never play hopscotch on the river rocks again, or gallop her horse across the flower-starred grass? He suspected that something inside her would shrivel when the connection was severed.

"You know, if you had any serious interest in opening a dude ranch here, I have a buddy who could give you some terrific firsthand advice."

"No, really, Alec had it wrong." She pulled her sweater tight. "It was a wild idea—a whim. I don't know anything about business, and, as Bree loves to point out, I am the least domestic person on the planet."

All probably true. But those didn't seem like deal breakers.

"I don't know," he said casually. "Might be more important to understand horses, and the land, and what makes people fall in love with the West. Nobody beats you at that."

She almost smiled, acknowledging that he meant it as a compliment. "Maybe. But it might also help to be able to cook some eggs and toast in the morning, so that the guests don't starve to death before they can pay the bill."

He shrugged. He knew better than to argue with her. Unless she'd changed a lot, the more pressure she felt, the more stubborn she turned. Dallas had once owned a horse like that. If you gave him a long lead, he would follow you anywhere. Pull in tight, and he'd dig his heels in so hard that a bulldozer couldn't move him.

"Well, obviously it's your decision. I just wanted to say that my friend Barton James used to own a dude ranch over in Crested Butte. He's retired now, but he'd be thrilled to pass along some tips."

"Thanks, but I don't think so. This really

is only a silly dream, and I wouldn't want to waste his time."

"He's retired, remember? He's got more time than he knows what to do with. And he loves to talk about it. He could answer any questions you have about—"

"Speaking of questions, didn't you say you have some?" She angled herself to face him, not seeming to notice that the position brought her knee right up against his thigh.

He noticed. "Yes."

"All right, then. Fire away."

He let the other conversation go without a struggle. He had said enough about Barton for the time being. And to tell the truth, he wasn't sure why he wanted to encourage this idea. His life would be a heck of a lot simpler if Bell River got sold to some nice grandma-grandpa team who were eager to babysit one nine-year-old troublemaker.

Besides, he'd waited a long time for this chance, and he didn't want to lose it. "Okay. I guess the first, or at least the biggest, question about what happened back then is...*why?*"

She frowned, as if confused. "Why did Johnny shoot you?"

"No. I think I get that. He caught me with his sixteen-year-old daughter, half-naked in the bed of my truck. Now that I have a kid myself, I understand fatherhood better than I used to. He went a little crazy."

She smiled coldly. "A *little* crazy?"

"Well, I hear he said he didn't intend to hit me. Apparently he just wanted to scare me."

She raised one eyebrow, signifying her skepticism, but she didn't argue. "So…what is your question, then? Why what?"

He shifted his leg, so that he didn't have to deal with the distracting awareness of her warm knee against his thigh. "Why did you set out to seduce me?"

She affected a small chuckle, as if the question amused her. But at the same time she pulled the edges of her sweater more tightly around her, and threaded her arms together on top of that. Maybe he should tell her how many suspects he'd interviewed who used that same defensive body language.

"That sounds like false modesty, Dallas." She tilted her head. "Be honest. From the day you hit puberty till…oh, let's say right up to and including *tonight*…have you ever met a female who *didn't* try to seduce you?"

"That's not the point." He wasn't going to be led down that path. "It was different with you."

"How?"

He considered his answer. The distinction was subtle, but deep. He'd spent far too many hours trying to put his finger on it.

From the moment he'd stepped into her kitchen that first night, she'd been entirely focused on trying to bewitch him. She played one-sided footsie under the table, her slim bare feet sometimes rubbing his thigh, and sometimes inching higher, until he didn't dare stand up, for fear her mother would see how helplessly turned on he was.

Other times, she'd sit across the table, eating succulent fruit in ways that constituted a primer course on oral sex. Same rushing heat in his groin, same tortured swelling in his jeans. And how it had amused her! She'd looked at him as if he were a lab specimen, curious about his reactions to various stimuli, triumphant when he behaved precisely as prompted.

He'd never felt so powerless in his life. He had hated it, and he'd been sure he hated her. At the end of every session, he swore he'd quit the job. But he couldn't do it. Like a moth hypnotized by the flame, he couldn't force himself to stay away.

And every night he dreamed the same helplessly vivid dream. They were in her kitchen. He was explaining conic sections in polar co-ordinates. And, then, with an evil smile, she would put down her much-abused banana and take him into her mouth instead.

He'd dreamed that dream for years after she left. Even after he got married. At the beginning, Allyson had been delighted when he woke up before dawn, hard and hungry, trying to transfer the fire to his wife, where it belonged. Later, when things went sour between them, he resorted to getting up and jogging the tension away.

"I think the main difference," he said, a little colder for remembering his humiliation, "is that you didn't like me."

A pause. "Well, that's blunt."

"Yes."

She shrugged. "Even if it's true, liking someone and being attracted to them don't always go hand in hand."

"Don't do that." He put his hand over her arm, forcing her to look at him straight on.

Her flesh was cool, her muscles rigid under his touch. "Do what?"

"Adopt shallow cynicism to avoid a real conversation. You know what I'm talking about. When you set out to become my lover, it didn't have anything to do with sexual attraction. You believe I've been chased by a million women? Well, at least give me credit for knowing the difference between a woman who wants me, and a woman who wants... something else."

She tried to meet his gaze boldly. But after a few seconds, she blinked, and gazed down at her hands. He thought perhaps her cheekbones burned a little pink.

"So what was it, Rowena? What did you really want? Was it a dare? A joke? Were you simply trying to make your father angry? Did you deliberately engineer our getting 'caught'?"

He waited.

Finally, she sighed. "No. I didn't stage that," she said, meeting his gaze again. "I swear. I knew he was crazy. And even if you think I'd risk your life, he could just as easily have shot me, too."

He'd have to take her word for it. She was the only remaining living person who could possibly know. The last thing he remembered from that night was pressing himself into her, and feeling the resistance that told him he was her first lover. He'd called out her name, and bent to kiss her, waiting for the pain to subside. He might have been the "good boy," but she was the only virgin in that truck. He'd been around enough to know he couldn't rush things.

He lifted his head, straining for control, and when he opened his eyes he saw her father stalking toward them, emitting a noise that sounded bestial, like a rabid dog. He was already less than ten yards away, and closing fast.

"Rowena," Dallas had choked out somehow. But it was too late. The moonlight glinted off the metal of Johnny Wright's rifle as he raised it. He pointed it toward Dallas.

With his last split second, he glanced down at her. She lay motionless beneath him, her shirt unbuttoned, her miniskirt hiked up over her hips. She stared up at him with dark, unreadable eyes. Tears glistened at their corners, and dripped silently into her hair.

Then he heard a loud noise, and he was aware of nothing but throbbing red silence. He woke up, three days later, in the hospital, with a bandage over his left eye.

Why had she been crying? Had he hurt her? Or was she anxious, emotional, maybe even a little guilty, as she waited for her father to explode?

He'd asked himself that question for years. He hadn't really thought she wanted him shot, or killed…but it did seem possible that she might have used him as a pawn in a larger game, whose one objective was to infuriate her father.

For some crazy reason, Dallas believed her now, when she swore she hadn't. It was a relief to finally get an answer.

However, she hadn't addressed the other half of the question. If it wasn't about her father, why *had* she decided to do her snake-charmer routine on Dallas in the first place?

"Okay," he said neutrally. "You didn't have a plan to get caught. So…"

She took a breath, and opened her lips.

But a loud rustling over by the stables interrupted whatever answer she'd planned to give.

They both turned toward the sound. Her horses whinnied, obviously alarmed. A human voice whispered loudly, hissing words he couldn't understand. And then someone giggled.

It wasn't an animal, then. It wasn't the wind. And it wasn't their imagination.

Someone was out there, watching.

Chapter Thirteen

"Wait here."

Dallas stood, and he took the porch stairs with as little noise as their age would allow. He crossed the patchy grass, going right through the defunct vegetable garden because it was the most direct route, and made it to the far side of the barn in less than a minute.

But even that was too long. Whoever had been there was gone, alerted by his footsteps, or by the squealing stairs. He heard the thudding of feet, and the echo of teenage laughter, over by the horse paddock, but it was too dark to make out details. He listened until the running sound grew faint, then faded away completely.

He turned back to the barn, and was relieved to see that no new message had been painted there. So...what had the intruders come here for? He scanned the ground quickly, and spotted a backpack tilted against the far wall. He picked it up, opened the top zipper and dug around, looking for identification.

Couldn't be that lucky, of course. But he did get his answer to the question of why they'd been on the property. The backpack was heavy, distended with their evening's supplies. He pulled it all out, tossing it on the ground. Six cans of beer, six foil packages of toaster pastries. A candle and some matches. A travel-sized Ouija board.

Cute. Get drunk and groggy on junk food. Then commune with the dead.

Apparently they'd planned dessert, as well. The side pocket, the one that usually held a water bottle, was full of condoms. So they'd get drunk and then have sex till they passed out, probably with the candle still lit. They wouldn't wake up till the stable caught on fire.

Brilliant. He swept the Ouija board aside

with the toe of his shoe, frustrated that the fools had gotten away. They could have used a scare.

"What is all that?"

He glanced up. Rowena had come to the edge of the barn, and stared down at the junk he'd found.

"It was just a couple of teenagers," he said, stuffing the condoms away, though he suspected she'd already seen them.

"Amateur ghost hunters," she said bitterly. She came toward the small pile of supplies and bent over, picking up one corner of the Ouija board. *"God."*

She dropped the board, then straightened, and once more whipped the edges of her sweater together angrily.

She lifted her chin, and suddenly a moonbeam caught on a tear glistening just under her eyes. "They actually think that if my mother could come back from the dead, if she could speak to someone, she'd waste a single second on morons like them?"

Her voice broke slightly, a helpless sound he'd never heard come from her lips.

He dropped the backpack and reached out to grab her shoulders. "Rowena, they're just kids." He smiled, trying to urge her to take it lightly, too. "Kids do stupid things. We know that all too well, right?"

She didn't resist his touch, but stood there, limply letting him hold her.

"They don't understand how it makes you feel." He ducked his head, trying to see her face. "Teenagers are selfish that way. They only think about what they want."

"Yes. I know," she said, her voice low and without expression.

Then she lifted her head, and for a long minute she gazed at him, a thin pencil line of a frown between her eyes. He waited, hoping she'd say more. It would do her good to talk it out.

But when she spoke, she seemed to have moved to something else entirely.

"Dallas, I want to tell you something."

He nodded. "Of course. Anything."

She swallowed hard enough for the movement of her throat to be visible even here in the shadows. Then she inhaled deeply and set her shoulders, as if she were preparing to move a boulder, or run a marathon.

"You asked me why I tried to seduce you, and I want to tell you, if I can." She met his gaze, and her eyes glittered, more black than green in the watery moonlight. "This isn't easy for me to talk about. Not if I'm trying to be…honest. But you deserve to know. You could have died that night, and you deserve to understand why."

"Okay." Then he waited, surprised by the frank, unaffected tone of her words. It was as if the sardonic mask had slipped a bit, giving him a glimpse of something entirely new beneath.

"Okay," she echoed. "So here goes. You said, a minute ago, that I didn't even like you back then. Well, you were right. In fact, it was worse than that. I *hated* you."

A small spasm ran through his nerves, as if she'd hit him. But he didn't let go of her shoulders. He could feel them trembling, and for some reason that mattered more than his wounded pride.

"Why?" He kept the question simple and nonaccusatory.

She glanced to the side for a moment, as if she were searching her mind for the right answer.

"I know how this sounds. So petty. But the simple truth is that I hated you because everyone else thought you were wonderful. Because everyone loved you. It made me feel like—something under your shoe."

He pressed his hands tighter. "That's ridiculous. I didn't—"

"Please. Let me tell it, before I lose my nerve. It may be ridiculous, but it's how I felt. You see, I had no idea how to be wonderful, no idea how to make people love me. All I knew how to do was be shocking. And I knew... I knew how to make boys want me."

Oh, yes. She had wielded that weapon like a master.

"It's strange." She seemed to gaze into the middle distance, just beyond his ear. "When I remember it now, it seems like another person who did all those things. But at the time it felt logical—and even justified, like straightening the scales a bit. I wanted to prove that you weren't so perfect. That all those people who called you a saint were wrong."

"They *were*."

"I had this idea that you needed to be taken down a peg. I hated the thought that you were always up there on your pedestal, looking down on me."

He hardly knew how to respond. When he'd asked for an explanation, he had never expected such unflinching candor. When had the proud, defiant young wildcat turned into a mature woman who could see herself with such brutal clarity?

In his memories, he'd always envisioned Rowena as a tiger, a mountain witch, a sexual sorceress. But now...

In this silly mismatched outfit, with her face washed in moonlight and her damp hair streaming messily down her back, she wasn't any of those things. Over the past couple of weeks, the extreme hollows in her face had filled out a little—and her new, softer contours contributed to this...this new woman before him.

She looked ten years younger. And a hundred thousand times more vulnerable.

Suddenly, with a lightning bolt of insight, he saw the truth she must always have been trying to hide with that abrasive bravado. Rowena Wright wasn't tough. She wasn't predatory or cruel or oversexed, or any kind of dangerous female archetype.

When stripped down to the base metal, she was a lonely, confused little girl. Fragile, lacking in self-worth and easily wounded.

Without even realizing it, he had hurt her back then, simply by being so different. Or at least *seeming* so different. She wouldn't have known about his father, and how being a "good" boy wasn't a choice Dallas made, but one that was forced upon him.

"Rowena. I'm—"

He wanted to say he was sorry, but what good would that do now? And so, instead, he pulled her in, and bent his head. His gut wanted something deeper than words, anyhow. He wanted the feel of her mouth against his. Her heartbeat against his.

He'd never forgotten how her heart had felt that night. Faster than his, and so powerful it seemed to vibrate against the pearly-white flesh of her breast. The heart of a tiger, he'd thought—aroused by the thought of making love to the wildcat. Arrogant and shallow as he was, he'd never once considered the truth.

Her heart had beat faster than his because she was more frightened.

When he touched his lips to her neck, he caught the faint scent of violets he'd noted earlier. Musky and sweet, barely teasing at his awareness, here for a split second, then instantly gone, as if he had imagined it.

Her throat was warm, and her pulse skittered at the edge of her jaw. He followed it up to her cheek, and then to her lips. He hovered there a second, stretching the sweet agony of anticipation. And then he descended with a low groan and covered her mouth with his.

For a heartbeat, she did nothing. But as the kiss went on, and heat gathered where their lips met, she softened, and slowly opened for him. Driven by a primitive need, he found the moist, darker honey inside, and savored that, too.

She lifted her hands to his shoulders and clung, as if his kiss somehow sapped her of the strength to stand alone. He pulled her closer, and, when she was pressed into him, her breasts hot against his chest, her pelvis tightly fitted around the swollen place between his legs, he groaned again.

A hunger he had pretended didn't exist came roaring out of his soul. He'd waited fifteen years to feel like this again. All that time, he'd searched for a substitute. He'd moved through a dozen lovers, and, like a fool, he'd taken a wife, thinking that might satisfy some deeper need. He'd even conceived a child, and for a while, in that paternal glow, he'd convinced himself that fatherhood was enough.

But this piece of him, the part that held poetry and fire, primal urges and physical bliss, had simply gone missing. He'd begun to reconcile himself to the loss. And yet, with one kiss and a whisper of violets, Rowena had brought the vanished piece back home.

On fire, he tunneled his hands into her wet, tangled hair and moved his lips down her throat again. He traced the line of her collarbone, and then, pushing away the sweater with his hungry mouth, he moved lower, to where the soft swell of her breasts rose and fell with rapid, shallow urgency.

Without hands, he couldn't find his way inside the nightshirt, so he nuzzled the pebbled tip of her breast blindly, from the outside. He took it between his lips and worked it hungrily, until the cotton was wet and hot, driving him mad. He ached to touch that puckered rosebud with his tongue, and feel it grow harder, tighter, more sensitive. He wanted to know that she was craving this as much as he was.

They should go inside…if he could make it that far. The fire between his legs was so painful the brush of denim across his skin felt like a knife. Did she keep a cot in the stable?

Before he could speak, she made a small, unhappy sound, and her grip on his shoulders suddenly changed. Instead of kneading her fingers into his muscles, she began to press outward with the heels of her hand.

Not violently, but firmly. The pressure meant *stop*.

Somehow he obeyed. It took all his willpower, but he lifted his head, the night air rushing in cold against his wet, raw lips. "What's wrong?"

"Nothing," she said, the word almost a whisper. "It's just that—I don't... I don't do this anymore."

He frowned. "Do what?"

"Have one-night stands."

He hadn't let go of her head. His fingers still were buried in her long, black hair. "You didn't do it back then, either," he said flatly. "We didn't get very far, but we got far enough."

"Far enough for what?"

"For me to see that you were a virgin. So don't tell me it was something you did all the time, Rowena. It wasn't. It was something about us, about the way we made each other feel. And we still do. You can't look at me and tell me you aren't feeling it right now."

She stared at him for several seconds, and he wondered if she would try to deny it. But then, without speaking, she turned her head, signaling that she wanted to be released.

He freed her, of course, with a half-numb

frustration. He let his hands drop lifelessly to his side.

Taking a step back, she lifted her chin. "I guess what I meant was... I don't have casual, short-term sex. The fact that you and I share a past doesn't mean anything. I don't take lovers with whom I have no chance of a future."

He kept his face immobile. "And we have no chance of a future because..." He stretched out the last word, making it a question.

For a minute, he thought she might laugh. "You're really asking? It would take the whole night to list all the reasons. But the simplest one, and the most powerful, can be expressed in five words."

"And they are?"

She wrapped her sweater around her moistened nightshirt. When she spoke the five words, she enunciated each one clearly. "I'm leaving in three weeks."

Monday the roofers finally got started. Thank heaven! Rowena was so tired of watching the weather report anxiously every night, fingers crossed that the sunshine would hold. Bonnie, too, was ecstatic, and sang out loud as she gathered all the emergency buckets positioned strategically around the house and stored them away.

To celebrate, Mitch brought chicken-salad sandwiches and lemonade when he arrived around noon. He set the goodies on the island. Today's chore, while the roofers pounded overhead, was to sort through the dozens of dusty boxes they'd lugged out of the attic to protect them from the leaks.

He seemed to be alone, which surprised her.

"No Alec today?"

Mitch shook his head, and Rowena felt an unexpected twinge of disappointment.

After last Friday's visit, the one that ended in the ice-cream fiasco, Mitch had brought Alec the next two days, both Saturday and Sunday. Apparently the Garwood nanny— a woman named Mrs. Biggars, who clearly wasn't Alec's favorite person—was still laid low by a nasty flu.

"Is Mrs. Biggars all better?"

Mitch shrugged. "Nope. She's still out, but Dallas took a day off so he could watch Alec. He said I've imposed on Bell River enough." He raised his eyebrows. "*Bell River.* That means you. You should see the knots he'll twist himself into, just to avoid saying your name."

She busied herself digging around in the bag of sandwiches, laying them on paper plates. She wasn't willing to meet his gaze yet.

Mitch was always trying to ferret out some info on where things stood between Dallas and Rowena, but she didn't intend to tell him anything about Friday night. She gathered that he didn't even know Dallas had been out to Bell River after his date with Fanny.

Maybe, like Rowena, Dallas had spent the whole weekend trying not to think about it.

"You're not imposing," she said. "You know we love having Alec here."

That was the polite answer. But it was also the truth.

"Well, we'll get twice as much done, if no one has to be assigned as guardian."

That was probably true. One of the three adults had to watch Alec at all times. No telling when the boy might shoot himself with the staple gun, or wear the new curtains as a matador's cape.

She smiled. "Yeah, but we'll have half as much fun."

Bonnie had been in the kitchen filling tumblers with ice, and she came out now, holding all three between her hands.

She paused by the island, clearly surprised to see Mitch alone, too. She obviously hadn't been listening to them talk.

"No Alec?"

Mitch shook his head again. "Hey, *I'm* here. Doesn't anyone care about that?"

"Not really," Bonnie responded with a smile. "I have some disgusting chores on my list today. I was planning to surrender reluctantly when Alec begged me to let him do them instead."

Mitch chuckled, but Bonnie glared at him. "Don't laugh. I'll probably end up making *you* do them."

Rowena had planned to skip lunch so that she could start on the boxes while Mitch and Bonnie took a breather. But the sandwiches looked so delicious, with fat green lettuce curling out of the edges. Bonnie had started to hum an old folk song as she poured out the lemonade, which sparkled like something magical in the light from the newly polished breakfast nook windows.

It was too tempting. Rowena compromised by dragging one of the smaller boxes over to the breakfast nook. She could nibble a little and work at the same time.

"I'm thinking of selling some sketches at the wildflower festival," Bonnie said after they'd chewed in appreciative silence awhile. Her tone was diffident, as if she were asking their permission, and she toyed nervously with the slab of dill pickle rather than look up.

"Oh, yeah. You definitely should!" Mitch offered his endorsement before the words were even fully out of Bonnie's mouth. If Bonnie had said she was thinking of putting sawdust in the lemonade, he probably would have agreed just as enthusiastically. But in this case, Rowena concurred. Bonnie's art talent was extraordinary, and Rowena had seen some of the wildflower sketches. They were gorgeous.

Bonnie would make more money in one day, selling those at the festival, than she would make in a month of domestic drudgery at Bell River.

"Would you like to see them?" Bonnie turned to Rowena self-consciously. "If you think we can spare the time, that is…"

"Of course we can. I have to look through these boxes on my own, mostly, anyhow. I'll get started while you show Mitch."

Bonnie bounded from her chair and dashed for the foyer. In a second, they heard her light footsteps tapping up the stairs. She'd been using the old playroom as a studio, though she still slept in the manager's apartments, as if she still needed the privacy.

Rowena took another bite of the wonderful sandwich, then picked up the box she'd brought over and began peeling off the tape.

"Rowena." Mitch leaned very close, and kept his voice low. "I've been hoping to get a chance to ask you. Do you know—I mean, has Bonnie told you anything about...about where she came from?"

Rowena shook her head. "Nothing. She clearly doesn't want to talk about it, and I don't like to pry." She pulled the top item out of the box, a book about fertilizers. *Charity box*. "So she hasn't told you, either?"

Mitch shook his head, his face slack and dejected. "Have you seen her hair?"

It should have been a strange question, but Rowena knew exactly what he meant. In the past week or so, Bonnie's hair had grown enough for the roots to offer a clear look at her natural hair color. It was an extraordinarily beautiful, shining color that had no easy name. Kind of like strawberry satin, fretted with gold.

"Yes. It's fabulous. Like something out of a fairy tale."

"Right. And she's obviously been to good schools." Mitch held up a hand, ticking off Bonnie's virtues. "She is refined—hell, she's twice as refined as I am. And she's rich, you know, the way you can tell with women. Their hands, their skin, their teeth. She's like one of those kids who split their teen years between cheerleading camp and etiquette class."

Rowena was surprised that Mitch was so observant, and so intuitive. It was only very recently, when Bonnie's fingernails had begun to dry out from being immersed in cleaning fluids, that Rowena had consciously registered how beautifully manicured they'd been when she arrived.

Of course, Mitch stared at every inch of Bonnie about a thousand times more often than Rowena did.

"So why leave all that pampering?" Mitch's voice dropped to an urgent whisper. "It couldn't have been anything trivial. She's young, I mean really young. But she's no drama queen. She's got a good head on her shoulders. I think she would have stayed, unless it was something…"

He screwed up his mouth, as if he didn't want to utter the words. "Something really bad."

Rowena picked up the next item in the box without even quite seeing it. She knew, of course, what kind of "bad" was haunting him. She had asked herself this same question so many times, and run through the same nightmare scenarios.

But now, as she witnessed his protective misery, a new question presented itself.

Almost without question, Bonnie had run away once. Was anyone chasing? If so, when would she feel the need to run again?

And what would it do to this sweet man who was falling in love with her?

Unable to bear looking at Mitch's troubled face any longer, she glanced down at the item she held, recognizing it for the first time. It was her father's pipe. An old bulldog pipe, with a huge rusty-brown bowl and a straight black stem.

He loved that pipe. Rowena could hear him now. "Where the hell did you put my bulldog, Moira?" She never could understand how he could possibly lose it, since she could hardly remember him ever taking it out of his mouth. He smoked a bowlful of tobacco every night, on the back porch. But all day long he walked around with the unlit bulldog clamped between his teeth, chewing on it the way some farmers chewed on a straw of oat.

Someone, probably her great-aunt Ruth, had packed this stuff away in a rush, because she'd wadded all Johnny's smoking things together in a towel. A tin of tobacco. His ashtray, coated with ancient white dust. His pipe stand, which looked like a little wooden cradle.

Even the bent, tarry pipe cleaner he'd used to clean the pipe after a smoke was in there. Rowena remembered with an internal shiver how he would wet the pipe cleaner with his saliva, then slide it in and out of the stem to remove the nasty gunk that apparently collected there.

Absently she ran her fingers over the mouthpiece, tracing the pits and grooves. And then she realized what those grooves were— a hundred tiny imprints of her father's teeth, which had made a pocked mess of the ebonite.

Shuddering, she dropped the pipe back into the box with a clatter. It felt almost too intimate to be holding it. And yet, as she stared at the dirty, ugly thing...

An idea formed.

Her father's saliva. Her father's teeth.

Was there a chance some of his DNA had survived on this pipe?

Was it possible that, if she sent these items to a lab, she could get some answers to the questions that were driving her insane?

Was she Johnny Wright's true daughter? Or was she the unacknowledged child of her young mother's athletic, outdoorsy lover, the mysterious, black-haired Rowan?

Which answer was right? Even more confusing, which answer did she *want* to be right? If she was a bastard child, foisted on Johnny Wright without his consent, what implications would that have?

The good news would be that her father hadn't killed her mother. True, she would be illegitimate. She would be the daughter of an irresponsible philanderer who probably had ditched the responsibilities of paternity.

But she would not be the daughter of a murderer.

On the other hand...if she wasn't Rowena Wright, her entire past, and all her memories, became a lie. Her famous "connection" to Bell River Ranch became a fraud. Her mother became…someone she hardly knew.

Her sisters became half sisters.

She felt suddenly dizzy, as if the floor had tilted under her feet.

"Rowena, did you hear me?" Mitch sounded frustrated, as if he'd been trying to get her attention.

She shook her head apologetically. "I'm sorry. What?"

"I asked whether you thought Bonnie—"

Mitch broke off abruptly as Bonnie danced back into the room, her arms loaded with the small canvases she'd been painting this week. The vivid pinks, purples, blues and yellows of Colorado wildflowers peeked out from the unframed, hastily stacked boards.

"Oh, please don't set the price on the larkspurs too high," Rowena said to fill Mitch's silence— and cover her own discomfort. "I want that one, and, as you know all too well, I'm stone broke."

Bonnie flushed, uncomfortable with compliments, but Rowena could tell she was pleased. She started standing the canvases up along the walls of the nook, explaining to Mitch which part of Bell River each one represented.

"And these are the goldeneye that grow over by Little Bell Falls. Have you seen them? They grow all the way down to the water's edge, and the yellow glows like a field of gold coins!"

While Bonnie chattered, and Mitch gazed, mouth open, obviously entranced, Rowena carefully folded the flaps of the box that held the pipe and then quietly slid it under the table. She didn't want them to ask about the contents. She couldn't talk about this to anyone yet.

She had to be careful. She'd need some time to think it over. To calculate what move she should make next. If any.

Her stomach felt slightly sour, and a mallet had begun pounding against her temples. She might need a *lot* of time.

Because, now that the truth might be within her grasp, she suddenly wasn't sure she wanted to know.

Chapter Fourteen

The sky above Little Bell Falls was draining daylight quickly, and Rowena knew she ought to head back to the house. But, hypnotized by the movement of the small but exquisite horsetail falls, she remained comfortably perched at the edge of the deep blue plunge pool.

Behind her, Flash whinnied softly.

"I know. We'll leave in a minute," she said. But when she turned, Flash had returned to grazing contentedly.

"Or two," Rowena added with a smile. "Or three."

The two of them, horse and owner, were

sharing a lovely harmony today. She'd trained Marybelle first thing in the morning. Ordinarily, after that, she worked on her own horse. But Flash had settled in so well that Rowena felt free to take the day off.

They'd spent the afternoon riding the Bell River property, visiting Rowena's favorite spots, all of which were fairly remote.

The actual Bell River ran diagonally through the property, but curved in a deep semicircle about halfway through—a shape that really did, from the air, look remarkably like a big, glittery silver bell.

The house, the stables and paddocks, the rings and other main outbuildings all nestled inside the big, protective skirt of the bell. That was where the Wrights had held their parties, trained their horses, taken their walks and cultivated their flowers and vegetables.

But for Rowena, the really cool stuff lay beyond the bell. She loved it out here, where her father buried their pets, and allowed downed trees to rot where they toppled.

Out here, disorganized streams burbled over rocks, appearing out of nowhere and disappearing into nothing. Jagged outcroppings thrust from the hillside like ancient faces, and gigantic trees linked branches to shut out the sun.

She had spent most of her free time here—on what she loved to call "the wrong side of the river."

On this cool early-June afternoon, though, it really didn't look like the wrong side anymore. Wildflowers in all colors of the rainbow carpeted the woods and fields, and the trees were green and alive with birdsong.

Funny, wasn't it? Her parents had tried so hard to tame the land. But all the carefully tended roses and topiary plants within the bell had withered away after the gardeners and landscapers had departed.

While out here everything flourished. Nature took care of her own.

In fact... She gazed around. This might be a great spot for an extra dude ranch facility—like an arts and crafts pavilion. Or a weekly campfire sing-along and cookout.

Or even, as long as she was dreaming, a small day spa, where guests could get a massage while they watched the falls through a picture window.

She closed her eyes, trying to stop the images from coming. She was thinking too grand. Any dude ranch they put here would have to be a small, bare-bones operation for a long, long time.

Bree and Penny didn't even know she was exploring the idea. And, depending on the results of the DNA tests she'd sent off to a nearby lab, she might never tell them.

She still wasn't sure she wanted to know the answer, but she'd mailed the samples—everything she could find that might have Johnny's DNA on it, including the heavily chewed pipe—yesterday. In about a week, she'd have the results.

Then, interrupting her thoughts, two things happened at almost exactly the same moment—Flash backed up, neighing nervously, and Rowena's nostrils were filled with a familiar scent. It was as if the air had suddenly turned cooler, sharply earthy, and moist.

She glanced up. Thunderheads crawled across the mountaintops. A storm was headed her way—and fast. It was still five miles or so out, but both she and Flash knew they had dawdled too long.

Sure enough, a minute or two before they reached the safety of the stable, the raindrops began to patter the top of her head. They fell lightly at first, then abruptly swelled to a downpour. Within seconds, it drenched her clothes, and cold water pooled on her lips and chin, and in her eyelashes.

Just as they got to the stable, the eastern sky flashed blue-white, and a thunderclap followed. A major lightning strike. And far too close for comfort.

Amazingly, Flash didn't react. Delighted, Rowena leaned over and stroked the horse's wet, silky neck.

"Good girl," she said warmly. "Good girl. We'll get you dry, sweetheart."

She slid off, and led the horse inside. They stopped first to say hello to Marybelle, and ensure that the other mare wasn't spooked by the storm.

"You okay, kiddo?" Rowena stroked Marybelle's forehead and gave her a kiss, but she could tell the mare was fine. She looked a little sleepy, actually, her big black eyes gleaming but slightly unfocused.

With the clouds blocking the remaining slivers of daylight, the stables were dim, with black shadows in the corners. Power had always been a problem out here. New wiring was part of this year's repair plan, but in the meantime Rowena had installed some solar fixtures in the stables.

Unfortunately, today had been overcast,

and hadn't offered enough sun to create more than a ghostly yellow glow here and there.

Still, she knew these stables by heart, and she had no trouble finding her way around as she removed the tack from Flash, and got ready to dry her off before shutting her in for the night.

It was one thing to let a wet horse roam an open paddock, walking herself dry. It was much more uncomfortable and unsafe for a horse to be stabled wet—and stay that way. She needed the polar blanket to wick the moisture away.

Rowena peered around. Where had she stored the hay wisp? Nothing got a horse dry faster—and it would bring a lovely gloss to Flash's coat, too.

She'd probably put it in the tack room, which, though small, had lots of useful shelving and drawers. She picked up the saddle and carried it with her. She remembered gratefully that she'd left a lantern in the tack room. The thunder made the walls rumble, and the lightning created strange bursts of brightness that made the stable look downright haunted.

She wasn't the nervous type. Still, a little light would be nice.

She'd just draped the saddle over its peg

when she heard a shuffling noise in the doorway behind her.

"Bonnie?" Without turning around, she moved to the shelves where she kept the polar blankets. That was the logical place to have put the wisp.

Ah, there it was. Now to find the lantern.

But the skin on the back of her neck prickled as she remembered that Bonnie hadn't ever responded.

"Mitch?"

She turned, holding the wisp up instinctively, before her conscious brain could remind her it was only made of hay and wouldn't bat away anything bigger than a horsefly.

Her breath caught as lightning sent a strobe of brightness through the room. Skinny, weird Farley Miller was inexplicably there, in the room, mere inches away from her, way too close for any kind of natural interaction.

"Well, hey there, pretty lady," he said, and laughed with a wide grin, sending a wave of liquor-sour air over her. His hair was soaked, and his sweater was plastered to his bony body.

And that breath… Lord, he was falling-down drunk, and apparently feeling amorous.

She considered simply lashing him across the nose with the wisp now, then discussing it later. Maybe, if she got enough air under it, she could raise at least a rope burn.

But he was already eyeing the wisp and starting to chuckle. "Ooh, look at that!" He steepled his fingers together under his chin, as if in prayer. "Don't hurt me, honey, *please!*"

Creep. She refused to flinch, although his breath...*wow.*

"What are you doing here, Farley?"

He grinned, which made his beady eyes look almost impossibly small. "Nothing yet," he said in a low tone he probably thought was seductive. "Want to help me fix that?"

"Sorry." She didn't smile, didn't blink. "I have to dry off my horse. She's wet."

"Oh, yeah? What's wrong with that?" Wiggling eyebrows. "I like wet."

Disgusting lecher. Rowena rolled her eyes, more annoyed than alarmed. She'd found herself in scenarios like this before. Such behavior rarely had anything to do with true sexual attraction. It was mostly cowboys bullying females to make themselves feel tough. They usually shriveled up and slithered away when she acted tougher.

She decided to take a maternal tone with

Farley—he undoubtedly had mother issues, and maybe it would subtly remind him that he'd just been a kid when she knew him last.

"Shame on you, Farley. I'd think a real man would have more self-respect than to talk garbage like that. Even drunk. Even you."

It was a good try. Unfortunately, turned out he wasn't one of the simple bullies after all. His hard eyes flashed with rage, and instead of shrinking he seemed to puff up and grow larger. He moved another few inches closer.

Aw, shoot. What now? Ignoring the way her heart had begun to race, she stepped backward. However, the darn room was so small. That particular maneuver wouldn't work for long. Mentally, without letting her gaze signal her thoughts, she did a survey of the items nearby.

Okay. Her mind settled on a plan. It wasn't much of one, but it was better than nothing. She should keep backing up. If she could reach the wall without triggering his suspicions, she might be able to grab one of the unused tack hooks hanging there.

A good swipe across the face with that, and he'd be singing a different tune.

"Come on, honey." He reached out and fingered her wet hair. "Why don't you play nice?

Give me a little kiss, and we'll see where it goes from there."

Not in this lifetime.

Two steps toward the wall. She put her hands behind her back. She hoped he would assume she was trying not to touch him. *Little weasel.* He'd probably seen revulsion in a woman plenty of times.

"Not a chance," she said, still cold, still holding his gaze with hers, as if she were hypnotizing him. With her middle finger, she had just located the tip of a tack hook. She hoped it would pull free easily. "Call me picky, but slimy toads aren't really my type."

"You bitch. Not your *type?*"

His face flushed. Good. She wanted him angry. Emotional people didn't think very clearly—so he was less likely to notice her hands working behind her back.

"Your type is anything with two legs and a—"

"Slimy, *drunken* toads are even less appealing," she said.

His eyes narrowed to slits. "You know what you are. You're the same as your mother. You want it, and you owe it to me. Why don't you just give it up, nice and easy, so we don't have to do it the hard way?"

She grimaced and tilted her head back. The motion closed the distance between her fingers and the wall. Her fingers wrapped themselves around the cool metal hook. It jiggled easily, and she knew it would come free without resistance.

Darn it, though. She didn't want to hit him. Not because he didn't deserve it, the slimy pervert, but because she dreaded providing the Dellians with another juicy Wright family sex scandal to gossip about.

"Come on, Rowena." Her apparent uncertainty emboldened him, and he leaned forward. He clumsily pressed both his palms against her wet shirt, and she felt her stomach spasm, pushing lunch toward her throat. She rocked the hook, trying to free it, but her legs had started to tremble, and her fingers were going numb.

Come on. You're not going to panic over this weasel. It's actually a pretty ridiculous situation.

Think about it. If word got out that first Dallas got shot and then this jerk got impaled on a tack hook, she'd never get another date as long as she lived.

"Come on, Rowena. It'll be fun. Why won't you—"

She narrowed her eyes. "Because, as I told you, Farley..." The hook was free. She swiveled it into her right hand for better leverage, and spoke with slow ferocity, every word its own sentence. "I. Need. To. Dry. My. Horse."

He frowned, but she didn't wait for a reaction. She ducked sideways, away from his grasp. At the same time she swung her right hand around in a hard, fast, looping arc. She squeezed her eyes shut at the last minute and said a quick prayer that she didn't kill him.

To her horror, although she put the force of her entire body behind the swing, the weapon connected with nothing but air. She nearly unbalanced herself, and the hook slammed awkwardly against the back wall.

She opened her eyes, bewildered. But what she saw was even more confusing.

Farley was no longer in front of her. He stood about two feet away, on tiptoe, held up by his shirt collar, which was...

She blinked. Which was clutched in Dallas Garwood's hand.

Farley's eyes popped, and he made strange snuffling noises, like a terrified rabbit snagged by a hunter.

She couldn't, for a minute, make sense of any of it. She sagged to a squatting position, her back against the tack room wall. Her legs didn't feel right.

"But... I didn't call for help," she said irrationally, as if Dallas's very presence challenged her courage, or her competence. "I had this under control."

"Yes. Of course. Absolutely you did." Dallas smiled. "Sorry to interfere. But I *am* the sheriff, and you *were* about to kill a man."

He glanced down at Farley. "Not that he doesn't deserve it."

She let the tack hook clatter onto the floor, because her hands were suddenly too weak to hold it, and stared at him. She had a feeling adrenaline was scrambling her brain.

"But...why are you here?" No, that was wrong, too. It sounded ungrateful, and she wasn't. She was stupidly grateful, actually. Throw her arms around him and weep grateful. She needed to keep a grip on...all that.

"I mean, how did you know that I needed... That Farley...?"

"I didn't." Dallas was utterly poised, holding Farley at arm's length as if posing for a picture with a big fish he'd just reeled in. "I'm here because my friend Barton James was eager to meet you. You remember Barton? I told you about him, and about his dude ranch up in Crested Butte."

He glanced over his shoulder, into the shadows of the stable. "Barton? You still there?"

Rowena really didn't have the strength to stand up, much less protest, even though she had a dim feeling that the already-mad situation had just grown impossibly bizarre.

All she could do was watch numbly as a very tall man—taller even than Dallas—with a handsome head of silver hair and a Gregory Peck face walked up to the doorway and grinned at her over Dallas's shoulder.

"Hi, there, Miss Wright," the stranger said in a mellifluous baritone. "I won't come in, because it seems a mite crowded. But I would like to talk to you about your dude ranch plans, when you have a minute. I think maybe I can help. In lots of ways."

"Oh, really?" She wasn't sure how to react, but being upright seemed like the bare minimum for courtesy. She forced herself to her feet, and dusted her jeans off smartly, in hopes that it made her look more alert and aware. "What ways?"

He didn't seem fazed by the direct approach.

"Well, advice, of course." He raised his

eyebrows and smiled sheepishly. "And, if I do say so myself, I am likely the best cowboy poet and singer west of the Mississippi."

"What the f—?" Farley made a strangled, disbelieving noise, and wriggled indignantly, though he failed to free himself from Dallas's grip.

"I'd audition for you now," the cowboy poet continued humbly, lifting his hand to show that he'd brought a guitar with him. "Except I'm sort of guessing this isn't a real good time."

Isn't a real good time...

She glanced at Dallas, whose blue eyes danced. He pressed his lips together so tightly she knew he was holding back hilarity.

Suddenly everything was simply too much, and she felt an involuntary laughter of her own, rising like champagne bubbles from her belly. From beginning to end, this whole situation was beyond surreal.

First Farley...and the feel of the hook in her hands.

Then Dallas...and her childish impulse to throw herself onto his chest and faint there, dead away.

And now...a job application from a stranger

who wanted to work for a dude ranch that didn't exist.

All at once, her laughter escaped, soft but uncontrollable. She tucked her head to her breast and felt her shoulders shake.

The dude ranch of her childhood dreams had no name, no cabins or guest rooms, no amenities, no programs, no employees or guests or money. But apparently it had the one thing she'd never thought of, even when she was ten.

It had the best cowboy poet west of the Mississippi.

Chapter Fifteen

The next morning, Rowena woke up tired and on edge. Definitely not in the mood to handle Marybelle. And yet, the lesson was on the roster, and Rowena never let her mood interfere with the training schedule.

Still, yesterday's deluge had left the training ring muddy and slow. Could she maybe postpone it an hour or two...?

Then she turned her head into the pillow and groaned. *Drat.* She'd invited Tina Blakeley to sit in on today's training. *That* was bad news. Communicating with horses wasn't ever really a strain, even when she was exhausted. People were harder.

A brisk shower helped, as did the first cup of coffee and one of Bonnie's amazing oatmeal parfaits.

Rowena noticed that her jeans were no longer as loose as they'd been a couple of weeks ago.

But when she looked in the mirror, her face was still pale, and her eyes shadowed. She hadn't slept but a couple of hours last night, and it showed.

After the fracas with Farley, Dallas had taken the creep down to the sheriff's department and booked him for trespassing. But, at Dallas's suggestion, Barton James had stayed behind to talk to Rowena.

Obviously, Dallas thought she needed a babysitter. She considered getting huffy and sending the old man away, simply to prove she didn't.

When she started walking back from the stables to the house, though, she realized her legs were still rubbery, and she dreaded the thought of sitting in the huge, silent rooms alone, trying not to think about Farley's groping hands.

So she made a cup of coffee for Barton, and a cup of hot honeyed tea for herself. They each took one of the big, tacky Barcaloungers in the great room, and settled down to talk.

And boy, did he know how to talk! He seemed to take it for granted that Bell River Ranch would someday become a dude ranch, and he waved away all her careful warnings about how, right now, the idea was nothing more than a pipe dream.

Dallas had been right about the old man. Barton possessed a gold mine of good advice. Plus, he was a born storyteller. He shared wonderful anecdotes about his own dude ranch and spun such beautiful, believable descriptions of what could be done here at Bell River that Rowena lost track of time.

At some point, Bonnie and Mitch got home from their movie and joined the conversation—and were equally swept away. Before they knew it, the grandfather clock in the foyer was chiming 1:00 a.m., and Mitch took Barton back home.

Rowena lay awake for at least another hour, turning over the new, intriguing ideas. Like turning the attic into small guest rooms, or inviting some of the Silverdell experts on local history, or wildlife, or flora and fauna, to give lectures to the guests.

She couldn't help being fascinated, though

she knew it was foolish to dwell on those tantalizing details. She already knew, from even the most preliminary research, that the project would take about ten times as much money as the three sisters possessed. Bell River Dude Ranch would never exist outside Rowena's own head.

However, Tina Blakeley's horse did exist in the real world, and so did the paycheck Rowena would earn for training it. So she finished the coffee, rinsed the cup and went out to face the day.

When Rowena reached the stables, Tina was standing at Marybelle's stall, stroking the horse's neck.

"Sorry—I just miss her so much." Tina shot Rowena an apologetic smile. "Plus, I came early because I wanted to talk for a minute before the lesson starts." Tina gave Marybelle one last pat, then joined Rowena as she gathered up the mare's tack.

"What about?"

"About the wildflower festival. I'm the chair this year."

Rowena groaned. "Ooh, sorry about that," she said with a smile. She could imagine what a headache that job must be. The two-day event was the biggest thing that happened in Silverdell all year. Everything from the bake-off to the music choices ended up causing controversy.

"It's going all right…so far," Tina said. "Esther Fillmore and Joanna Madison can't agree on anything, of course. They *both* want to sell flower garlands for the girls' hair. But I've scheduled them at booths at least five hundred yards apart, so I'm optimistic that we'll all make it out of this alive."

Rowena laughed. "I don't remember Joanna Madison. But Esther Fillmore would start an argument with a rock, if she couldn't find anybody else, so I'm not surprised."

Tina sighed, nodding. "Oh, you must remember Joanna. Used to be Joanna Truewood? She married Jimmy Madison. It was their daughter, Mabel, who fell into the show ring the other day."

"Oh, okay. I was glad to hear she's doing fine." Rowena did remember Joanna Truewood, of course. Head cheerleader, spoiled rotten. Her family owned Tall Trees Ranch, the biggest spread for about a hundred miles. *She* had married Jimmy Madison, the geeky, disheveled president of the chess club?

Guess that proved it. The labels you wore in high school didn't stick with you forever.

"So anyhow, I know you probably don't want to get embroiled in all the local nonsense," Tina went on, "but I am desperate to find someone to handle the pony rides."

Rowena put the saddle over her shoulder and led the way to Marybelle's stall. "I don't know. I'd be happy to help out, but Esther doesn't exactly approve of my being here at all. And she may not be the only one. I wouldn't want to make things worse."

Tina's smile could have lit the whole stables. "Oh, thank you! You'll be perfect for it. It's from noon to six, both days. Can you handle that many hours?"

Rowena stroked Marybelle's glossy side, then lay the saddle pad over her back. "You probably should think this over, Tina. As I said, I'd love to help, but I'm not exactly the most popular resident of Silverdell. Half the town thinks I'm as mad as my dad, and the other half thinks I'm gutter trash, like my mother. You sure they'll put their kids in my care?"

"Of course they will." Tina put her hand on Rowena's arm. "Really. You're wrong about what they think, Rowena. Well, I can't vouch for Esther, of course, but there are a lot of people in this town who would like to see you happy. After everything you've gone through—"

Rowena turned away, breaking the contact before it could become too uncomfortable. Tina didn't know her well enough to realize that this wouldn't help. The idea that a bunch of self-satisfied Dellians were sitting around pitying her was even worse than the idea that they were despising her.

"Well, I'll be there if you want me," she said. "But for now, I want you to watch how I put the saddle on Marybelle, okay? Never drop it on her with a thud. She should learn that taking the saddle is normal and comfortable, nothing to worry about."

Tina, who obviously adored her horse, instantly focused on Marybelle. Relieved to return to a subject she understood, Rowena demonstrated some of the changes she'd made in the horse's routine.

Tina caught on quickly, and after a few minutes Rowena decided to let her do the riding. She stood to the side, by the paddock rails, and made small suggestions whenever Marybelle started to balk.

"Marybelle's a pretty horse," a voice said from somewhere around Rowena's knees. "But not as pretty as Flashdancer."

She looked down. Alec squatted beside her, just outside the paddock. His hands looped around the fence, and his head poked through the rails for a better view. His black cowboy hat dangled down his back, the stampede strings knotted at his neck. He was a mess. Crescents of dirt rimmed his fingernails, and bits of hay sprinkled across his thicket of rumpled blond hair.

"How did you get here?" She kept her gaze on Marybelle. "And why do you look as if you've been wrestling a hay bale?"

"Uncle Mitch brought me. He's over there talking to Bonnie, but he'd better stop pretty soon, because we're going swimming."

"Oh, yeah? Isn't this a school day?"

"I had a stomachache this morning," Alec said. "Uncle Mitch said I could stay home."

Rowena raised one eyebrow, and Alec flushed.

"Yeah. Well, it went away. I'm all better now. And swimming isn't as hard as school, anyhow."

Rowena managed not to laugh. "I see. So where will you swim?"

"The hole at the bottom of Little Bell Falls," he said blithely, reaching up to pick the hay out of his hair but not offering any explanations for its presence. "It's cold as the devil in there, but you get used to it."

She smiled. "Yes. I know."

He looked up guiltily. "Oh. Right. Uncle Mitch said we had to ask you if it was okay first. Sorry. I keep forgetting this place is yours."

"It's okay," she said, chuckling. "It's not as if you can use it up. Just be careful. It's deeper than it looks."

"Yes. I know," he said, echoing her words with a smile. He watched Tina and Marybelle for a while, and when he spoke again, he was onto another subject entirely. "I saw a horse that is so awesome. It's a Welsh mountain pony. It's exactly what I always wanted. And it was selling for cheap. I've got almost that much saved up already."

"Oh, yeah?" Rowena was only half listening. She noticed that Tina was still holding the reins too tightly. They'd have to practice that. "Are you going to buy it?"

Alec stood, adjusting his jeans so that they fit more neatly into his boots, and then dusting off his knees. He plucked another piece of straw out of his hair and chewed on it, not answering.

"Hello?" She tousled his hair. "Alpha Base,

do you read me? I said are you going to buy it?"

"I would. But I can't."

Something in his tone made her look more closely. His mouth drooped at the corners, and his eyebrows knitted together in some strong emotion.

"Why not?"

"It's complicated." He looked away, pursing his lips, and kicked at the fence post without much energy. Every few seconds he'd look back at her, and draw in a breath, but then he'd turn away again and pretend he was watching Marybelle.

Obviously, he wanted to tell her. And he probably would, as long as she didn't drive him into a corner by begging for it. So she remained focused on Tina and Marybelle, as if she were indifferent to the whole subject.

After a few seconds, she called out, "Loosen up the reins a little," and then, when Tina obeyed, she applauded. "Excellent. Perfect."

Sure enough, when Alec saw he'd lost Rowena's attention, he suddenly spilled the truth.

"I can't buy a horse here," he said. "Because I won't be living here very long."

She gazed down at him placidly. "Oh, yeah? Where will you be living?"

He climbed on the lower rail, hooking his arm around the top rail for balance. He didn't meet her gaze when he answered, messing instead with a splinter of wood that had come free from the rail. "In France. With my mom."

She tried not to show her shock. She hadn't heard anything like this—not from Dallas, or Mitch, or Alec himself. "Oh, okay. Well, that'll be exciting, I guess."

"Yeah. Superexciting." His words were positive, but after he said them he sighed. His profile looked so somber that she wondered whether perhaps this was part of the divorce agreement, and he would be living a split existence, trading off between his parents. The school year was almost over, so it made sense that he might be required to spend his summers in France.

Crummy way to live, but better, she supposed, than trying to live with two people who no longer cared for each other. She'd done that, and she could vouch for its own special brand of hell.

"Well, I mean it's *definitely* exciting." He kicked the post again. "But the problem is… there's one little hitch."

She had thought there might be, judging from his expression. "Yeah? What?"

"My mom said I have to stay here and live with Dad, like forever. She says she's got her new husband, and her new babies. But Dad is all alone, and he needs me to keep him company."

"Oh." Rowena truly couldn't think of any more intelligent response. It didn't sound like a "little" hitch to her. It didn't even sound like anything a real mother could bring herself to say. What was this woman thinking, putting that kind of responsibility and guilt on an eight-year-old child?

"Yeah." Alec heaved a sigh. "Crummy, huh? But I've figured out a way to fix it. I have to find him a girlfriend."

She hadn't even glanced at the training circle in several seconds. She couldn't stop looking at Alec. "A girlfriend?"

"Well, yeah. I mean, he's gotta start by dating them, before they can be his girlfriend. But it's working. Remember when we saw him with Fanny Bronson?"

Of course she remembered. But surely that had been a casual date. After all, he'd come out to Bell River to see Rowena later that night. And he'd kissed her, and he'd wanted more...

"Tell you the truth, I kind of hope it's not Fanny," Alec said, still picking at the splinter.

"Why?" Rowena wondered, for an idiotic, completely self-centered moment, whether Alec might be hoping that she would be his dad's choice. "Who do you want him to pick?"

"I was hoping he'd pick my math teacher, because I like her." He gazed out across the training circle, his face set and grim. "But I guess it doesn't really matter, since I won't be here, anyhow."

Before Rowena could think of an answer, Mitch loped up and grabbed his nephew. He called out encouragement to Tina, and sweetly asked Rowena's permission to swim on her property with all the good manners Alec had lacked. She granted it, smiling at his mischievous charm, and sent them on their way.

When they were gone, Rowena tried to concentrate on Marybelle and Tina. But in her heart, she had to laugh at her own vanity. Obviously it had never occurred to Alec that Rowena might be a suitable "girlfriend" for his dad. At home, he'd probably heard plenty about what Dallas thought of the wild Ms. Wright.

She understood that. But, if she were honest, she'd have to admit it had stung to realize the little boy wasn't exactly pining at the thought of leaving the country and never seeing Rowena or Bell River again.

Oh, get real, Rowena. She forced herself to banish the hot, unhappy feeling that had settled into her chest. Why on earth should he pine? He had known her only a few weeks. Just because she had grown inexplicably fond of him didn't mean he returned the feeling.

She was a novelty in their lives, not a permanent fixture. She wasn't a permanent fixture in *anyone's* life, by choice. So why whine about the price of that choice now?

As for the dude ranch… She hardly knew her sisters, and they didn't trust her enough to partner with her in the purchase of a stick of gum, much less the building of a business.

And that was now, while they believed she was their full-blooded sister. When the DNA tests came back—probably just after the festival—how shaky would that bond be then?

She kept lecturing herself, determined to scold until this absurd, teary feeling went away. She didn't belong in Silverdell anymore, if she ever really had in the first place. She didn't belong anywhere, thank goodness. Belonging to someone or someplace only meant they had the power to hurt you. The power to kill you, even.

It was high time she put aside these stupid delusions—the ones about the dude ranch and the ones about Alec and Dallas, too—and remembered that.

It was almost dusk, only half an hour before Chad arrived to take over the office, when the phone rang. Dallas glared at it. Swear to God, if it was Esther Fillmore again, with more crap about her neighbor, he was going to send the men in white coats instead.

"Dad?"

Hearing Alec's voice was almost a relief, though Dallas knew his son never phoned unless something was wrong. For Alec, though, "wrong" meant Mrs. Biggars wouldn't let him watch TV, or he'd forgotten to get a permission slip signed.

"Dad, I'm really, really sorry to bother you at work, but I have a *huge* problem."

Two red flags in the first sentence. One, Alec was being ultrapolite, which meant he thought his dad would be angry and so was trying to score some advance points. Two, he was talking in italics and exclamation points, which meant he truly believed he had a problem.

Dallas glanced at the clock on the wall of the simple office. Chad was usually a little early, so maybe Dallas could get free to handle whatever this was.

"What's wrong?"

"Well, you know how superhard I'm trying to get my math grade up. And you know how you said Mitch and I couldn't go swimming at Bell River unless I had my homework done."

Oh, brother. Dallas tapped his pen against his desk. "Right."

"Well, I was going to do it at the swimming hole. Honest. I brought my book with me and everything. But then I forgot to do it."

"So do it now." Dallas wasn't sure why Alec had admitted this, instead of rushing through the work before anyone realized he'd slacked off.

"Well, see, that's the huge problem. I left my book at the swimming hole."

Dallas groaned, dropping his pen. *"Alec."*

"I know." Alec's register rose an octave. "It's awful. Seriously. I'm going to be in huge, gigantic trouble if I don't get that book. I already called Danny and Mark, and I even called Helen. I was that desperate. But they all did their work at school, so they didn't even bring home their books."

Dallas didn't bother asking why, if time had been provided in class, Alec hadn't done his there, too. He just cut to the chase.

"Where, exactly, did you leave it?"

A brief silence. Then, in a subdued voice, Alec answered. "In the tree."

Of course. Dallas ran his hand through his hair, trying to hold on to his patience. "Which tree? Surely there's more than one."

"The biggest one. It was the only one that had a branch wide enough to hold it safely." Alec, who Dallas decided really should become an actor when he grew up, put on his angelic voice. "See, Dad? I was trying to be responsible. I was trying to protect it, and keep it from getting wet."

For a second or two, Dallas tried to think of a way out of going to Bell River. But there wasn't one. Mitch was off with Bonnie tonight. Mrs. Biggars didn't drive. And he never asked his employees to do personal errands.

Of course, he could refuse to help, and make Alec face the music tomorrow. But Alec really had seemed to be trying harder in the past few days. Veronica Darren had even sent home a note, praising his improved attitude.

Dallas didn't quite have the heart to crush that newborn effort so soon. So he agreed to go look. The minute Chad arrived, he took off, hoping he could get out there before it was pitch-dark. Trying to find one math textbook in a tree, using nothing but his flashlight, could take all night.

On the way, he phoned Rowena. He had already sent Chad out to check on the place this afternoon, and he had scheduled two more drive-bys between now and 5:00 a.m., so he was pretty sure things were quiet on the ranch. But he didn't want her to glimpse his truck, or hear his footsteps, and wonder even for one split second who it was.

She didn't answer, so he left a message. He hoped she wasn't gone for the night, because he was going to need directions to the falls. Unlike his son, he didn't make himself at home on other people's property, so he'd never seen them.

She didn't answer when he knocked at the house, either. But her car was there, so he walked out toward the stables. The horses both watched him with large, gleaming eyes as he entered through the main door.

"Hey," he called. "Anybody home?"

She was in the tack room. She came to the doorway, her hands full of bridles and bits. The weak solar lights caught her pale face, and he almost had to stop breathing for a minute. How was it possible that, after fifteen years, she was more dramatic, more stunning than ever?

"In here," she said. "Just organizing some equipment. Is everything okay?"

"If you mean Farley, everything's fine. Since you didn't want to press charges, I had to let him go. But I laid it out for Perry, and I think he finally gets it. He tells me he's planning to send Farley to live in North Carolina for a while. He thinks some hard work might do him some good. Turns out they have elderly relatives there who own a pig farm."

She laughed, and the sound made the horses nicker softly. "Well, a pig farm will be a perfect fit."

The laughter didn't sound a hundred percent normal, but he had to admire her grit. Frankly, he wouldn't have expected to find her out here, alone in the dark, so soon after Farley. He wondered whether she might even have concocted some reason to work in the stables tonight, simply to prove she wasn't spooked.

She tilted her head. "So did you come all the way out here to tell me that?"

"No. Truth is, I'm here to ask a favor."

Instantly her face grew guarded. "What kind of favor?"

"Apparently Alec left his math book out by the swimming hole today. The way he makes it sound, his teacher will roast him alive if he doesn't do his homework. Would you mind if I drive out there, to see if I can find it?"

She frowned. "It's pretty dark. Are you familiar with the spot?"

"Not really. I was hoping you could give me directions."

"Well…it's not as if there are street signs. I've never even clocked the exact distance with my car or anything. It's just something I find by feel."

All these years, and she still knew every inch of this place by heart. Once again, he wondered what it would do to her to sell it.

"It isn't that far, at least by car, but it's hard to describe." She hesitated. "I could ride with you, I guess."

The way his pulse jumped, he had to admit this possibility had been lurking in the back of his mind all along. And yet he heard how tentative her offer was. She obviously wasn't sure it was wise to wander off into the dark, wild edges of Bell River with him.

"I'd appreciate it," he said. "I won't keep you long. If I can't find the book quickly, I'll give up. I know you have work to do."

She shifted uneasily. "It's not that. I mean, I don't want you to think that…"

She didn't seem to know how to finish the sentence. But he did.

"I don't. I heard what you said the other night. You're leaving, and you don't intend to get involved in anything short-term while you're here. I heard it, and I respect it."

This was definitely a first for him…essentially having to promise a woman that he wouldn't accost her if she agreed to get in his truck. But then, everything about Rowena—and his reactions to Rowena—had always been unique.

And it was no use denying she had a point. The chemistry between them was damn near irresistible, at least for him.

He'd have to work hard to keep the promise he'd just made.

Chapter Sixteen

As Rowena climbed into the truck, she knew she was taking a risk. She didn't doubt for a moment that Dallas would live up to his word, but she wasn't all that sure about herself. Something about this man kept her keyed up, thrumming with sexual tension.

And if she faced the truth, he always had. It was her desire—not her hatred, not her jealousy or even her born-bad bitchiness—that had really made her seduce him fifteen years ago. She'd told herself it was a game, but deep inside she'd always been hopelessly attracted to him.

She could handle it, though. She was older

now, and...well, maybe not wiser, but stronger.

For the first few minutes, they drove under a round, creamy moon that lit the land and made the hilltops glow. If he really needed to find this textbook, too bad he hadn't come earlier, because as they went on the trees gathered around them more densely, and the dirt paths grew harder to distinguish.

By the time they reached Little Bell Falls, they were cocooned in darkness, except where the shafts of shimmering white projected by his headlights would suddenly illuminate a rough brown tree trunk, or a shocking flash of purple columbine.

They didn't talk much. He seemed to understand that she needed to focus on her senses, without any verbal static. Though her route was oddly serpentine, he never once questioned her ability to get them there. He turned right or left, sped up or slowed down, exactly as she suggested, without complaint.

She navigated mostly by lowering the windows and listening for the faint hiss of the waterfall. The temperature seemed to drop another degree every minute, and she rubbed her arms, wishing she'd brought a sweater.

"There it is." She had to admit she was relieved not to have directed them off course.

He found a clearing large enough to accommodate the truck, and parked. For a few seconds, they simply sat there, listening to the murmur and splash of the water, drinking in the beauty of the spot. Just enough moonlight seeped through the trees to turn the falls into a magical ribbon of white, twinkling with sparks of silver.

This wasn't where they'd been, that terrible night her father had found them. Stupidly, they'd been in the small poplar grove that night, only a hundred yards from the stables. If they'd come this far out, they might have been safe.

But something about the crisp air, the sweetness of the unseen wildflowers and the pale moonlight reminded her of that night, anyway.

She remembered how terrified she'd been when she realized he wasn't going to stop this time. Tension coiled like a snake, just below her stomach, and she felt strange—edgy and strung out, as if she wanted to scream, but at the same time tearful and disoriented, as if she couldn't focus on anything but the tightening throb between her legs.

Then he was on top of her, large, male, heavy and shockingly real. She could see the moon over his shoulder as he guided himself into her. The coiled snake of tension sent sparks out through her body as flesh touched flesh. She lifted her hips instinctively, craving more of that sizzling thrill.

He pushed. And then the moon turned red for an instant of blinding pain. Trying not to cry out, she fixed her gaze on Dallas. He was backlit by the moonlight, and she couldn't read his face.

She gripped the truck's door handle now, trying to stop herself from sinking completely into the past. She remembered it all so vividly that she felt the same tightening tension in her belly now.

Back then, she hadn't completely understood what should have come next. But she knew now, and she felt suddenly as if her body had been waiting fifteen years to be released from that one relentless coil of tension.

"Dallas." She turned to him, confused. But then she couldn't say anything else. He wouldn't remember the night that way. He might not remember it at all. Maybe, because of the gunshot wound, he'd never transferred those moments to his long-term memory.

And, even if his brain had retained the facts, he still had every reason to want to block that night from his memory. Besides, he had obviously moved on. He'd recovered, except for that one rakish scar. Then he'd spent the next fifteen years enjoying all life's most profound pleasures: a home, a career, a marriage, a son.

"Dallas." She tried again.

He smiled. "I know. I should go get the arn book."

She didn't know whether he had misread er tone, or had simply chosen to ignore it. ither way, she knew she should be glad. The intensity of that sudden, blind craving for him had already begun to recede, and she could think more clearly.

"Do you want me to help look for it?"

He gazed at her a long minute. "There's a lot of paradise and poetry out there tonight. It's probably smarter if you stay here." He raised his eyebrows. "Don't you think?"

She flushed. She knew what he meant. Out there, with the water roaring past them, full of wet, sensual urgency, and with the moon silvering them into romantic ghosts instead of people, they would never be able to resist touching. And then kissing.

And then…

"I suppose so," she said, nodding. He was right. He was right. She took a long breath to relax her muscles, and pushed all those dangerous thoughts out of her mind.

By the time he opened his door and got out, she was herself again.

He seemed to know where he was headed, so Alec must have given him directions. He moved sure-footedly over the stones and mosses and ferns, all black and gray and silver tonight, until he reached the large oak. The tree must be a hundred years old, but it had never been pruned, so its big fat outstretched limbs were low to the ground, inviting people to turn them into chairs.

The dark was too deep for her to see anything, but he obviously believed the textbook was there, because he circled the tree, ducking his head into the leafy canopy to check every branch.

The sight was oddly touching, and she felt herself melting again—but in an entirely different way. He might look like a Nordic god, and as sheriff he might have the power of a local overlord, but he was first and foremost a father.

And he clearly loved Alec. Deeply. Unalterably. Every thing she'd seen him do since she arrived, whether it was strict or tender, infuriated or amused, had been designed to protect and nurture his gutsy, goofy little boy.

But why was that perversely even more attractive than his obvious physical charms? She pressed her hands against her rib cage, trying to stay relaxed. She needed to think right now, and clearly.

It would be so hard for him, if he ever lost his son. Should she tell him what Alec had said this morning? It wasn't really any of her business. But if he knew, he might be able to think of something to do about it.

Funny that she didn't seriously consider the possibility that Alec's mother might have an equal right to her son. But it simply wasn't conceivable. The woman had chosen to divorce Dallas Garwood. She was either a fool or a lunatic, and neither one would be good for Alec in the long run.

A couple of minutes later, Dallas climbed back into the truck, a large, dark textbook in his hand. He tossed it on the bench seat between them with a chuckle. "Of course, it was black. I think I passed it four times without seeing it."

She smiled back. "Sorry."

But he didn't seem upset, really. He turned the key to start the engine, then backed out of his makeshift parking space, throwing one arm over the bench seat so that he could swivel and look behind him. His fingertips almost grazed her shoulder.

"Dallas, there's something I think I ought to tell you."

She paused as he cut a quick glance in her direction. "Yeah? What's that?"

"It's about Alec."

He had turned the truck around, and began retracing their route.

"What has he done now?" Dallas smiled. "You should know I'm already ready to box his ears blue. You don't want to send me over the edge."

"No. He hasn't done anything wrong. It's just…something he told me today, when he came over to go swimming."

Dallas kept his eyes on the road, maneuvering the overgrown path of nettles and rhododendron. "What was it?"

She couldn't quite think how to put it. "Well, it's really not my business, and I thought at first I should stay out of it. But it was a little disturbing, and I wonder whether maybe you should know."

"I should." He flicked a glance at her. "I'm his father. If something disturbing is going on, believe me, I should know."

"Okay. The way he was talking, it was clear he's determined to go to France to live with his mother. He's already making plans."

Dallas laughed, just one abrupt sound that was entirely without mirth. "Is he, now?"

"Yes." She eyed him, confused. She hadn't expected him to like her news, but she saw a strange bitterness on his face that was unfamiliar. "Apparently he feels there's only one serious obstacle preventing him from going to live with her, and he's creating a plan to overcome it."

He tightened his hands on the wheel, but he didn't look at her this time. "And did he say what that obstacle is?"

"Well, what he *says* is that…he says his mother told him you need someone to take care of you."

"What?" Dallas whipped his head around, glared at her, then turned back to the road. "That's ridiculous."

"Perhaps. But he says that's what she told him. She told him to take care of Daddy, so that Daddy won't be all alone."

He didn't respond, but she noticed that his grip had tightened on the steering wheel.

She moistened her lips nervously. "And this is where it gets awkward. I don't know whether you've noticed that Alec is extremely eager for you to…start dating."

"I realized that a couple of weeks ago," he said dryly. "Guess I was the last to know. But how is my social life—"

He broke off, going utterly silent, as if blinded by the light bulb that had finally fired up in his brain. "Oh, *hell*. You mean he thinks that if I…"

She nodded. "Apparently Alec has decided that the only thing standing between him and his mother is finding a girlfriend for you."

Dallas was so enraged he couldn't see straight.

But somehow he found his way back to the sheriff's office. He was off duty, but he had a telephone call to make, and he wasn't going to make this one from home. He couldn't risk letting Alec overhear him.

He blasted in, slamming the office door behind him. Chad glanced up from the front desk, where he was doing a sudoku puzzle. "Bear chasing you, Sheriff?"

"I'm not here," Dallas barked. He moved through the front room, into his private office, and slammed that door, too, just because it felt good.

He grabbed the phone and went through the convoluted process of making an international call but charging it to his home account. He had to be civil to the operator, of course. By the time it was ringing, he was a little calmer.

A very little. But calm enough to realize it was only three in the morning in Paris.

Well, tough. What he had to say couldn't wait.

He wasn't sure why he was so surprised by Rowena's news. He'd learned long ago how manipulative Allyson could be. But to play this wretched, selfish guilt game on her grieving son? That seemed too low even for her.

At first, he'd wanted to believe Rowena had it wrong. Alec couldn't really think this was the answer to that basic question…why couldn't he be with his mother?

But as soon as Dallas uttered the denial in his mind, he knew better. Alec's will was absolutely strong enough to reinvent reality. And since Dallas had never spelled out how impossible that scenario was…

Dallas sat back, a small flare of fury going up inside him, as it always did when he thought about this.

Apparently he feels there's only one serious obstacle preventing him from going to live with her, Rowena had said.

Yeah, there was an obstacle, all right. A big one.

Allyson didn't want him.

His ex-wife had made it clear to Dallas. Under no circumstances would she allow her first son, the fruit of her disappointing first marriage, to move in with her new, picture-perfect second family. Maybe later, when her infant twins were older, Alec could come for a week, or two....

The twins were eight months old now. It was pretty obvious that the extended visit was unlikely to happen, either.

However, he hoped Alec had no idea about any of that. Dallas had always made excuses for Allyson, and Alec seemed to accept them.

Like a few weeks ago, when Mrs. Biggars had warned Dallas that Alec was pining for a letter from Allyson. Dallas had shot her an email sharp enough to guarantee that an overnight delivery arrived within a couple of days.

He drummed his fingers on the desk. *Come*

*on, damn it. Answer. Where can you be at
three in the morning except at home?*

Surely her new relationship hadn't soured
in only two years.

A sleepy, elegant alto finally answered the
phone. "Hello?" She must have peered at the
caller ID, because he heard a rustling sound,
and then her throaty voice came again. "Dallas, is that you? Do you know what time it is
here? Is everything all right?"

He gripped the phone hard. "That would
be a yes, a yes and a resounding no."

"What?" Her voice lifted a few notes. "Is
there something wrong with Alec?"

"Damn straight there is," he responded
curtly. "He's physically well, but emotionally he's about as messed up as a kid can get."

"What?" She never had been very sharp
when she was sleepy. "What do you mean?
What's happened?"

"Apparently his mother has been playing
some nasty mind games on him. Apparently
she's been telling him that the only reason he
doesn't get a spot in her shiny new life is that
he's responsible for taking care of his lonely,
needy old man."

The other end of the line hummed with silence.

"Dallas," Allyson began. "If you'll let me explain—"

"You bet I will. But not over the phone, and not to me."

"What do you mean?"

"I mean…you're going to get on a plane, and you're going to come back to Silverdell, and you're going to explain this to your son. Honestly, for once in your life. He truly believes he's just one successful blind date from jetting to Paris to live with you."

"Well." She hesitated, and he could imagine her sweeping her silky blond hair out of her face. "Isn't that easier than knowing it'll never happen? I thought that, this way, he'd come to accept it gradually, and it would be easier all around."

"Easier for you, you mean." He was so sick of her self-obsessed denial. She hadn't wanted to confront the disintegration of their marriage, either. She'd simply slept around until, as she put it, he'd "come to accept it gradually."

"No, I—"

"Look. You've as good as told him that I'm the only thing standing in the way of his idyllic life. And, of course, he deeply resents me for that. If you don't want a relationship with him yourself, at least be strong enough to get out of the way and let the two of us work things out."

"But...but how? If I tell him the truth, he..."

"He'll know his mother is a shallow, selfish woman who uses people up and then tosses them out like trash? It doesn't have to come to that. I'm sure you can find a way to put it that saves your face, at least a little."

"Dallas, I can't—"

"Yes. You can. You're a writer, Allyson. Wasn't that why you had to live in Paris? Pretend you're one of your fictional characters, and write yourself a beautiful little speech."

Another silence. She put her hand over the phone. Clearly she wanted to explain to Chance, her husband, what the ruckus was all about.

"All right." She came back, her voice weary, but resigned. "When were you thinking I should come?"

"Next Tuesday."

She groaned. "Next Tuesday? That's pretty short notice, Dallas."

"I don't think I'd call it *short notice*." He

was so angry he feared he might splinter the phone into pieces. "What I'd call it is...*his birthday.*"

Chapter Seventeen

If you could pick just one month to live in Silverdell, Rowena figured it would have to be June.

The weather had usually leveled out by then. Snow was only a memory—good or bad, depending on whether you were a carefree kid or the adult who had to make sure everyone made it through the winter. Skies shone blue and clear, nights were crisp enough for cuddling, and the afternoons were balmy. Even the rain eased up in June, except for the occasional thunderstorm that played out like an exciting melodrama against the mountaintops.

And, of course, you got the wildflowers.

This year, the Silverdell Wildflower Festival celebrated its twenty-eighth birthday, and apparently the event had grown bigger and grander as time passed. It had been exciting enough to Rowena as a child. But as she reported for work at the pony ride booth on her first day, she'd caught her breath.

The whole downtown area had been transformed into a botanical fairyland.

Every door had, at the very least, a wildflower wreath. But most stores had redone their window displays and street fronts to look like blooming mountainsides, or fairy gardens.

Elk Avenue was closed to auto traffic for both days of the festival, and the streets teemed with pedestrians—almost everyone from the city, and hundreds more from towns more than fifty miles away. It was definitely worth the trip. Huge garlands of wildflowers looped between streetlights, and sometimes, when the wind gusted high enough, people walking beneath were showered with aromatic petals.

On Sunday, the second and last day of the festival, Rowena showed up early so that she could stroll slowly to her post, taking in the beauty. On both sides of the street, colorful booths sold every imaginable craft that could be made of wildflowers.

Lots of booths had paintings, of course. Last night, Bonnie had reported with glee that she'd sold more than half her works already.

But the paintings were only the start. Other booths offered photographs, homemade papers, luminary candles, place mats, fairy houses and, of course, the always-popular wildflower garlands.

Rowena paused at Joanna Madison's booth, partly to be polite, and partly because, no matter how silly it seemed, she still loved these beautiful wildflower crowns, just as she had when she was a kid.

She'd never dreamed of being a princess in a castle—that was the game Bree liked to play. But she had secretly loved to imagine herself as the queen of the forest, reigning wisely over all the birds, bunnies and deer.

"Rowena! Hey!" Joanna seemed thrilled to see her again. Yesterday, when they had first run into each other, Joanna had thanked her so profusely for "saving" Mabel that Rowena had been almost embarrassed.

"Are you sure you won't let me give you one?" Joanna's hand hovered over the colorful display of wildflower crowns, revisiting the argument she'd lost yesterday. "Please? I would love to find some little way to say thanks. And I have a few that would look fabulous with your dramatic coloring."

She picked up one of the larger head-dresses—big white marsh marigolds with yellow centers that gleamed like gems in a real crown, surrounded by a riot of wide, glossy green leaves. Bold yellow and green ribbons streamed from the back in glittering spirals.

This was a far cry from the dainty phlox and pastel candytufts that bedecked most of the other crowns.

"Oh, yes! This would match your eyes exactly." Joanna beamed. "What do you think?"

Rowena hesitated, torn between not wanting to encourage the other woman, and not wanting to seem surly. And besides…she loved it.

"Thank you," she said, giving in. "I couldn't possibly accept it as a gift, though." She hoped she'd brought some cash, and slipped her purse from her shoulder to look.

But Joanna wouldn't hear of it. She wouldn't take a penny, no matter how emphatically Rowena insisted. Joanna seemed so thrilled to have found a concrete expression of her gratitude that Rowena eventually surrendered.

She walked away from the booth feeling strangely buoyant. She waved as she passed Tina Blakeley, who was racing around like a madwoman, keeping the festival running, but still took time to run over and hug Rowena. She declared the new headdress perfect, and plucked it from Rowena's hand, and placed it on her head.

"Oh, gorgeous! You look magnificent! The children will love it!"

Though Rowena touched the flowers self-consciously, feeling a bit foolish, she realized Tina was right. Most of the girls who came to ride the ponies would be wearing them, as well—and so would their friends, mothers and even their grandmothers. Actually, around here Rowena looked more odd without a crown than wearing one.

So she didn't take it off when Tina rushed away to deal with another crisis across the avenue. She kept ambling down the street, enjoying the booths and exchanging pleasantries with the vendors.

Surprising how comfortable she felt among the Dellians, after all this time. She waved at Fanny Bronson, who was selling nature books at her own table near her store, and got another shower of smiles and compliments on the headdress.

And, miraculously, even Esther Fillmore, whose own wildflower crowns decked a booth at the far end of the street, refrained from open warfare when she spied Rowena wearing her competitor's creation.

It was as if the festival had turned everyone tolerant for forty-eight hours. Come to think of it, not one bit of the hostility Rowena had been expecting had presented itself.

Yet.

"Ro?"

Caught in her own thoughts, Rowena only half registered the nickname—a name no living soul in Silverdell had ever used, except her family. She turned, completely unprepared.

"Yes?"

"Oh, Ro! Don't you even recognize me?"

Recognize...?

She froze. The woman standing in front of her was Penny.

"Penny?" she said, not because she wasn't sure, but because on some level her paralyzed mind wouldn't take it in. "What on earth are you doing here?"

Penny shook her head, tsking. "First things first!" Without warning, she wrapped her arms around Rowena and hugged her, laughing and swaying, until Rowena's rigidity eventually began to soften.

"I'm so happy to see you!" Penny pulled back to examine her sister. "And you look wonderful, Ro, really you do. So much better than when we talked on the phone. You must be eating well."

The sweet, powdery perfume Penny wore was the same scent their mother had always worn. Bal à Versailles. The fragrance had brought a hot rush of jagged pain into Rowena's throat, and for a moment she couldn't answer.

Overcome, she tightened her grip on her sister's delicate shoulders. The wind blew Penny's silken, baby-fine brown hair across Rowena's fingers. It felt exactly the same as it had when Penny was a child, and she had come to Rowena for comfort in the night.

"Bree's here, too," Penny said, edging back slightly, as if she thought it might hurt Bree's feelings to be ignored. "Bree, I told you it was Ro!"

Rowena met her other sister's cool, elegant gaze. If Bree was in any danger of succumbing to reunion emotion, she certainly didn't show it.

"Hi, Ro." She leaned in and touched her cheek to Rowena's. She even let one graceful hand land on Rowena's shoulder briefly, like a butterfly touching a flower.

Bree looked Rowena over just as Penny had done, her blue eyes appraising. Rowena forced herself to remain outwardly at ease, though she had the feeling Bree could calculate her weight to within a couple of ounces.

The verdict came in. "Penny's right. You look great."

Both of her sisters seemed to feel a carefully muted surprise about that fact. Rowena understood why, of course. They all knew that Rowena didn't eat when she was under too much stress.

Well, she couldn't explain her full, rosy cheeks, either. Maybe it was Bonnie's cooking—and her simple, unconditional friendship. Maybe it was mending fences with Dallas, after all these years. Maybe it was the dude ranch dreams she'd been indulging in secret.

Or maybe it was simply being home again—without her father's cruelty to poison it.

"Thanks," she said. "I can't believe you guys are here." She pulled off her crown, smoothed her hair, then raised her eyebrows. "Out of curiosity…why *are* you here?"

The motive couldn't possibly be sisterly love, or a hunger to see her again. Rowena and her sisters had laid eyes on each other only three or four times in the fifteen years since they'd been split up. And those meetings were mostly mandated by events…like their father's funeral.

"We wanted to take a look at Bell River," Bree said, her voice calm and unapologetic. "We're spending a lot of money. Do you think it's odd that we might want to see for ourselves exactly where it's going?"

Penny glared at Bree, then reached a hand out to touch Rowena's arm. "Plus, we thought you might like some moral support. We know it's been an enormous burden to carry alone."

"It's been fine." Rowena straightened her shoulders. "I've had plenty of help."

For some reason, that comment seemed to make Penny uncomfortable. She glanced at Bree, who looked fairly odd herself. She looked… Rowena searched for the right word.

She looked angry.

Why? What on earth did they think Rowena had meant by "help"?

"I'm not kidnapping local children and forcing them to rebuild the basement," she said irritably. "There's a young woman who was looking for a job. Her name is—"

"Bonnie," Bree supplied. She smiled without opening her lips. "Yes. We've met Bonnie."

"Ro." Penny rushed to explain. "We went by the house first. We thought you'd be there. It never occurred to us that you would be working here."

Penny pulled on her ear, a habit she had apparently never broken. It meant she was worried. "But Bonnie was there, and of course she let us in, and…"

She couldn't finish the sentence, clearly distressed.

But Bree could.

"And when we went in, we saw the renderings."

Rowena's heart kicked double-time, like a bucking horse. Oh, hell. The pictures were all over the great room, as if it were a museum. Bonnie probably guessed that Rowena wouldn't have wanted her sisters to see them, but she probably hadn't been given enough warning to clean up.

And that wasn't all. If Bree had been nosy enough, she probably had even looked at the mess of paperwork on the breakfast table. It included the rough draft of a business plan that Barton James had delivered yesterday, endless printouts from other dude ranch websites, a loan application from Silverdell Fifth Third and a book of floor plans she'd borrowed from the library.

But she refused to be cowed. She hadn't spent a dime of Bree and Penny's money on any of that. Who was Bree to dictate how Rowena spent her own time, and her own money?

She set her jaw. "Okay. So?"

"*So*...we know what you're really doing at Bell River." Bree's smile was brittle, and her voice was hard. "And whether you like it or not, Rowena, it's time you and I had a talk."

By the time dusk fell around 8:00 p.m., the tension in Bell River's great room was so thick Rowena wondered whether anyone could breathe.

The "talk" Bree demanded wasn't going well.

The chances of success had been low from the start, because Rowena had insisted on remaining at the festival through her shift at the pony rides, which Bree thought was ridiculous.

"I'll be back around six," Rowena had insisted stubbornly. And then she'd added, with a caustic note, "Feel free to prowl through anything you find in the house."

"I will," Bree had said, a dangerous glint in her eye. "It is my house, too."

So by the time Rowena got home, everyone was already on edge. Clearly Bree and Penny had been arguing. Penny looked pale and drawn, which was her sign of stress. All the color bled out of her face—cheeks, lips, even the rims of her eyes. It was as if, when her spirits sank, she turned immediately anemic.

Then Bree made everything even worse by starting out with an insult. Approaching the minute Rowena entered from the kitchen door, she held out a sheaf of papers.

"You've already gone pretty far with this dude ranch scheme, Ro," she said without preamble. "That can't have been cheap. Whose money did you use to do it?"

Instantly, Rowena's blood felt hot in her

veins. *Whose money?* Bree thought Rowena had taken the sisters' pooled kitty for the new roof and used it on her own pet project?

Was she honestly accusing Rowena of being a *thief?*

Rowena almost didn't answer. It was beneath her to respond to a charge like that. But, for all her gregarious charm and personal grace, Bree had a bulldog streak. She could gnaw on a topic till you wanted to scream.

So Rowena swallowed her anger and answered.

"My *own* money," she said without inflection. "Don't worry. I can, and will, provide receipts for every cent that came from you or Penny."

Penny cast a glance toward Bree that mutely said, *See?*

Bree didn't acknowledge the glance. She stood by the ugly fake black leather couch, ramrod straight. Her arms crossed across her midsection. Hands clutching her elbows. Angry eyes staring at Rowena.

One part of Rowena's mind could hardly process the emotional dissonance this scene created in her. She hadn't stood in this room with these people in fifteen years. And now that they were here, nothing was the same. Every detail jarred.

"I thought we'd decided the dude ranch was a bad idea." Bree frowned, still gripping her elbows. "I thought we were putting the ranch on the market."

"We did. We are. So what exactly is your problem here, Brianna? The roof is repaired, the basement is shored up, and the house looks pretty darn good. If I want to play around with an idea for a dude ranch in my spare time, what business is it of yours?"

"It's not just *a* dude ranch." Bree gestured stiffly toward Bonnie's painting of Bell River's renovated exterior, with a parking lot where the pole barn used to be. "It's *this* dude ranch. It's Bell River. And the reason it's my business is that I own one third of this place."

"Which means I can't do a darn thing without talking to you first. So what's the problem?" Rowena took a couple of steps toward her sister, to show she wasn't cowed. "I mean...let's get past the nonsense about the dude ranch. You've had an undercurrent of hostility toward me for years. What's *really* the problem?"

"Ro, no," Penny interjected from where she sat at the breakfast nook. She perched on the edge of her chair as if she might need to spring up and pull her sisters apart at any moment. Taking over their mother's role, maybe?

"Please," she said. "Let it go. We don't need to dredge up old—"

"No, Penny," Bree responded. "She wants to know. I guess I'm just tired of how secretive you always are, Ro. You're always so distant, and remote, and inaccessible. Even with this. Why couldn't you have told us you were still exploring the dude ranch idea?"

As Rowena suspected, Bree had been waiting years to unload on her, and it all came pouring out now, like mud out of a long-clogged pipe. Well, let her. She couldn't hurt Rowena, because Rowena had already cut the ties. She didn't expect to be loved by these people, any more than you'd expect support from an arm or a leg you'd cut off years ago.

Rowena shrugged. "I didn't mention it because you'd already made it clear how you felt about it."

"Yes, but...your emotional inaccessibility... it's more than that. I mean, some families that have been through what happened to us would have become closer than ever. They would have banded together. Not you, though. Oh, sure, you send Christmas cards. Sometimes you remember a birthday. But mostly you're just...not there."

That stung. "Not there" was the way Rowena had always described her mother. She might have sat at the table, slept in the bed, but emotionally she was always remote. Inaccessible.

Had Rowena inherited that inability to connect with the people she should have loved?

"I'm sorry. I guess I didn't get the memo on how *families like ours* are supposed to behave. I assumed we were all doing the best we could."

Bree's fair skin flushed easily, and two deep pink circles appeared on her cheeks now. "That was your best? Ignoring your sisters as if they are little more than strangers? And was it your *best* when you packed your bags in the middle of the night, and left Penny alone with Ruth? That is your *best?* Abandoning your little sister when she needed you most?"

"Bree, please." Penny stood and held out her hands. "I was fine. I am fine. It doesn't matter anymore."

But it clearly did. Rowena could hear the old pain still coloring Penny's sweet voice. Vulnerable, artistic, introspective Penny had been scarred by that year, every bit as much as Rowena had…and maybe more.

Rowena's skin went cold, as it did every time she thought back on what a coward she'd been. She had no excuse, really. Not one that Bree would accept, anyhow. And not one that she was willing to lay at Bree's feet, like a sacrifice to an angry god.

Her only explanation was humiliating. She wouldn't, couldn't, mortify herself in front of this judgmental iceberg who was her sister in name only.

"You know how frightened Penny was, right after Mom died," Bree said. "I couldn't be there with her. But *you could have.* You just *chose not to be.*"

Blindly, Rowena took two steps toward the kitchen, instinctively trying to put space between herself and Bree's disdainful words.

She put her hand on the granite bar, seeking support because her knees seemed to want to liquefy.

Bree's gaze flicked to the movement, and she laughed bitterly.

"Oh, that's right, Ro. Leave." Bree narrowed her eyes. "And you wonder why I wouldn't trust you to commit to Bell River for the long haul? You can't even commit to one honest conversation. So go ahead. *Leave.*"

Bree's voice had grown thick, as if she might be fighting tears, but she aimed that coolly dismissive smile at Rowena and waved her hand toward the door.

"Run away—again. That's the only thing you're good at."

Chapter Eighteen

"Hey, Sheriff! You're here mighty late." The old man walking toward the parking lot smiled, his cane tapping the sidewalk irregularly, like a heart skipping a beat. "Keeping an eye on the stragglers and miscreants?"

"Something like that. So if you'll just go on home, Harper, then maybe I can, too." Dallas winked at Grayson Harper, who might be the richest, meanest old coot in Silverdell, but who had a pretty good sense of humor.

Harper laughed and tapped on toward his limo. Beside the gleaming black machine, his sexy chauffeur—Dallas didn't know her name, as Harper had a new one every month or so—waited, cap in hand.

When Harper got himself situated, and the limo finally purred off, Dallas leaned against the ancient maple that marked the edge of the lot. He held Rowena's marigold headdress in his right hand, hooked on the edge of his fingers, the spangled ribbons trailing to the ground. The sheriff's department had taken custody of about fifty lost-and-found items tonight, but this was the only one he'd accepted responsibility for.

He'd seen her wearing it, earlier, the green leaves matching her eyes exactly. The sight had nearly brought him to his knees.

He wasn't sure what he planned to do with the crown now. Maybe he'd give it to Mitch, and let him return it when he reported for work tomorrow.

Or maybe…

No. That would be dumb. Seriously dumb.

He gazed down Elk Avenue, which was misty in the streetlights. The festival had officially ended at six. The tower clock at the south end of the street had just struck nine, and very few remnants of the festivities remained, except about a million wildflower petals the wind had blown like confetti across the asphalt.

Most of the vendors had broken down their booths, and only a few die-hard merrymakers still trickled down the avenue, clearly reluctant to leave fairyland behind and return to their normal lives.

Dallas could sympathize. He'd been at the event all day, and he ought to be tired, but he kept hanging on. That stuff about keeping an eye on things was only a smoke screen. Bartlett and two other deputies on duty had security covered.

Plain and simple, he felt restless, and he wasn't in the mood to be alone. Mitch had taken Bonnie to a movie, and Alec would sleep over at Benny McAvee's house, so nothing waited for Dallas at home but a plate of Mrs. B.'s leftovers and a few miles going nowhere on the treadmill.

He twirled the wildflower crown absently. He could drop by the Grille and undoubtedly pick up a friend or two who would help him kill the evening. Or he could see if he could get a real date. He tilted his watch into the cloudy moonlight. Only about nine-fifteen, not too late for a quick bite to eat.

But who? The date with Fanny Bronson

hadn't started any fires, but maybe... Gina Teasdale, the pharmacist? She was a nice woman who got divorced about the same time he did.

And Sally Hathaway, the vet who had replaced old Doc Gunter, had hinted she was available whenever he felt ready to get back in the dating game.

But damn it...no. He made an irritable sound under his breath. They were nice women. Attractive. But dating any of them would simply be another kind of treadmill.

Maybe he should drive around till this rotten mood lifted. Because Mitch had borrowed the truck, Dallas had been stuck with the motorcycle. That had annoyed him, at first, but now he saw that the situation had possibilities.

A lot cooler than the sheriff department issues, Mitch's bike hunkered by the curb like a big, black insect with silver armor. The chrome glinted as the wind swept the elm branches, blocking then revealing the shine of the nearest streetlight.

Maybe he'd head out onto the open roads and see what the bike could do. Maybe, if he was lucky, the roar of the wind would clear his head.

Maybe he could stop thinking about Rowena.

Instantly, he heard a scrape of tires behind him. Looking back, he saw that Rowena had pulled into the parking lot, as if his brain had the power to materialize his thoughts.

She parked jerkily, then killed the engine and the lights. He watched, but she didn't emerge. Could she be waiting for someone? But the street was empty now. Everyone else was gone.

And then he wondered if she really was alone.

He frowned, a wave of jealousy moving through him, catching him by surprise.

Jealous? Of whom?

And with what right?

Still, if she was alone, he didn't like the idea. Farley Miller had left Silverdell yesterday, according to his dad, but airplanes flew both ways, and a man who left yesterday could always have returned, unannounced, today.

He'd better go check. As he straightened, leaving the cushion of the tree trunk behind, he felt the tickle of the wildflowers between his fingers. Even better. He had a genuine excuse.

As he approached, her car door opened, and she got out. She still wore the green, off-the-shoulder gypsy blouse she'd had on earlier, with embroidered flowers around the gathered neckline, puffed sleeves and full, rippled hem. It was perhaps the girliest thing he'd ever seen her wear, and she looked amazing.

He assumed, at first, that she got out because she'd seen him approaching. But then she shut the door and turned to drop her forehead against the hood. He realized she was crying.

"Rowena?"

She lifted her head with a jerk. The streetlight hit her obliquely, and she swiped her hands across her face, trying to obliterate the tears.

He moved quickly, reaching her in two seconds.

"What's wrong?" He didn't touch her, not even to emphasize his concern. He would have been just as cautious with a lost child, or a kitten hit by a car.

Up close, he could tell she'd been crying a long time. Redness rimmed her puffy eyes, and her nostrils looked painfully raw, as if she'd blown too hard and too often.

A dozen ugly scenarios raced through his mind before he could stop them. More graffiti? Stupid teenagers with Ouija boards?

Farley?

His heart thudded. *Not Farley.* Please, not Farley, while Dallas had been slacking off here, being the stereotypical bored, useless cop.

"Rowena, tell me. What's the matter?"

"It's nothing. I mean, it's Bree. She's here, and—" She blinked. "It's nothing. Nothing more than I deserve, anyhow."

"Bree is here?"

She nodded.

"What does she want?"

"I don't know. Well, I guess that, among other things, she wants me to admit that I'm a terrible person." Her mouth trembled, making a mockery of her attempt to sound scornful. "No problem. *I'm a terrible person.*"

Instinctively, he reached out. He stopped himself just short of touching the silver wetness on her cheeks.

"That's ridiculous," he said. "Beyond ridiculous. It's insane."

"It's true. Everything they say I did is true."

He didn't believe it. But she clearly did,

and that was what mattered. "All right. What did you do?"

She bent her head, her brow furrowing with emotion. "I left Penny. That's what Bree has never forgiven me for. I ran away a few months after Mamma died, when we were sent to live with Ruth."

This couldn't be all of it. He waited for the rest.

"I took off in the middle of the night, even though I knew Penny needed me. I didn't even tell her I was going. They never found me, until after I turned eighteen, and then it was too late. They couldn't make me go back."

She swallowed awkwardly. "So, you see? Bree says I abandoned Penny, and she's right. I did."

He still didn't really understand. "Is that so terrible? Was your aunt Ruth a bad woman? Was Penny physically or emotionally at risk while she was there?"

She shook her head. "Ruth loved Penny. I was the one she couldn't stand."

"And that's why you left? Because you didn't feel wanted there?"

Rowena tried to laugh, but none of her normal affectations were working right now. It sputtered out on a half sob. "Wanted? Are you kidding? She hated me. We fought constantly. The night I left, she told me she'd decided I was 'ungovernable.'"

He felt a chill. That sounded like a legal term. "What exactly did *ungovernable* mean?"

Rowena lifted her chin, and she met his gaze with the bleakest eyes he'd ever seen. "It meant she was planning to return me to the State of Colorado, so that they could put me into foster care."

His breath stopped, instantly and painfully. It wasn't possible. Could anyone be so cruel?

What kind of fool had Ruth Garnett been? A girl of sixteen had just lost her mother, her father, one of her sisters and the only home she'd ever known...and Ruth was surprised that she was hostile and difficult? If Ruth couldn't handle a traumatized teen, why on earth would she have taken Rowena in the first place? Surely Ruth knew the road out of tragedy would be rocky. Months, maybe years, of therapy, patience and love would be needed to guide those girls safely to the other side.

"Does Bree know?"

"That Ruth was going to kick me out?

No." She blew her nose softly with a wadded-up tissue. "It doesn't exactly make me look very..."

After a brief silence, she set her jaw. "I won't ask Bree for sympathy. Even Penny doesn't know, unless Ruth admitted it, which I doubt. I've never told anyone. In fact... I'm not sure why I told you."

"Maybe because you realize how unfair Bree's being. Maybe you realize it might be time to tell them both the truth."

"No." Her refusal came quickly. "Why would I? Penny doesn't hold it against me anyway. And it wouldn't change Bree's opinion. She would only say I should have stayed and fought for Penny, no matter what. And maybe I..."

"Rowena, listen to me. I know it feels as if you failed somehow, but I promise you the failure is one hundred percent on the other side. Your aunt should be..."

He tried to think of some relatively civilized punishment to suggest for Ruth, but he was so angry that everything he could conjure up involved boiling oil and bullwhips.

"She should be ashamed." Not exactly medieval torture, but he said it with enough fervor that he felt sure Rowena understood how he felt.

She gazed at him a moment in total silence. And then, to his surprise, she laid her fingertips against his cheek.

"You are a very good man," she said softly. "You may be the kindest person I've ever met."

He didn't respond. He wasn't sure he could. Her fingers drifted up, across his cheekbone, past his lashes and then slowly along the jagged white scar that separated his right eyebrow into two pieces.

"But surely you know better than anyone," she went on, "just how terrible I can be."

He hesitated, sensing that only honesty would help at a moment like this. But what was the truth? His feelings about her were so complicated—contradictory and ever-changing. And yet, in spite of everything, he had never once believed she was wicked.

"What I know," he said finally, "is how unhappy you've been. All those years ago, I think you needed…something that you weren't getting at home. Love. Or freedom. Or both."

"That's very sweet, too," she said. "But it's

just an excuse. Every teenager feels like that. They don't all do what I did."

"I'll ask you again. What did you do?"

Her mouth twisted cynically.

"No, I'm serious. *What did you do?* Let's see…you flirted with me."

Another wry smile, and this time he smiled back. "Okay, you flirted *hard.* Still, lots of girls had flirted with me before that night. I didn't end up in the back of my truck with any of them. Even eighteen-year-old boys are capable of saying no, Rowena. What I did was my decision. My fault. Not yours."

She didn't seem to have an answer for that, so he pressed on. "And when you left your aunt's house—that was sheer survival. Your sister wasn't in danger. *You* were."

Again, no answer. She wasn't crying anymore, but something in her posture told him he hadn't found the right words yet. She seemed calm, but oddly empty.

"Anyone would have—"

"Dallas." She shook her head. "Are you going to try to rationalize every sin I've committed in my entire life?"

"I'm not rationalizing anything. I'm saying that your view of reality is warped by this crushing guilt you carry around. I'm trying to make you see that there's another way of looking at it."

She sighed, and glanced at the wildflower-strewn avenue, empty now of all the people. She squared her shoulders, seemingly unaware that the gypsy shirt had fallen low on her left arm, and turned back to face him again.

"All right, see if you can give me another way of looking at *this*. My father didn't just inexplicably fall into a pointless rage the night he killed my mother. He was furious with her because he'd learned that she'd lied about where she was all day. And he learned it from me."

His heart sank in his chest, all at once, like a dropped anchor.

"That's right," she said. "I'm the one who really caused my mother's death."

Chapter Nineteen

Rowena wasn't sure what she'd expected to happen when she uttered those terrible words. She'd guarded that secret for fifteen years. She never spoke of it, rarely thought of it and didn't even allow herself to dream about it.

Her only hope, she'd believed, was to bury the fact deeply, like nuclear waste. It would remain toxic forever, but at least if she kept it underground it wouldn't be as dangerous.

As she stared at Dallas, waiting for his response, she realized her shoulders were tight, as if she had braced for some kind of physical reaction. How absurd! He might despise her, after hearing this, but he would never strike her.

Would she always, for the rest of her life, confuse every man she met with her father?

She hated that thought. *Hated* it. It made her feel...broken. Emotionally damaged beyond repair.

But she wasn't. She wouldn't let the past define her.

"Rowena, I'm so—"

"No." She interrupted before he could say *sorry.* She hated pity, too.

And then, suddenly, she couldn't stand here another minute, dwelling on the whole sordid thing. She pointed to the only other vehicle in the lot. "Is that Mitch's motorcycle?"

He glanced over at the bike. Its chrome twinkled in the shifting light. "Tonight it's mine."

"Will you take me for a ride? I need...to get away. I need to stop thinking about this, if only for a little while."

He gazed at her a long moment. And then, as if making a difficult decision, he yanked the keys out of his pocket. "Okay. Let's go."

The first thing he did was thread her wild-flower crown over his arm, so that its streamers didn't dangle far enough to be dangerous. Then he handed her the helmet.

He straddled the seat, scooting as far forward as his long legs would allow. He balanced the bike, and then glanced over his shoulder to see if she was ready.

Gingerly, she climbed up behind him. She put her hands on his shoulders, but the minute the bike took off, she realized that wouldn't be enough. Instead, she wrapped her arms around his waist, and she felt the involuntary tightening of his muscles in response.

After that, the landscape flew past her, dreamlike. It was as if the world were liquefying into an impressionist painting, softened with pearly mist and lit with intermittent streaks of glowing yellow streetlamps.

He didn't ask her where she wanted to go. He seemed to understand that she wanted to go nowhere, and think of nothing. They simply growled through the night without purpose, taking the main road out of town, and then angling onto one of the long, two-lane county roads that no one ever used.

After a few minutes, she laid her head against his back. If she shut her eyes, she could imagine that they were no longer two separate bodies. The vibrations that coursed through his shoulders passed into her, and when they skimmed over a rocky patch of road, they rose and fell together.

A long time later—ten minutes or an hour…time lost its shape out here—she felt the icy kiss of raindrops against her arms. At first it was exhilarating, and she raised her face to the cloudy sky. But very soon, with only a cotton shirt to cover her, she grew cold. When she shivered, he obviously felt it. In this intimate embrace, he would have known every single move her body made.

Instantly, he slowed down, so that the needles of rain didn't strike with such force. Then, when a roofed structure came into view, he pulled over.

The building was a very old, very small covered pedestrian bridge, with a red metal roof. It must allow some remote ranch owner to bring his horses over the creek that passed through this land. The milky-gray rippling water was some tributary of Bell River, no doubt, but Rowena no longer had any clear idea of where they were.

Dallas glided the motorcycle into the sheltered area, dropped his feet for balance and finally turned it off.

The sudden absence of engine roar made

her ears ring a little. She removed the helmet and shook her hair free, sighing with the pleasure of being released from confinement.

Within a few seconds, though, she became awkwardly aware that she was still sitting so close to Dallas that her thighs cradled his hard hips, and her breasts pressed against his shoulder blades.

"I should get off, I guess," she said, trying to laugh. She straightened self-consciously, tucking the helmet under one elbow. While he held the bike steady, she swung her leg over and managed to dismount without crashing to the ground.

"I'm sorry," he said. "I should have thought of this. It's been threatening rain for hours now."

"I don't mind," she said. And it was true. This primitive, remote spot, surrounded by poplar trees and unmown grasses, pleased her. Closed in by the rain and fog, they seemed a million miles from anywhere, or anyone.

But, as her hearing returned to normal, she heard music all around them. The soprano plink of the rain on the metal roof. The deep murmur of the creek that rushed past below them. Nearby, probably on one of the creek banks, a couple of bullfrogs croaked lazily, unbothered by the weather.

Dallas put the bike on its kickstand and walked over to where she stood. He peeled a couple of strands of wet hair from her face. Then he slipped the wildflower crown from his arm and arranged it on her head.

When he had it centered and the streamers untangled, he stepped back and considered his work. "I'm not sure the wind did it any favors," he said, smiling, "but you look beautiful."

She touched the crown self-consciously. "Thank you for saving it."

"No problem." He stepped to the edge of the shelter and looked up, as if evaluating exactly how much rain the clouds held tonight. "This may last a while. I hope your sisters aren't going to be worried. I have my cell. You could call if you like."

"No, thanks. They'll be asleep. They won't even notice I'm not there. When I left, things were... They were sort of..."

Leaning back against the wooden slats of the bridge's walls, she shut her eyes and shook her head. "They were bad."

For a moment, Dallas didn't respond. But then, even with her eyes closed, she heard his footsteps on the rickety bridge, and she knew he was walking toward her.

"I assume Bree and Penny don't know about…about your father's reason for—"

She shook her head again. "No. I've never told anyone."

"God, Rowena," he said in a throaty voice. He was so close to her. If she'd stretched out her hand, she would have touched him. "You've carried this all alone, all these years."

"Yes," she said. She felt a stinging along her lids, warning her that the tears might not have finished falling yet. A year ago…a week…a day, she couldn't have imagined crying in front of him, much less telling him any of these painful secrets.

How did he do it? How did he strip away her defenses? And why, in a strange and terrifying way, did being exposed feel almost… good?

She knew that, before they left this shelter tonight, she would tell him exactly what had happened, and why she felt responsible for her mother's death. And, even while she feared it, she felt the tempting pull of confession. Release, even a temporary one, would be such bliss.

"Rowena." His warm fingers touched the

chilled skin of her chin. She opened her eyes and looked into his. "Do you want to tell me?"

She swallowed hard. But she didn't answer. A tear slid down her cheek, another heat against the cold.

He moved his hand and softly erased the tear with his fingertips. And then, slowly, he reached out and gathered her into his arms.

She didn't resist, but she didn't return the embrace, either. Numbly, she stared over his shoulder at the poplar branches that swayed restlessly in the rain.

But somehow the warm strength of Dallas's muscled chest slowly drew the tension from her, and she felt herself relaxing into his embrace.

She shut her eyes again, and let her cheek rest against his shoulder.

Inhaling, she felt the low thrum of recognition. His body was harder, more manly, rippling with muscles he'd been too young to dream of back then. And yet, he smelled the same. Clean, a hint of lime and an undertone of something sweet, like currants or pears. How was it possible that, while everything else in the world had changed, Dallas Garwood smelled exactly the same?

His arms tightened. She felt his chin against her hair.

"Tell me," he said.

She wanted to...wanted it so much her throat burned with the need to speak.

But when she tried to think of which words to use, she knew they would all sound like limp, self-serving excuses. Who would believe that Rowena hadn't intended to betray her mother? Who could imagine that a loving daughter could be so self-absorbed, distracted, caught up in her own fear and shame about Dallas, that she would forget to cover for her mother, as she'd promised?

"Please." His lips touched her hair. "Tell me."

And so, perhaps because she felt safer in his arms than she had felt for so many years, she did.

Telling meant reliving—which she hadn't done in so long she wondered whether she'd remember the details. But soon she was right back in the moment. Fifteen years ago. Alone in her bedroom at Bell River. Boiling with anger and despair, the day after Dallas had been shot.

"Did your mother do laundry today?"

It had seemed like such a simple question.

Her father had appeared in her doorway, looking exhausted and half-mad, his hair uncombed and his shirt covered in blood from trying to revive Dallas. The police had questioned him all night, and again in the morning. He hadn't had time to change.

Rowena had hoped they would *never* let him go. She didn't want to see him, or talk to him, ever again. She hated him with every ounce of her being.

If she'd been smart, she would simply have mumbled a quick "No," or "I don't know," and let him move on down the hall to take his shower.

But instead she'd lashed out, hoping she could maybe hurt him a little, too.

"*Laundry?* You'd love to think all your slaves have been hurrying around here, making sure you have everything you need, wouldn't you? Well, Mom hasn't spent a single hour in this house today, and I wouldn't have, either, if I had anywhere else to go."

The slow narrowing of his eyes and the deep furrows that appeared on his forehead had brought her to her senses.

Oh, no... She'd promised...she'd make sure her dad never found out...

A claw of shame and fear held her heart in

its grip. Would he put two and two together? What would happen now? Would they fight? Would they maybe even break up? Would her mother ever forgive her?

Amazingly, he hadn't reacted at all. The claw relaxed. Maybe her mom hadn't contended she was at home in the first place. Or maybe he was too tired to think it all through.

After a late dinner, which had been tense, but calm enough that Rowena dared to hope her father had forgotten about what she'd said, he told the girls to go outside and check on the horses. He and their mother needed to talk about what the police were planning to do.

That made sense. Rowena wanted to believe all was well, and so she made herself believe it. The three sisters lingered in the stables an hour or two, unable to fathom their good luck. Away from the grown-ups, they could grill Rowena for details about Dallas and the shooting.

By the time they returned to the house, it was almost midnight, and her mother lay dead on the floor. Her father was upstairs, burning photo albums and smashing perfume bottles and mirrors and frames—and mumbling noises that weren't even really words.

The memory was so vivid that for a second

Rowena's nostrils stung with the acrid smell of smoke. She returned to the present slowly, like someone waking from anesthesia. Her mouth felt dry from talking without pause. And she felt a damp spot on Dallas's shirt that told her she'd cried a little, too.

His heart beat against her ear, and she let that be enough for a minute or two. But when he didn't speak, she grew nervous.

"I know what you must think of me," she said. She didn't look at him. She didn't want to see how his expression had changed. "But please know that it can't be worse than what I already think about myself."

He made a sound in his throat. And then, with those strong, gentle hands, he moved her out an inch or two, so that he could look at her.

"I'm sorry, Rowena. But you don't have a clue what I think of you." His voice was husky. "You never have."

She peered up at him, wishing suddenly that the covered bridge were lit. His face was distorted by shadows, and his eyes were very dark. The electric blue was only a momentary flash as the moonlight sparkled on the falling rain.

She could determine nothing from his expression. So why did she suddenly feel so breathless? From the start, his embrace had been comfort, not seduction. The tale she told had been agonizing, not erotic.

Why, then, was her heart beating so fast? Why was her midsection twisting in on itself, as if he had already begun to undress her?

"Tell me, then," she said, consciously repeating his earlier words. "What do you think?"

"I think..." He took a jagged breath. "I think you are the most amazing woman I've ever known."

"In spite of what I just told you?"

"Because of it. Because of *all* of it. Because you have fire, and courage, and great, undying love. Love for your mother, and your sisters, and even the land itself." He tightened his arms. "And because, somehow, after everything you've endured, you have survived with that passion intact."

She began to tremble, and she didn't even care. Unshed tears, a lifetime of them, it seemed, burned behind her eyes, but she burned everywhere suddenly, and one place seemed no more important than another.

"No," he said harshly. "I didn't mean to

make you cry. I was just trying to say that you are brave, and beautiful, and—"

"Dallas." Before he could say another word, she rose to her tiptoes and wrapped her hands around his head, burrowing her fingers into the thick silk of his hair.

She pressed her lips to his hungrily, and drank from them. She didn't take a breath, couldn't seem to quench the need. She kissed, and nipped, and tasted him, releasing all the aching desire she'd held inside for so long.

When his lips opened, and he finally returned the kiss with a hard, driving thrust of his own, any hope of controlling herself vanished.

Murmuring his name against his lips, she ran her hands down his chest, and found the buckle of his belt. Her fingers tripped over themselves trying to free the clasp. Every time she grazed against the hard swell beneath, she stopped breathing.

Finally the belt opened, separated and revealed the button fly beneath. She groaned... A zipper would have been so much faster, so much easier for her trembling hands to manage.

If only he would give her one clear moment to think, to remember how buttons and buttonholes worked. But he seemed determined to keep her breathless and confused. He tugged down the gathered elastic neckline of her shirt, until he pulled it over her elbow, across her wrist and then away from that arm entirely.

He pushed aside her bra, too. The breast that he exposed to the chilly air tightened, even as it seemed to swell with desire. He placed the warmth of his hand over her, then dipped his head and took her breast between his teeth.

Crying out, she lost track of what her fingers were doing. As his tongue circled, and his lips tugged, she tilted her head back, fighting for air. Lost in the sensation, she hardly realized that his hands were free now, free to slide, hot and hard, up her thighs and deftly release the zipper of her own jeans.

Before she knew it, he had opened the clasp, and the zipper practically freed itself. He skimmed the denim, and the panties beneath, down her legs in one velvet motion. His fingers cupped her behind first one knee, and then the other, lifting, so that she stepped free of the cloth.

It only took an instant. Suddenly, she was

bare to the night, except for her crown and the flowing gypsy cotton shirt.

She ought to be ashamed. They were outside, where anyone could see.

But there was no one for miles. The covered bridge was its own world, behind a curtain of secrecy created by the mist and rain. And besides, even if a dozen people came marching up to the bridge right now, she wasn't sure she could stop.

He sank to his knees, and before she quite understood what he intended, he began performing the same agonizing ministrations on the fiery, pebbled spot between her legs. She tunneled her hands into his hair, trying not to cry out, trying to somehow survive the blindly spiraling pressure without losing her mind forever.

"Wait," she whispered, and she tugged on his hair, desperate. She couldn't hold out much longer, not unless he stopped right now.

He bent back his head and looked up at her, with gleaming eyes.

"Why?"

"Because… I want more than this." She shut her eyes again as a wave of heat pulsed through her.

"We'll have more," he promised. He started

to lower his head again, but she pushed him away with the heels of her hands.

"Please," she said, her voice thin from lack of air. "The first time... I want us to be together."

He hesitated a second, as if it was difficult for him to relinquish what he'd just found. But then he nodded. He rose quickly and stood before her, his hands at his side. She could see the thick, hard line pressing at his jeans, and she reached out instinctively to free him.

He let her work unimpeded this time, and her fingers were deft and true. Within seconds, she had peeled the denim away. He took one step toward her, closing what little distance there was, and placed the palm of one hand against her buttocks. With the other hand, he lifted her right leg and wrapped it around his hip.

The position embarrassed her at first, but then she saw how perfectly it opened her to him. When he guided himself urgently inside her, it seemed as if they had been designed from the start to fit exactly like this.

He was large, and she was inexperienced, and she felt him holding back, going slowly, giving her time to accommodate him. She tried to relax, though every muscle seemed to want to tighten and clench and ride him until somehow the agony went away.

Finally, he groaned, and tilted his hips one last time.

Oh... She couldn't keep from moaning. She tingled everywhere, as if she were being slowly electrified. Though they remained perfectly still, he had moved all the way in, stretching her until she felt helplessly, beautifully impaled. She heard herself panting, and she felt tiny nerve endings twitch and pulse where he filled her.

She needed more. Instinctively, she wrapped her other leg around him, too.

"Yes," he breathed. He put both hands around her hips, and then, in a dance so complicated she could only follow by instinct, he began to make love to her at last. He guided her hips up and down, his own hips thrusting and withdrawing, then thrusting again.

She tilted back against the wall, so that their joining was more complete. Her breast still rose from her shirt, a naked, pink invitation, and, laughing, he bent his head to take it into his mouth again.

It was too much.

"Dallas," she cried out, her senses overloading. The aching part inside her that was filled with him began to spasm, and she lost her ability to cooperate with the intricate rhythm. She jerked awkwardly, her feet digging into his back, a reflex that shoved him into her so far she felt a hot stab of pain in her deepest core.

And then she cried out one more time, louder than ever, as ripples of searing, shivering firelight exploded all over her body. She arched her back, and bucked gracelessly against him, utterly, terrifyingly out of control.

At the very last minute, she finally felt his masterful rhythm stutter. His fingers ground into her hips. He whispered her name and then, with a groan that might have been pure pain, he seemed to explode inside her.

A wet heat gushed against her, filling her with a shockingly primitive bliss.

Panting and weak, she leaned her head against the wall, aware that her cheeks were striped with tears again. She closed her eyes, hoping he wouldn't ask her why.

She couldn't answer, because she honestly didn't know.

She was crying either because she had

waited so long for this heartbreakingly beautiful experience…

Or because she knew that it would never happen again.

Chapter Twenty

They had barely caught their breath when Dallas heard a distant hum that sounded ominously like a car. He turned his head toward the road, realizing for the first time that the rain had stopped. The only drops falling now were from overladen branches.

But the worst part was that he also saw two hazy halos of white-gold light moving rapidly toward them. *Damn it.* Out here, halfway to nowhere. A car.

He lowered Rowena gently to the ground. "Someone's coming," he said. "We should be ready in case they stop."

She glanced once toward the opening, saw

the car, which was only a hundred yards away now, and nodded. She slipped her arm back into her shirt and centered the loose neckline across her collarbone, as modestly as possible. Then she picked up her discarded jeans and pulled them on.

She ran her fingers through her hair, and when they snagged on the ribbons of her headdress, she reached up and tugged it off. She held it loosely behind her back, as if somehow it might betray them.

The headlights kept coming, and Dallas suddenly realized that this tiny bridge they had borrowed might have been built for more than only pedestrian traffic. It might be the route the owner used to access his ranch at all times—whether on horse, or in a vehicle.

"We need to get out of here," he said, grabbing Rowena's arm and walking quickly toward the back end of the bridge. That side was much closer anyhow, but it also made more sense to walk away from the oncoming car, buying whatever extra seconds they could. The motorcycle, which he'd parked along the wall, would have to fend for itself.

They made it out, and onto the open land behind, just as the car entered the covered area, still going at an ungodly clip. The tires rumbled over the wooden slats, the sound echoing under the roof like trapped thunder. Apparently whoever drove that car hadn't for an instant imagined that anyone or anything might be in his path.

At the last minute, as the driver barreled out of the shadows, he obviously saw Dallas and Rowena standing at the mouth of the bridge. The sight must have nearly given him a heart attack. He stood on the brakes, attempting to go from forty to zero in one second flat. The back of the car fishtailed slightly in the soggy ground, and Dallas wondered if the guy might be going to end up in the creek.

The brakes won the battle, though, and when the car settled, the driver's window opened, and a man's head thrust out. "Goddamn it, what the hell are you doing on my bridge? I nearly killed you."

Dallas positioned himself so that he obscured Rowena as much as possible without looking suspicious.

"I'm sorry," he said evenly. "We got stuck in the rain and took shelter here. We were just about to get back on the road when we saw you coming."

The man seemed to be calming a little

with every passing second. He frowned. "Oh. Well, sorry. You say your car broke down?" He swiveled, looking in all directions. "Where is it?"

"No, nothing broke down." Dallas smiled, hoping the old guy didn't hate bikers. "We're on a motorcycle, and the rain was too heavy to keep riding. The bike is back on the bridge."

The man craned his neck in vain, then settled for peering into his side-view mirror. Of course, the bridge was too dark to reveal anything. "Your motorcycle is in there right now? For God's sake, get it out of there! I could have smashed the darn thing to a pancake."

"I definitely thought you would," Dallas said, laughing as if they were sharing a joke. "And while I wouldn't mind that very much, my brother owns the bike, and he would have been heartbroken. I'm Dallas Garwood, by the way. Sheriff Garwood. Pretty solid driving there, Mr....?"

"Harkness." The man seemed to recognize Dallas's name. "Shady Nook Ranch." He cleared his throat, perhaps realizing that he'd been speeding, and this was a cop. "Well, then I guess everything's fine. You'd better get back home, though, before the rain starts up again."

"Absolutely." Dallas smiled. "Thanks very much for the use of the shelter. We'd have drowned without it."

Harkness smiled, too, but Dallas noticed that he watched them in the rearview mirror, all the way back down the bridge. The car didn't move even after they mounted the motorcycle and started the engine, brake lights gleaming, and headlamp lighting their way forward.

In fact, the man's car was still parked there in the mud when Dallas maneuvered onto the road and rounded the curve that would point them back toward Silverdell. By then, he'd completely lost whatever chance he'd had to talk to Rowena while she was still caught in the afterglow of good sex.

She undoubtedly had already retreated back into her emotional cave. She'd probably hidden deeper, rendering herself more inaccessible than ever, if he understood her correctly—and he believed he finally did. He had learned so much about her over the past few weeks, and he realized that her trust issues were enormous. She probably was regretting having spilled so many secrets to him.

She *definitely* was regretting that they had made love. He could feel it in the way she sat, stiffly and as far back as the motorcycle's seat would allow.

He could imagine the loop of denial playing even now in her head. The decision to have sex had been unfortunate, but not fatal. It had meant nothing. It committed her to nothing. She had given him no power he could use to hurt her. She was still free, and safe, and in control.

A comforting lie. But a lie, nonetheless. He had seen her face as she fell apart in his arms. She had been in control of nothing—all body, no mind. And, in that abandoned state, she had sparkled with pure, elemental joy.

When he drew the motorcycle up to the festival's parking lot, which was eerily motionless, like a black-and-white art photo of an abandoned field roiling with mist, she climbed down quickly and pulled off her helmet.

He got his first clear look at her new face. The *after* face.

He had completely underestimated just how far she had withdrawn. She might as well be gazing at him from another planet.

"Rowena," he began urgently, though he knew it was futile. That face... Nothing could touch her tonight. She had encased herself in a protective shell of ice and stone and steel. If he tried to break through now, he'd bloody them both in the process...and maybe destroy his chances forever.

But how could he let her go?

"Rowena," he said again.

"No." She shook her head slowly and firmly. "Look... I appreciate what you did tonight, Dallas."

He frowned. She sounded like a teacher, thanking a parent for the brownies.

"You were, as I said, extremely kind," she continued in the same overly formal tone. "And your...your generosity helped me get through a very difficult night."

Generosity? Was that what she really believed? That this wild, wonderful, unwise... and, by the way, *unprotected*...encounter had been nothing more than pity sex?

"Look, Rowena, I know you're scared—"

Oh, hell. What was wrong with him? Did he have oatmeal for brains? *Scared* was the one word he should never have uttered.

She'd hate him for sensing her vulnerability, when she wouldn't even admit it to herself. Her pride, her fierce, unbreakable pride, had been the only crutch she could trust, through all these years of exile.

"I'm not scared," she said, instantly haughty, as he should have known she'd be. "What I am is tired. I thank you for everything you did. But right now, I'm afraid the only thing you can do for me is let me go."

When she got home, Rowena dropped her mangled wildflower crown into the outside trash can. Then she let herself into the house as quietly as she could. She put her purse down on the kitchen counter, took off her shoes and was tiptoeing through the great room when she saw Penny, curled up on the sofa, half-asleep.

"Hi," Penny said softly. She raised herself to a sitting position and brushed her hair out of her face. "I'm so glad you came back."

Rowena felt a pang. It hadn't occurred to her that Bree and Penny might think she wouldn't return. Where could she have gone? Did they think she'd squander money on a hotel simply to avoid talking to them?

"How come you're sleeping down here?"

"I was waiting for you. I wanted to tell you about Bree." Penny rubbed her ear. "She left, Ro. She was really upset. In spite of what she said, I don't think she really believed you'd leave. You know how she is."

"I don't understand. The rental car is still out front. Where did she go?"

"Home. When you drove off, she called a cab. She left the car for me. I think she was going to Montrose, to see if she could get a plane out in the morning."

Rowena stared, unsure what to say, or how to react. She wondered if she were simply incapable of absorbing another shock tonight. She heard Penny's words, and technically she understood them, but she didn't really *feel* anything.

Somewhere under the numbing, gauzelike layer of exhaustion, she might be sad, or hurt, by Bree's abrupt departure, but the emotion couldn't force its way up to her conscious mind.

Her legs felt flimsy, though, and she let herself plop down on the sofa beside her sister. "I'm surprised she didn't try to make you leave with her."

"She did." Penny's face was somber. "But I wouldn't do it. Not so soon. Not in anger. I have to go back home tomorrow anyhow—Ruth isn't well. But I couldn't leave without saying goodbye."

Penny's cheeks flushed, as she realized what she had said. The whole argument had started because Rowena *had* been able to leave Penny, just like that, with no goodbye, and no explanation.

"Thank you." Rowena reached out her hand, and took her sister's. "Standing up to Bree is no mean feat. You always were tougher than you look, Pea."

"Maybe." Penny smiled. She glanced toward the doorway that led to the staircase, and squeezed Rowena's hand. "Not tough enough to sleep upstairs alone, though."

"Oh." Rowena squeezed back. "Penny. It's okay."

"I know. I know it's childish, but I haven't been in this house alone, not since Mom died. And for the life of me, I just can't stop seeing…"

She didn't finish the sentence. She obviously knew she didn't need to. Instead, she let her tousled head fall against Rowena's shoulder, and stared blankly down at their joined hands.

With that warm, familiar pressure against her, Rowena's numbness finally broke. A wave of protective love swept through her.

"She's not here anymore, Pea. I've been living alone in the place for weeks, and I promise you there are no ghosts. Not even *his.* It's just a house now, and we can sell it without any regrets."

"I know." Penny didn't sound convinced, though. She had always been the most sensitive of the sisters. Rowena wondered whether Penny still painted. She wished her sister could stay long enough to get to know Bonnie. The two artistic spirits would like each other, she felt sure.

But staying wasn't really an option for any of them now. How long would Rowena herself be here? The Austin job started a week from tomorrow. And if she wanted to, she could leave even earlier. Why hang around here any longer? The main repairs were finished, and Bree had stuck the final pin into the bubble dream of a dude ranch.

Maybe Rowena should take a few days and see some of the countryside between Colorado and Texas.

She'd wait for the DNA results, of course, because they were being mailed to this address. But they were due next week—as early as tomorrow, perhaps. That was really the last piece of unfinished business, wasn't it?

In a spur-of-the-moment decision, she told herself that, if the results confirmed she wasn't Johnny Wright's child, she'd leave immediately.

Would she tell Penny and Bree?

Maybe she'd have to.

Because Johnny had never rewritten his will, the document had still named Moira as the primary beneficiary, with the provision that, if she predeceased him, the estate would be divided equally "per stirpes," which the lawyers had concluded meant the three sisters.

But what was the exact definition of that piece of legalese? If it meant *divided equally among his bloodline...*

Where would that leave Rowena?

Was it enough that he was listed on her birth certificate as her father? And, even if that was enough to satisfy a court, was it enough to satisfy her conscience?

"Where did you go tonight?" Penny's voice sounded sleepy, and she yawned behind her hand. "We had such a bad storm. I was worried about you."

"I went to see a friend," Rowena equivocated. But she didn't like to lie to Penny, so she amended that. "I was with Dallas, actually."

Penny raised her head from Rowena's

arm. "Dallas? You're kidding! I would have thought he hated all of us, after what happened."

"No." Rowena discovered that the subject of Dallas made her even more uncomfortable than any other, even the DNA issues. "He's too nice for that. We've talked it out, and it's all fine. We... I guess it's fair to say we've found some closure."

Closure?

Though it sounded like something out of a psychology textbook, she decided she liked that word. It felt sensible, and nonthreatening. Way back then, they had started an emotional fire, but they hadn't had the chance to put it out. Her father's violence had interrupted them before any resolution, literal or figurative, could be reached. It had left them both hanging—and it had given their past far more power than it deserved.

She felt a little better, now that she'd hit on this way of looking at it. Tonight's lovemaking might have been extraordinary, but it hadn't meant anything particularly profound. It had simply been scratching a fifteen-year itch.

"Well, that's nice of him." Penny returned

her head to Rowena's shoulder and yawned again. "Is he still gorgeous?"

Rowena pictured him, silvered by the moonlight.

"Yeah, he's pretty cute," she said. Then, to avoid further questions, she reached behind her and pulled out a couple of the ugly cushions. She tossed one to the far end, and propped the other up against the armrest on her side.

"But enough talking, Sweetpea. It's late. Let's get some sleep."

Penny smiled gratefully, obviously relieved to have Rowena beside her tonight, as she had so many nights in their childhood. Though the sofa was large and overstuffed, easily big enough for both of them, Penny stretched out the other way, so that they lay head to toe, as they used to do in the tiny twin bed.

Rowena kicked off her shoes, lifted her legs and placed her head on her armrest, as well. She shut her eyes. She knew she wouldn't get any sleep, not tonight. But maybe Penny would.

Within minutes, though, the room began to float around her, and the ticking of the grandfather clock in the foyer seemed to come from far away.

When she suddenly heard Penny's voice, Rowena wasn't sure whether the sound was real, or the beginning of a dream.

"I guess Bree's right, but…still." Though Penny's sleepy lips slurred the words, otherwise she spoke quite naturally, as if continuing an ongoing conversation. "Bell River would have been a wonderful dude ranch, wouldn't it?"

Chapter Twenty-One

At midnight, when the rain finally stopped, and a smudgy moon appeared in the low-hanging gray sky, Alec sat outside on Benny McAvee's front stoop, waiting for his dad to pick him up. He wished his father would hurry. He'd made a cushion of his backpack, which protected him from the wet concrete, but he'd packed some of his action figures in there, and they poked annoyingly into his rear.

He knew Mrs. McAvee was watching him through her living room window, but he pretended he didn't. He wanted to be alone. It was kind of embarrassing to have to go home from a sleepover. No matter what terrible disease you faked, everyone probably thought you were just homesick.

But he wasn't homesick. Not exactly. The official story, the one he told Mrs. McAvee when he came out into the living room, was that he had a bad stomachache. The truth was more complicated and didn't have an easy name.

Here was the situation. It was Sunday—the day after the wildflower festival was always a school holiday, so everybody had sleepovers. His birthday was on Tuesday, only a couple of days away. Right before Uncle Mitch had delivered him to the McAvees' house, Alec had received an email from his mom, telling him that she was flying home for the party.

Ever since then, he hadn't been able to settle down and feel normal. His stomach did hurt, but not from too much cotton candy at the festival, which is what Mrs. McAvee believed. It was more like…a kind of emotional sick.

And the weird part was…it wasn't regular happiness, like when he got too excited before some cool thing, like a trip, or a hike with his dad. It wasn't sad, either, like the knot he got before a math test.

It was a little of both. It was really tight, and swoopy, and strange.

Mostly he just wanted to be at home. He wanted to see his dad.

He heard a rumble, and then he saw the headlights. He jumped up, grabbed his backpack and slung it over one shoulder, then bolted down the steps to greet his father. He reached him just as he got out of the truck and came around toward the house.

"Dad!" He hugged his father, which he hadn't done for a long time, not since he was a little kid. He wasn't sure why he did it. It was kind of risky. For all he knew, Benny and the other boys were spying on him from their window, too.

His father tousled his hair. "Hey, buddy. You okay?"

"Yeah, it's just that—"

Wouldn't you know it? Mrs. McAvee had to come out right then, probably so that she could make sure Dad knew it wasn't her fault Alec was sick.

Or maybe she came because she was divorced, and he'd heard her say Dad was handsome. Alec tilted a look up at his father, trying to see what the women saw. But he just looked like Dad.

Alec wondered if, when he grew up, he'd be handsome, too. Partly he hoped so, and partly he hoped not, because it seemed annoying to have girls flirting with you all the time. Sometimes, at recess, he had to insult Katie Landringham simply to make her go away.

"Dad, can I go sit in the truck?"

"Sure." His dad opened the passenger door, and Alec tossed his backpack in, then climbed up as fast as he could. He got the door shut just in time. Mrs. McAvee had reached the sidewalk and had already started gabbing.

Good thing the window was closed tight. Alec heard only her first words, "I think he's a little homesick, Dallas—"

He turned and stared the other way. He didn't want to hear any more.

Amazingly, his dad got Mrs. McAvee to shut up pretty fast, and sent her back inside. Within a couple of minutes, they were on the road. He liked driving with his dad, who didn't talk all the time like Uncle Mitch did. Sometimes, sure, Alec was in the mood for talking. He was a big talker—everyone told him that.

But when he wasn't, his dad's easy silence was comforting. It gave him time to think.

So for a while he just listened to the quiet hum of the truck skimming along the shining roads. Everything looked different late at night. The headlights seemed to eat up the strange, swirling mist, and he could imagine that they were in an intergalactic capsule, rolling through deep space.

It started to make him sleepy.

"Did you hear about Mom?" He didn't want to fall asleep before he talked about this with Dad. Maybe that was why he felt tight and weird. Maybe he was secretly worried that Dad might not be okay with her showing up.

"About her coming for your birthday?" His dad kept his eyes on the road. "Yep, I heard. That's great, huh?"

"Yeah!" But Alec still didn't feel pumped up and happy. He still felt weird. He fiddled with the straps of his backpack. "I wonder why she's coming."

His dad glanced at him this time. "What do you mean? She's coming because she wants to see you on your birthday. She wouldn't want to miss the party. You know how she loves Mrs. B.'s cakes."

"Well, she didn't come for my birthday last year." Alec chewed on his lower lip, where a piece of dry skin had started to lift up and become really annoying. "Or the year before that."

His dad's hands gripped the wheel tightly. Alec could see the bunched-up muscles in his shoulders.

"I know," his dad said, his voice a lot calmer than those shoulders. "And she felt horrible about it, both times. Sometimes a person just can't make things happen, though. No matter how much he wants to."

Alec nodded automatically. He didn't want to sound whiny, like a baby, but those birthdays had been spoiled, completely ruined, because his mom wasn't there. Even worse, the presents she sent were so cool, but when he called to say thanks she sounded embarrassed, and he knew she'd probably sent cash and let his dad pick them out.

"Hey." His dad laid his palm over Alec's knee and jiggled slightly. "You're not worried that she'll cancel, are you?"

Alec shrugged. "Who knows? Sometimes a person just can't make things happen, right?"

His dad laughed. "Right. But this time is different, I promise."

"Why?"

"Because this time, if she can't make it,

we're going to get on an airplane and fly over there instead."

That was a big deal, his dad promising something major like a trip to France. His dad never made promises he didn't mean to keep. Alec's stomach settled down a bit, and he relaxed against the leather seats, closing his eyes.

But then, suddenly, he bolted upright. "Oh, Dad. I meant to ask you something, but I forgot."

"Yeah? What?"

"I wanted to know if it's okay for us to invite Rowena to my party."

His dad's jaw tightened, and his grip, which had relaxed, squeezed the wheel again.

"What's wrong? It's not okay?" Alec tried to read his expression. "Why? Don't you like her?"

"Hey, settle down." His dad smiled, and he stretched out his fingers, one hand at a time, as if he had noticed how he was gripping the wheel. "I didn't say it wasn't okay, and I definitely didn't say I don't like her."

"You do like her?" Instantly, Alec's mood lifted. "She looks pretty now, I think, don't you? Did you see her at the festival? She's really nice, and not in that fakey way. And you should see her when she trains the horses. She's awesome. She should be on TV."

His dad lifted one eyebrow. "Wow, that's a hard sell, buddy. You're not trying to set me up with Rowena this time, are you?"

"No!" Alec denied it automatically, but then he reconsidered. If Rowena became his dad's serious girlfriend, she'd want to stay in Silverdell. So she probably wouldn't sell Bell River. That would be great. Whenever Alec came back from France, he could visit them.

Out of nowhere, as soon as he thought those words, his stomach twisted. He touched it instinctively, wondering what was going on. Was he maybe a little afraid of living in another country, or something?

"No matchmaking?" His father cut a glance at him, and Alec let go of his stomach.

"Well, I don't know. Maybe." Alec tilted his head. "Would you go for it?"

His dad didn't answer for a few seconds. And then, to Alec's surprise, he nodded. "Yep. I would definitely go for it."

When Alec started to make a whooping sound, his dad held out a hand. "Hold on. I said *I* would go for it, but that's only half the battle. The real problem is… I'm not sure *she* would go for it."

Alec considered this. He was pretty sure Rowena liked his dad. She didn't talk about him a lot, and she never put on that icky gooey voice like the other women did. But there was something in the way she looked at him....

"Want me to talk to her for you, Dad?" Alec's sleepiness and stomachache had disappeared. Suddenly he was all energy and focus. "I mean, she and I are pretty good friends. Maybe she thinks you're...you know...kind of stuffy. She probably isn't the kind of person who is all swoony and impressed just because you're the sheriff."

His dad's smile was odd. "I'm pretty sure you're right about that."

"But I could probably talk her into giving you a chance," Alec said. "I mean. If you want me to."

They were almost home. Alec watched his father closely, waiting for the answer. It was a long time coming. His dad had already pulled into the driveway, parked the car and stopped the motor before he turned back to look at Alec.

"You really think you could talk her into it?"

Alec nodded vigorously. "I do. I'm serious, Dad. She and I are like...tight."

"Well, that's lucky for me." His dad chuckled softly. "Because frankly, I am pretty sure I'm going to need all the help I can get."

Penny was set to leave just before noon. She had a lot of ground to cover. The Montrose airport didn't fly directly to San Francisco, so she'd have to transfer in Chicago, and it would take her all afternoon to get home. She had promised Ruth she'd be back that night. Ruth's congestive heart failure, which Rowena had heard about since the sisters were all in grade school, got worse every year.

In the past couple of years, apparently Penny had become her full-time maid, nurse, companion and housekeeper. When Rowena expressed dismay about that, Penny assured her it was fine.

"It might be hard for someone as outdoorsy as you, or as social as Bree," she said, smiling. "But it suits me perfectly. I like to live quietly, and I get a lot of time to read and paint."

Rowena subsided, well aware she didn't have any right to pass judgment on Penny's

choices. They were who they were. Penny
was a sticker. Rowena was a runner. Those
patterns had been established aeons ago, and
it was too late to change them now.

Still, parting from Penny was hard this
time. They stood by the car, going over a few
details about the real estate listing, and talking about Rowena's new job in Austin. They
stalled as long as they could, and then, finally,
they hugged goodbye.

Penny clung as if she feared they might
never see each other again. Which, given Rowena's past disappearing acts, wasn't exactly
impossible.

Suddenly, with Penny's arms around her,
Rowena felt herself on the verge of tears. She
moved back, blinking roughly.

What on earth was wrong with her? Maybe
selling this place was the smartest move, after
all. Something about being here made her
weak. She'd teared up more times living in
Silverdell the past few weeks than she had in
the entire fifteen years of exile put together.

"Do you think it's possible that, once the
ranch is sold, and all the old memories are
gone, we might be able to start over?" Penny's gaze drifted over the front drive, which
led down to the gate and the twisted pines.

Rowena didn't see any pain in Penny's expression, as if parting from this land broke her heart. Maybe the five years between them made the difference. Maybe, because Penny had been only eleven when they left Bell River, her attachments hadn't run as deep.

What she did see was a new maturity in her baby sister's sweet, fairy-tale face. Penny was twenty-six now, all grown up. Hard to believe.

"What I mean is, I've always felt the past, dragging us down, dragging us apart. Haven't you?" Penny hesitated, watching Rowena, waiting for her answer.

"I suppose so," she said, because what else could she say? She couldn't begin to put words to the cacophony of emotions that always clamored just beneath her conscious mind.

Penny nodded. "So I guess what I'm asking is…do you think that, now that Daddy's gone…and all the memories this house holds… Do you think that, once we're free, it might be easier for us to see each other more often? Do you think there's any chance we could be more like family again?"

Family?

Rowena thought of the secret pictures of her mother and the mysterious Rowan—and the DNA tests being performed on her father's pitiful few remaining possessions.

But no matter what the results of those tests said, Rowena suspected that the only way she could handle the loss of Bell River, and Silverdell...and Dallas...would be to close the door on her past forever. She'd have to become a different woman, and that woman would have no home, no roots, no family. No heart, no pain.

"I don't know," she answered. It was as close to honesty as she could come without being cruel. "I only know I want you to be happy, Pea. No matter what happens. Will you promise me that?"

"Of course," Penny said, but her eyes were sad. They hugged again, and then, because it had to be done, she got in her car and left.

When she made it through the gate and turned onto the main road, Rowena heard the faint echo of her horn, signaling a short double-beep goodbye. Rowena waved stiffly for far too long, though she knew Penny could no longer see her.

Then, turning so abruptly dirt scuffed into her shoes, Rowena jogged straight to the stables and began to saddle Flash. She would not just sit around and fret. The morning was beautiful, the bright air washed clean by last night's storm. The wildflowers had loved the rain, too, responding by shooting up another six inches. In the distance, the western fields seemed carpeted in thick purple fluff.

The vista called to Rowena, deep in her blood. Besides, Flash needed some exercise—the festival had eaten up too much of Rowena's time these past two days. She and the horse could both use a nice, long run in open country to clear their heads.

Before she could mount, though, Bonnie appeared in the stable door. Dressed in the cutoff jeans and T-shirt she always wore to clean house. She looked about sixteen—and absurdly beautiful.

She held a large white pasteboard envelope with bold red letters that announced it had been hand-delivered.

"Hey," she said, strolling in to give Marybelle a pat, obviously well aware of how jealous the mare got when Flash was chosen for a ride. Bonnie held up the envelope. "This just came for you. It looked important, so…"

Rowena glanced over. It was the DNA results.

Instantly, her heart slowed down to the point that she couldn't quite feel it beating anymore. She'd known it was coming, but knowing it was *here,* knowing it was tangible, solid and irreversible... That was shockingly different.

The testing company promised results within a week in a case like hers. It could have been sooner, except that she had provided such marginal samples. She'd ended up sending everything. The pipe and pipe cleaner, Johnny's electric razor, an old hairbrush and a toothbrush, and even a pair of fingernail clippers.

Apparently, somewhere in that odd assortment, the lab had found the DNA it needed. So now, in that white packet, lay the information that would tell Rowena who she really was.

Or wasn't.

"Thanks," she said. She took the envelope, which seemed slight, not substantial enough to hold her future inside. She almost dropped it, because she'd expected something heavier.

She stared down at the letters on the envelope. Express Overnight, it said—no other identifying marks except her name and address. It might have been anything. Bonnie would have no clue what Rowena was reading, even if she opened it right here in front of her.

But she needed to be alone when she learned the truth contained inside. Whatever it said, she might be flooded with emotions she couldn't quite hide.

"Would you mind taking Marybelle out to the paddock for me? I think they're both feeling a little cabin fever, after being ignored this weekend."

"Sure." Bonnie loved to walk the horses, though she never rode. "Come on, Mary, we're going for a walk" she said, nickering to the horse, who happily nickered back.

Rowena waited while she slipped the halter and lead rope around Marybelle's head, opened the stable door and guided the obedient horse toward the yard. Bonnie had learned well, and performed the task efficiently, but even so…to Rowena their departure seemed to take forever.

When she was finally alone, she sat on one of the three-legged stools and quickly pulled the tab that unsealed the packet. She didn't give herself much brooding time. The way she felt, she might brood herself right into tossing the whole thing in the trash.

She pulled out two sheets of paper, then

opened the mouth of the packet wider, to see if she'd left something behind.

No. Two pages. That was it. One chart, and one explanation page, which consisted of merely one paragraph. She looked at the first page, the chart. For a few seconds, what she saw there swam like black, squiggly tadpoles instead of letters, and she had to blink several times to clear her vision.

Even then the black symbols were no more useful than hieroglyphics. Genetic markers, numbers, phenotypes, something called allels, and AMELs...it made no sense to her. But then, finally, at the very bottom, real words.

One large field, separated from the others:

Probability of Paternity.
Zero.

The second page was even simpler:

The results indicate that the alleged father, Jonathan Scott Wright, is excluded as the biological father of the child.

Rowena's blood rushed strangely in her ears, sounding like an internal wind, and for a split second the stable floor, with its scattered bits of hay, seemed to tilt, as if it might swoop up toward her.

She touched the wall behind her, to steady herself. Thank goodness she was sitting down.

When the room was still again, she slid the pages back into the envelope carefully, as if they were some volatile mixture that might explode if mishandled. She sat there, staring at nothing, her mind blank, for several minutes. She had a million things to do, but she had to wait until her legs were steady enough to hold her.

At some point, Bonnie returned. She paused in the doorway, backlit by the beautiful June sky. "Rowena? Are you okay?"

"Yes." Rowena nodded, though she didn't dare stand yet. "But I need to talk to you, if you have a minute."

Bonnie entered, her manner wary. She obviously could see that something quite serious had happened.

"What's up?"

"I am going to have to leave Bell River earlier than I expected," Rowena said as calmly as she could. Maybe Bonnie would assume that the letter had been from the Austin ranch. "I want you to know, though, that you are

welcome to stay here as long as you like—
until the place sells, of course. In fact, you'd
be doing me a favor. It's never good to leave
a house unoccupied for long."

Bonnie's blue eyes widened. "When do you
leave?"

Rowena thought it through. She had already contacted the livestock transport company about getting Flash to Texas. They had
seemed flexible, so they probably could move
up the date without too much trouble. Or, she
could buy a cheap truck and trailer, and take
Flash herself.

Or she could sell the horse.

Ignoring the pinch around her heart when
she articulated that thought, she tried to think
rationally. Maybe she'd been foolish to buy a
horse at all. Owning tied you down—which
is why she hadn't done it in years.

And besides, obviously if she was going to
make a clean break, it would work best if she
left everything and everyone behind.

It should be possible. Since Rowena had
begun training Flash, obviously quite suc-
cessfully, several people had expressed interest, including Tina Carpenter. Which
reminded her—Rowena would have to contact Tina, and tell her to pick up Marybelle.

The mare's training was almost complete, anyhow.

"I might leave as early as tomorrow," she said, and she tried to ignore the hurt surprise on Bonnie's face. "If I can get everything together. Wednesday, at the latest."

Bonnie made a soft sound of dismay. "So soon. I thought you'd be here all week, at least."

"Well, you know what they say about plans," Rowena said briskly. "But I'm serious about my offer. The Realtor says that the market is so glutted right now that it might take up to a year to sell the ranch. I really would be very grateful if you'd agree to stay on...kind of like a caretaker. Paid, of course."

And if Bree didn't approve of that, well, then, tough. Rowena was not going to leave Bonnie homeless—or jobless.

She stood, relieved to discover that her legs felt perfectly steady. Action always helped. Action and anger. Though she wasn't sure whom she was angry with, she definitely felt a banked rage awakening deep inside.

No wonder she'd always felt that Johnny didn't love her—didn't even like her, really. She'd spent all those young years trying to earn an affection she could never, ever get.

And all those teen years rebelling against a man who should have meant nothing to her.

How could her mother have allowed Rowena to wander in that emotional wilderness for so long? Why hadn't she ever told her the truth?

But she couldn't think about this now. She tucked the envelope under her arm and moved into Flash's stall to start removing the saddle. She didn't have time for a ride today.

As she worked the straps, she sensed Bonnie standing behind her, motionless, as if the news of Rowena's departure had stunned her into paralysis. That was an overreaction, surely. The two women had met only a few weeks ago. As much as they'd enjoyed each other's company, they'd both known the arrangement was temporary. And Mitch would still be here.

So, realistically, how big a hole could Rowena's absence leave in Bonnie's life?

"What do you think?" She glanced at Bonnie over her shoulder as she loosened the saddle. "Would that work for you? Being Bell River's caretaker, for a while?"

To her surprise, Bonnie looked more than merely disappointed. She looked...worried.

Her brows knit furrows over her beautiful eyes.

"I appreciate the offer, more than you can ever know," Bonnie began in a low voice. "But I… I don't think you ought to count on me."

Rowena lifted the saddle off Flash's back. She tucked her forearms under the skirt, and held it in front of her, smiling as naturally as she could.

"I already do count on you for just about everything that goes on under Bell River's roof. You cook, you clean, you supervise every repair. Why should it be any different when I'm gone?"

"Because…" Bonnie took a breath that sounded slightly unsteady. "Because, you see… I can't actually promise to stay. I'm not really free to commit. Things…things could happen that would mean I had to leave."

Things? Words like that—words that meant nothing or everything—were designed to dodge true communication. Rowena used words like that.

What unmentionable truth lay in Bonnie's past? She considered the sad-eyed beauty who had dropped into her life as if out of no-where. As always, she noted the details that didn't fit. The grace, the quiet charm, the education. The faint hint of an old-world Southern accent.

Her skin didn't belong out here, in the harsh, open country of the West. That peaches-and-cream complexion came from somewhere shaded and slow, with porches and oaks and large-brimmed hats.

And her hair. Rowena had begun to take it for granted, but now she saw anew the strawberry-satin roots emerging from the clumsy dye job. Sunlight sparkled on that inch of amazing color, picking out golden threads.

She remembered her earlier analysis. This woman had run from something. And now she was saying, as straightforwardly as she could, that she might have to run again.

Well, Rowena knew all about running, too.

"Bonnie," she heard herself asking, "is there any way I could help you?"

She hadn't intended to say any such thing. Here she was, preparing eagerly to sever the last true emotional and physical ties she had in this world, so that she could finally be free. So that she could finally be safe. Why would she get involved in Bonnie's problems?

Besides, she could hardly help herself these days—what could she possibly do for anyone else? And yet, there it was. She'd already said it.

Bonnie shook her head slowly. "Thank you, but I'm afraid there is nothing to be done," she said in a polite monotone. "Is there any way I could help *you?*"

Rowena almost smiled, but got only as far as a dry, ironic lift of one side of her mouth. She got the point. Sometimes all the goodwill in the world meant nothing. They both were locked in battles that had to be fought alone.

"Okay." Rowena nodded. "But I'm not asking for a commitment. I'm simply telling you that, until someone buys this place, you're welcome at Bell River."

She set down the saddle. Then, squaring her shoulders, she turned and laid her hand lightly on the young woman's arm.

"Stay as long as you want, Bonnie. And leave whenever you must."

Chapter Twenty-Two

Monday was hectic, which wasn't all bad, because it kept Dallas from driving himself half-insane, trying to decide what to do about Rowena.

Post festival, Dellians often got cranky, and had small fender benders and domestic dustups. Dallas and Deputy Bartlett were in the car all day, putting out those little brushfires.

Then, in the evening, he and Alec used one of the department's sedans to pick Allyson up at the airport. When she appeared at the gate, looking as stunning as ever, but with a new chic Bohemian look, Alec was clearly shocked to discover that his mother had brought the twins with her. Her arms were so full her son couldn't even get a proper hug.

Dallas, too, was surprised. She hadn't mentioned this. But of course no selfish act of Allyson's really *shocked* him anymore.

Dallas, at least, was glad she had brought them. After a few minutes of Alec's excited babble, conversation lagged. Allyson looked very tired, and she was clearly not in the mood for light chatter. She sat in the backseat, with the twins in two incredibly heavy baby carriers they'd dragged off the luggage carousel.

Now and then, Dallas glanced at her in the rearview mirror. Her pursed lips and tight jaw told him how much she still resented being strong-armed into making this trip.

The long ride back to Silverdell might have been damned awkward, with the three of them struggling to find common ground, except that the twins began to squall about the time Dallas reached the Highway 92 bridge, and didn't stop until he pulled up at the house.

"Can you call Mrs. B.?" Allyson bounced the crying babies on her shoulders as Dallas and Alec hauled the luggage out of the trunk. "I'm going to need help. If she could sleep over, that would be even better."

"Sure," Dallas said easily. "I can ask."

His gaze met Alec's briefly as they both reached for the same suitcase, but neither of them allowed any flicker of communication to pass between them. They looked away quickly, and kept unloading.

When they got inside, Allyson excused herself, saying she had a migraine—those must be new, either an affectation of the Bohemian lifestyle, or a result of the twins. She absolutely had to go to bed, she was so sorry, she'd see Alec in the morning, and they'd have a grand chat.

Alec seemed to accept that promise. Within half an hour, though, he quietly announced his decision to turn in, too. Dallas, who ordinarily had to muscle Alec to bed in a headlock, ached at the sight of his son's empty face.

"Hey," he said impulsively. But when Alec turned, he realized there was nothing to say, really. It probably wouldn't help for Dallas to tell him "I'm sorry I saddled you with a spoiled bitch for a mother."

But he was sorry. When they met, he had thought Allyson was beautiful, idealistic, romantic. Her childish enthusiasms and playful pouting had seemed like signs of a charming innocence. After the dark, fiery and dangerous experience with Rowena's volcanic personality, Allyson had seemed like a sip of water from a spring-fed fountain.

Now, of course, he knew better. But now was about ten years too late.

"Dad?"

"Nothing," Dallas said, giving up. "Just sleep tight."

And then he was alone in the living room, sleeping on the sofa because, of course, Allyson expected to be given the master bedroom. She could have it, but he'd be damned if he'd displace either Alec or Mitch.

The sofa, still the same one his father had owned years ago, on which he "counseled" troubled parishioners, was wretchedly uncomfortable. That had been deliberate, of course. His father's brand of counsel always included giving you a little taste of how a sinner's afterworld would feel.

When Dallas finally got out of the hospital, after the episode with Rowena, his father had made him sleep sitting up in one of the straight-backed dining room chairs for two weeks. So that Dallas, as Preacher Garwood had intoned, would glimpse, in some small way, what happened to degenerates who succumbed to filthy pleasures of the flesh.

Mitch had sneaked him pillows, and a few nights he'd even sat sentry at the dining room doorway, so that Dallas could stretch out on the floor and really sleep. If Dallas needed aspirin, he smuggled it in. When the pain stopped, he'd brought chips and beer instead—absolutely verboten in the Garwood household. Since Mitch had been only about ten at the time, heaven knew where he got it.

But it had been exactly what Dallas needed to climb out of his funk. He didn't let Mitch drink, but *he* had gotten a little tipsy. Together they lampooned their father's absurd rhetoric and cliché mannerisms.

He'd been damned lucky to have a brother like Mitch, who knew how to laugh in the face of almost any terror. He wished with a sudden intensity that he'd been able to provide a sibling for Alec.

But he hadn't. So he would have to be the one who ensured Alec had to face as few terrors as possible. He'd sleep in the doorway forever, guarding against dragons, if he had to. And he was going to start with Allyson, who by God had better come down in the morning wearing a big smile and a brand-new attitude.

He rolled over on the lumpy couch and tried to sleep.

It didn't work. He was up, off and on, all night. And he spent most of it thinking about Rowena, still wondering what to do.

By Tuesday morning, when he had to hoist his exhausted body up and get himself dressed for work, he wasn't one bit closer to a decision than he'd been the day before.

He felt like a professional safecracker, sitting in front of a lockbox full of priceless treasures—except that it had been rigged to explode if the wrong key was inserted. His mind constantly circled the problem, trying to figure out how to get in without destroying the prize he was trying to reach.

Should he be patient, for fear pressuring her would trigger her commitment phobia? Should he push, for fear restraint was interpreted as indifference? Should he call? Should he show up? Should he send an invitation to Alec's party via Mitch?

He frowned at the dithering idiot in the mirror. *To hell with this nonsense.* He jammed his razor back into its charger, and pulled a comb through his hair.

He was going over there. Now. He called Bartlett and warned him he'd be late. He stayed at the house long enough to see Mrs. B. arrive, and to be sure Allyson was going to share some of that maternal attention with Alec, who'd taken the day off school to be with his mom. Breakfast seemed to go well, with Alec lively and natural again, jabbering to Allyson about horses. And Allyson at least pretended to listen attentively.

They'd agreed she wouldn't talk to him about the France thing until they could do it together, tonight. So Dallas felt free to take off.

Once in the car, he could barely stop himself from gunning the accelerator. The sun flickered through swiftly passing trees like a strobe light as his tires sped over the asphalt. Now that the decision was made, he couldn't get to Bell River fast enough.

He didn't really have a game plan. He'd have to find the right words when he saw her. Surely, if he simply told the truth and spoke from the heart, he could break through whatever anxieties tormented her.

But… His foot eased off the gas as he suddenly asked himself the one question he'd forgotten to ask, even while he fumed and obsessed about everything connected with Rowena.

What *was* the truth? How did he really feel about her?

He admired her intensity and her fire, which helped him reclaim some of his own that he thought his father had smothered forever. He enjoyed her intelligence, her wry jokes, her unique perspective on people and places. He pitied her past. And, of course, he lusted after every mind-bendingly sexy inch of her.

But what he felt was more even than the sum of all that.

With a ferocity similar to his passion for Alec, he also wanted to see her smile, and to hear her laugh. He wanted to make her happy because he wasn't sure he could be if she wasn't. He wanted to help her recover from the wounds she'd never even admitted the existence of.

He wanted to make her whole, and well, and safe.

And he wanted to make her his.

There was a word for all that, of course. It was a word he didn't toss around lightly, not since the hideous mistake of his marriage.

Love. He forgot to hit the gas at all, and the

car almost coasted to a stop. The car behind him honked.

But… God help him, he had fallen in love with wild, untamable Rowena Wright.

And he had no reason on this earth to believe she felt the same way about him. She'd never denied that she was leaving this town, or that she had no interest in a long-term relationship. She'd been as brutally honest about her gypsy soul's preference for a rootless existence, and she hadn't really cared whether he liked it.

He took a deep breath and hit the gas again. He might well be in store for a great big mess of hurt. Or he might finally find that little piece of heaven. Might as well find out which one it was going to be.

When he reached Bell River's front drive, he saw the one thing he hadn't expected. The place was crawling with cars and trucks and horse trailers.

He parked toward the back, though he couldn't get very close to the house. He didn't recognize most of the cars. No, wait, there was Tina Blakeley's Mercedes. He'd given her husband about a dozen parking tickets in the past few months.

And there was Mitch's motorcycle.

As Dallas emerged from his car, Mitch came loping toward him, clearly trying to head him off.

"Hey," Mitch said, slightly breathless, when he reached the car. "I was going to call you."

"Why?" Dallas watched as Ethan Stills, a local transporter, loaded a horse into his trailer. Tina Blakeley followed beside the horse, patting it on the head and supervising carefully. "What's going on here? Is everything all right?"

"Not really." Mitch ran his hand through his hair. He looked pale, and his freckles stood out the way they used to when he was a kid. "She's leaving. I mean, really leaving. Like...for good."

Dallas glanced toward the house, where Bonnie stood, watching Mitch, her hands pressed together in front of her stomach.

"Who?" Inexcusably selfish, he momentarily wanted to believe Mitch was talking about Bonnie. But he knew better.

"Rowena." Mitch frowned as another car pulled up beside them. It was Judy Oppenheim, the town's one Realtor. She got out, smiled at them, then rounded the back of her vehicle to extricate a large for-sale sign from the truck.

"I'm sorry," Mitch said. "Bonnie tried to talk Rowena out of it, and so did I, but—"

"When?"

"Tomorrow. She wanted to go today, but she had too many details to…"

Dallas didn't hear the end of that sentence. He had already started to move toward the house. Behind him, Mitch called out, "She's in the stables. She's selling Flashdancer."

His feet paused themselves, without his command. She was selling her horse? She adored that horse.

But then, he knew for a fact that she also adored Bell River. And she had seemed pretty fond of Alec, and Bonnie, and even Mitch. And the other night, when they made love, he'd allowed himself to believe that maybe…

Hell. This wasn't simply leaving town. This was scorched earth. She was redrawing the map of her life, and when she was finished, Bell River wouldn't be on it.

He could almost smell the bridges burning from here.

When he reached the stables, he heard her voice. He'd been imagining her angry, or agitated…or any excess of emotion that might account for this hectic departure. But to his surprise, she sounded calm, melodious, even amused.

"I'm just taking bids right now, Grayson," she was saying. "I'll decide who gets her later."

Grayson? As far as Dallas knew, Silverdell possessed only one Grayson. Old Grayson Harper couldn't be here, though. He didn't ride anymore, and besides, Dallas would have noticed his limo, even in that packed yard.

"I know you have more money than God, Grayson, but—"

Rowena broke off as she saw Dallas enter the stables.

"Good morning," she said, sounding genuinely pleased to see him. He frowned. After the way they'd parted, that had to be a facade. When had she become such a good actress?

It was indeed Grayson Harper who stood in the stable with her, leaning heavily on his cane. His face bloomed red. He wasn't used to being thwarted.

Flashdancer watched them all from her stall, chewing on hay the way a kid might munch on popcorn at a mildly boring movie.

Grayson scowled at Dallas, too rich to bother feigning anything he didn't really feel.

"I'm buying the paint, so you can head on home, son."

"I'm not here to buy a horse," Dallas responded curtly. "Rowena, do you have a minute?"

"I'm sorry," she said. "I wish I could, but I'm so busy. I have to decide today who will be buying Flash, and I've got three more people to see—"

He took another step in. "For God's sake, Rowena."

Clearly surprised by his tone, she flicked a glance at Grayson, as if to remind Dallas that they had an audience. But Dallas didn't give a plugged nickel what Grayson thought.

"Rowena," he said again. "We need to talk."

She must have decided it was more dangerous not to agree than to give him a few minutes.

"Will you excuse me, Grayson?" She smiled at the older man. Then, without looking at Dallas, she moved toward the stable door. For a minute she was just a slim silhouette against the sunlight, framed by the rectangle of the doorway. As he followed, she came into focus again outside, with her feisty green eyes lit like emeralds on fire.

"This must be very important," she said. "I have to find a good home for that horse, and I don't have much time to do it."

"Why?" He shook his head. "Why are you doing this?"

She lifted her eyebrows. "Doing what? Leaving Bell River? I told you from the start I was leaving. I have a job waiting in Austin. I'm only moving the schedule up by a few days."

Everything she said was rational…and true. But those few days had been the most important days. He had deluded himself that perhaps, in those few days, he could persuade her to stay.

"Fair enough. But what's the hurry? If it's about Sunday night—"

"It's not," she broke in. For the first time she looked flustered. The breeze gusted, and she smoothed her hair away from her face, as if the tickling strands irritated her. "I promise you, Dallas. It's not."

He didn't believe her. She had felt something that night—something bigger than sex. He would stake his life on it. But it had obviously scared her, and she was doing what she always did. She was running away from her fears instead of facing them.

She was running away from him.

"Look, if you regret what we did that night, I understand. And if you don't want it to happen again, then it won't. You don't have to sell everything and disappear for another fifteen years simply to avoid me."

She smiled, the movement very small and dry. "I know the timing makes you think that. But it's a coincidence, honestly. In fact, when I thought about it, I realized that we probably needed to do that, if we were ever going to fully move on with our lives. I think of it as sort of a healthy…well, you know. Closure."

"Closure?" His voice was hard, and he took an instinctive step forward. "Are you trying to fool me, Rowena, or are you fooling yourself? That wasn't the close of anything. It could have been—*should* have been—the beginning of something damned special."

She was shaking her head, denying the words he uttered even before he was finished speaking them.

The automatic rejection was maddening. He looked her hard in the eye. "But you can't let anything special come into your life, can you? Because, deep inside, you don't believe you deserve it."

She flushed at that, and he felt a quick laceration of guilt. She probably thought he was using the secrets she'd confided to him that night as a weapon to hurt her with. But he'd always known, deep inside, that she didn't value herself very much. He just hadn't understood why.

"Are you through?" She straightened her shoulders. "Because I have a lot to do, and frankly, if you drove all the way over here to talk me into staying, you're approaching it in a very strange way."

His temper subsided as quickly as it had erupted. This wasn't her fault. She had warned him. He had known all along it would come to nothing. He had fed his hopes and fantasies on bits of smoke and air, and the occasional amazing smile.

Still…he hadn't come to Bell River with the intent of talking her into staying. When he drove over this morning, he hadn't even realized she planned to leave.

He had come to invite her to Alec's birthday party.

But now he knew he couldn't do that. And he couldn't go on trying to persuade her to stay, either. Because even if he could, by some miracle, convince her to give their relationship a chance, how long would it be before some other incident spooked her, and she decided to run again?

He loved her. If she left him a month from now, or a year, it would break his heart. That was his problem. His risk to take, and his burden to carry.

But Alec had begun to care about her, too. Sweet, spunky Alec, who wanted a mother's love so badly, and who had already been viciously cheated once.

If she stayed, if she and Dallas became lovers, Alec would latch on to her. He would pour into her all that thwarted adoration his biological mother didn't want. And then, when she bolted...

Dallas simply didn't have the right to risk letting this woman break his son's heart.

If she didn't want to stay, if she wasn't ready to commit, to put down roots and be a part of a healthy family, he couldn't beg her to.

And obviously she wasn't even close.

He felt defeated, and oddly hollowed out.

"You're right," he said numbly. He pulled his keys out of his pocket, so that he could make a quicker exit. "I shouldn't have shown up here today, and I shouldn't have said what I said just now."

He smiled and shrugged his shoulders. "Apparently," he said as he turned to go, "where you're concerned, I can't stop making stupid mistakes."

He had to stop by the department, but he left as soon as he could and went straight home. He dreaded it, but he had to tell Alec about Rowena.

He'd been praying that Alec had a good morning, so that he'd be happy enough to handle the news well. He should have known better. Alec didn't seem to remember how stormy the house had been back before the divorce. Distance and longing had painted an idealistic picture of his mother in his head.

But Dallas remembered. He should have known.

When he arrived, the house was in chaos. Mrs. Biggars had made Alec's birthday cake for tomorrow's party, and she'd placed it in the center of the kitchen table, the official place of honor. She'd outdone herself this year. The cake was three layers high, and its green icing had been spiked to look like wild grasses. A brown path curved around the side of the cake, and at the top a plastic horse munched on sugared wildflowers in bright reds, yellows and blues.

"He touched it! I saw him! He put his dirty fingers right here, in the icing on the side!" Alec was bent over, inspecting something on the cake's bottom layer. He sounded half-crazed with anger.

"No, he didn't. The cake is fine." Mrs. Biggars held one of the twins, who screamed bloody murder, as if the housekeeper's hands were made of molten lava.

Allyson perched on the edge of a chair beside the kitchen table, holding the other crying baby. That one kept tilting with all his might toward the cake, arms extended, fingers wiggling and stretching, trying to reach the wildflowers.

Dallas had no idea what had really happened with the icing, but Alec was right about one thing. That kid's fingers were disgusting.

"Dallas, thank God." Allyson pulled the baby's hand back one more time, only to have it pop free almost instantly, and begin waving over the cake again. "Dallas, can you please tell Alec that the twins are not plotting to destroy his birthday?"

Alec reared back and glared at his mother.

"I didn't say they were. I said he put his grimy fingers in my cake!"

"His fingers are not gri—"

"Yeah, they are," Dallas broke in. "Why don't you take the babies upstairs and give them baths? I need to talk to Alec."

"But they had a bath this morning, and I was going to—"

"They need another one." Dallas kept his voice calm, which wasn't easy. The impulse to scream louder than the twins, just so that he could be heard, was almost irresistible. "Please, Allyson. Take them upstairs."

Grudgingly, she and Mrs. Biggars gathered the babies' things and eventually departed. Thankfully, the screaming faded as they climbed the stairs. The house wasn't big enough to muffle the noise entirely—hell, the White House wasn't big enough for that. But eventually Allyson shut a door, and it was once again possible to hear yourself think down in the kitchen.

He dropped onto the chair Allyson had vacated and wondered how he was going to make any of this right. Could he really add another piece of tough news to Alec's crummy morning?

"I'm sorry, buddy," he said. "Can we cut

the gross part out? Or do we need a whole new cake?"

Alec had his hands in his pockets, and he screwed up his mouth. "I don't care. It's just a dumb old birthday cake. But it's *my* dumb old cake, not theirs. It was the principle of the thing."

Dallas almost smiled, hearing his own words echoed back to him. Nice to know Alec sometimes listened, even when he didn't seem to.

"I agree. It's rotten luck. But babies are hard to control, even when there's only one. When you've got two at once, it's pretty stressful, I'm sure."

Alec shrugged. "I guess. It's just that Mom thinks he's perfect, and she won't hear a word I say. But I'm telling you. I saw him put his hand in his mouth, and drool all over it. Then he put it in his hair, and even in his diaper!"

Dallas decided on the spot that, unless they switched cakes, he was sticking to ice cream. He closed his eyes, as if he felt sick, then made a ridiculous fake retching sound.

As he hoped, the dumb noise made Alec smile. He grabbed his stomach and emitted a similar sound, except nastier, because kids were just plain better at fake vomiting. Then he plopped into the other kitchen chair and grinned at Dallas.

"Babies," he said, and shuddered dramatically.

"Watch out," Dallas said with a wink. "You had some pretty revolting baby moments yourself."

Alec laughed. "I did? Was I as disgusting as Trevor?"

"Every bit. Actually, more, I'd say."

Ironically, Alec preened a bit, as if suddenly being disgusting was an Olympic event, and he'd taken the gold. Dallas's shoulders relaxed as his son relaxed. But then he decided this was probably as good a mood as he was going to find today, and his shoulders went rigid all over again.

It was time to tell Alec about Rowena.

"I'm sorry to hit you with something else right now, buddy, but I'm afraid I've got some crummy news."

Alec's brow lowered. "What?"

"Rowena is moving to Texas. They've definitely decided to sell Bell River. Looks as if she'll be gone before the party tomorrow, so I'm afraid she won't be able to come."

Alec's face hadn't moved. It was as if the

words bounced off him, instead of sinking in. He just stared at Dallas for a long time.

"She doesn't want to sell Bell River," he said, finally. "She wants to turn it into a dude ranch. It's her dream."

"Maybe." Dallas knew this was probably an important life lesson. But damn it. Sometimes learning life's lessons really sucked eggs. "But dreams can't always come true. Sometimes they have to stay dreams."

Alec's frown had deepened, and his face began to turn red again. "You've got to be wrong, Dad. We're, like, *friends.* She wouldn't leave without telling me. She wouldn't just move to Texas forever without even saying goodbye."

"Well, she told me to say goodbye for her," Dallas lied.

"No." Alec scraped his chair back and stood up, as if he might have to defend his truth with his fists. "She wouldn't do that."

"I think she has to, Alec. You have to think about how she feels. You know what happened to her mother there, in that house. You know about her father. And the place is really run-down. She needs to sell it to someone else. Someone who doesn't have the bad memories. Someone with enough cash to fix it up right."

Alec was breathing heavily. He fixed his eyes on his father, and the intensity of the gaze shook Dallas more than he could have imagined possible. How attached had Alec actually become to Rowena?

If it hurt him this much for her to leave now, how much worse would it have been in a year, or two…? In spite of the dull ache in his chest, Dallas felt vindicated. He had been right—he couldn't have risked letting Alec be rejected by a mother figure all over again.

"I thought you liked her, too," Alec blurted. "I thought you knew she was special."

"I do." Dallas put his hands on the table, palms down, and stared at them for a minute, trying to find the right words. "I do like her. In fact, I feel even more than that. In some ways, Rowena was my dream."

Alec nodded vigorously. "Right! So then, obviously you have to—"

"But there's a catch, Alec. She doesn't feel the same way about me. So my dream won't be coming true, no matter how much I'd like it to. It happens to every one of us, at some point in our lives. It hurts, but you can get over it."

In the middle of that speech, Dallas realized he was, in some indirect way, trying to prepare Alec for what his mother would tell him tonight. He wanted his son to understand that even the things that hurt a lot could be endured. And sometimes, it was for the best.

Alec recoiled, his nose wrinkled, his gaze incredulous. "So you're going to let her go?"

"That's not how it works with people," he said. "She wants to go. She needs to forget about Silverdell and all the terrible things that happened to her here. She needs to be free. If I took her freedom away from her, would that be right? If I forced her to stay, could she ever be happy with me?"

The logic was irrefutable, and even Alec saw it. But knowing his dad was right didn't soothe his fury. He made a few starts at a retort, but they all sputtered out as he realized he had no argument.

Finally, he fell back on the tried and true response to an unbearable situation. "I hate you," he said.

"Dallas, come quick!" Allyson's voice rolled down the stairs like a sea of hysteria. Dallas considered ignoring her, because he didn't want to leave Alec on this note. But when she yelled again, he knew he had to respond, just in case something was wrong with the babies.

"Wait here," he said to Alec firmly. "We need to sort this out when I get back."

Chapter Twenty-Three

The minute Alec was alone, he opened the kitchen door and scurried down the porch stairs, trying not to make noise. He felt sure his dad would open an upstairs window any minute and yell a booming command at him—*you'd better not leave this house, young man.*

But as he rattled his bike out of the little metal stand by the garage, he didn't hear anything but the chick-chick of their next-door neighbor's sprinkler system.

Even when he pedaled as fast as he could down the driveway and onto the sidewalk, no one followed. He hoped everything was okay with the babies, but he did sort of appreciate them providing a distraction at the perfect moment.

Alec had ridden to Bell River many times over the past year—his dad would pop a vein if he knew exactly how many. So the two miles didn't seem very far anymore. His legs were used to it.

Today, though, he raced as fast as his bike would go, for fear of being too late. By the time he tackled the loose dirt of the long, uphill front drive, he was huffing and puffing. His forehead felt sweaty, and his legs burned like fire.

Uncle Mitch's motorcycle was parked around back, and somebody else's car, too. For a minute, he was afraid Rowena's car wasn't there, but at the last minute he saw it, over by the barn.

Beside it, the little vegetable garden had begun to sprout green leaves everywhere. At first, he thought that must be a good sign. Who would plant vegetables if they didn't expect to be around to eat them? But then he realized she probably hadn't put these down herself. The rows were uneven and had gaps, like an old person missing a bunch of teeth.

The green, growing things must be either weeds or leftover plants from long ago.

He dropped his bike in the dirt, and ran over to peek in her car. Several boxes were piled on the backseat, but thank goodness Rowena wasn't in there, keys in hand, prepared to drive away.

So where was she? He scanned the property. He hoped she wasn't inside with Uncle Mitch and Bonnie. What he wanted to say, he didn't want anyone else to hear.

He checked the outbuildings first. Not in the stables, or the pole barn. But then he got lucky. He found her on the far side of the main barn, kneeling on the ground, playing with the kittens. She had the two yellow ones in her lap, and the two black ones were playing with her boots. The mother cat lay nearby in a bright patch of sun, probably relieved to have a babysitter.

Rowena didn't look like a person who was about to rush off and move to another state. But he'd seen the for-sale sign in front of the house. And he knew his father didn't lie.

"Hello," he said loudly. "Were you even going to say goodbye?"

He hadn't meant to begin in an angry voice,

but that's what came out when he opened his mouth.

She lifted her head, obviously startled. Then, instead of looking relieved that it was just Alec instead of an axe murderer or something, she looked sad.

"I wanted to come see you, Alec, but..." She put the kittens back into their box, as if she couldn't handle the distraction while she talked. "The move is happening pretty fast. If I didn't get to talk to you, I was going to write you a letter."

Yeah, sure. Like his mother was always going to write him a letter. He knew what promises like that were worth.

"Well, I'm here now. And I'm not here to say goodbye. I'm here because I think you should know you're making a big mistake."

She lifted her hair away from her face. "Oh, Alec. You don't understand."

"No, *you* don't understand." He was really mad now. Why did everyone assume that, just because you were a kid, you couldn't have anything to say worth hearing? "You don't understand at all."

"Okay," she said, resting her hands on her knees and looking right at him, to show that she really was listening. "Maybe you should tell me, so that I *will* understand."

Oh. Okay. His steam eased up. He'd forgotten for a minute how different she was from other grown-ups. She had always listened to him, if he asked her to.

"Well, the important thing is that you don't really want to leave Bell River. You *think* you do, because you feel like everything is all messed up, and you have bad memories, and you hope maybe you'll be happier in this other place."

She nodded. "You're not far off," she said, with one of those sad smiles.

"Yeah, but here's the thing. You *won't* be happier there. This is where you belong. And I'm not just saying this because I want you to stay. I'm saying it because I know! I almost made that same mistake myself."

She frowned. "You did? How so?"

He felt a tiny bit disloyal telling anyone about his mom, but Rowena wasn't really *anyone.* She really needed to know.

"Well, you know how I wanted to go live with my mom in France?"

She nodded.

"Okay, well, the thing is, my mom is here now. She came for my birthday, so she's staying in our house. And I'm glad to see her and everything. But I found out pretty quick that I don't really want to live with her."

Rowena's eyebrows went up, and she tilted her head. "You don't?"

"No. I love her and all, but she's different. Or maybe *different* isn't the right way to put it. Maybe she was always like this. But it's been two years since I saw her, and I had forgotten. I was thinking she was always sweet and would let me do whatever I wanted. I thought she was like a hundred times nicer than my dad. But she's not."

"Oh." Rowena's face wasn't as easy to read now. She almost smiled, but her eyes still looked sad. "If you're disappointed, I'm sorry. But for your dad's sake, I'm glad. He would have missed you a lot."

Alec moved closer, pleased that she seemed to catch on so quickly. He was close enough now to hear the kittens squealing softly in the box and see them writhing and climbing over one another. "I know!" He smiled. "That's exactly what I'm trying to say!"

Rowena looked confused. "What is?"

"That I would have missed Dad, and he would have missed me. Luckily, I realized I was wrong before it was too late. My mom came to visit, and I was able to see for myself. But you won't know, and you'll sell Bell River, and you'll move away. And then, when you find out you were wrong, you'll be sorry, but it'll be too late!"

He was pleased with how logically he'd been able to lay it all out. Surely she had to see the sense in it.

But she didn't respond for a long time. She looked at him awhile, and then she turned her head and seemed to stare out at the field of wildflowers instead.

Finally, she turned back to him. "I understand what you're saying. I really do. And if that were the only problem, I might even take your advice. But there are a lot of reasons why I have to leave Bell River. Even if I'm not happier in Texas, I still have to go."

The finality in her voice made him feel like crying, which made him angrier than ever.

"Why? Because you had a crummy father? Because your mom died? Because you have bad memories in this house? All that stuff isn't going to go away just because you move to Texas. You'll still have bad memories, and a crummy dad. But everybody else has stuff like that, too, and they don't run away."

She wound her fingers together so tightly

the ends went white. "Alec, it's truly not that simple."

"It could be. Look at my dad. His mom and dad are dead, too. Plus, my mom left him. He was really sad when that happened. You think he doesn't have sad memories in our house? But that doesn't make him sell it and run away. He stays, and he loves me, and he loves Uncle Mitch, too. He takes care of us. And we make new memories, happy memories, to make the old ones go away."

She shut her eyes briefly. When she opened them, they were dull and didn't sparkle the way they usually did. "Your father is a better person than I am, Alec. A stronger person. He always has been."

Her skin looked pale, even though she was in the sun. And her voice sounded kind of... frozen. If he weren't so mad, he'd be worried.

But he was mad. Everything in his chest seemed to be burning up with anger and defeat.

"Okay, then, go! I don't care. But you're going to hate it, and you're going to wish you could come back to Silverdell and Bell River and my dad and me. But it'll be too late, because some other person will own the ranch, and my dad will marry somebody else, and

I'll grow up, and I'll be off at college or something."

She didn't speak. Maybe she was angry, too. Or maybe her voice had finally completely frozen over.

He started to leave, kicking up dirt as he went. He wished he could think of one last, perfect line, something so brilliant that it would make her change her mind—or at least make her sorry, every time she thought back on today.

But he couldn't think of anything like that. So he settled for turning around one last time, giving her his angriest look and saying, "When that happens, Rowena, don't forget. *I told you so.*"

Rowena always traveled light, so she hadn't brought much with her when she came to Bell River. A suitcase of clothes, a bag of toiletries, a couple of books and her computer. But somehow, during the weeks she'd been here, she'd accumulated so many things she didn't know how she'd fit them all in her car.

She'd have to leave most of it behind. Okay. That was fine. She needed to get back to traveling light, anyhow. Material possessions became a ball and chain. Like the cliché said, you started out owning them, but eventually they owned you.

When it came time to decide what to discard, though, it hadn't been quite as clear-cut.

The horse supplies and tackle, of course, could stay. So could all the cleaning supplies and office junk and new towels and linens and pots and pans.

She'd bought a few new clothes, and those she'd keep, even the gypsy shirt that would always remind her painfully of Dallas.

She'd also bought two of Bonnie's wildflower paintings. She had no idea where she could hang them in Austin, but she couldn't bear to leave them behind. Alec had made her a bracelet at school, out of colored threads, and an ashtray of lumpy red clay. Those didn't take up much room, so why not keep them?

But she hadn't realized how many books she'd bought while she was here. Local subjects, mostly—history and wildlife and flora and fauna and pictorial essays of the region. She'd bought a Colorado Beauty DVD, and had impulsively purchased Barton James's CD of cowboy poems and ballads, which he'd recorded himself at a local pay-by-the-hour studio.

When she looked at them, stacked together

in boxes, she'd seen how obvious—and how pathetic—it was. She was trying to take Colorado with her to Texas.

Absurd. She put those boxes aside, in the corner. If Bonnie didn't want them, some charity or hospital or library undoubtedly would.

She'd also packaged some cuttings of flowers and shrubs around the property—and that was the most ridiculous acquisition of all, because where on earth could she plant them? She picked that box up, and emptied it into a large black garbage sack.

She carted the remaining boxes to her car, two or three at a time. Overhead, the moon was round and brilliant and steady, like the tallest lighthouse in the universe. It shone on the mountaintops at the horizon, and it made the wildflowers on the flatlands glow with eerie blue-white phosphorescence.

She didn't look over at the manager's apartment, where Bonnie had long been sound asleep. They'd said their goodbyes already. And she didn't look toward the stable, either, where Flash seemed to be restless. Every now and then she'd hear the horse stamp her feet, or blow hard through her nose, as if she couldn't settle down.

Horses were sensitive like that. They often intuited when big changes were coming. Luckily, Rowena wasn't worried about Flash's future. At the last minute, Mitch had made an offer. Much lower than all the other offers, it was still the one she accepted. Though he'd have to find somewhere to board Flash, and Dallas probably wouldn't approve, Mitch was still the one she trusted.

So Flash would be fine. Rowena, on the other hand, struggled with the idea of leaving the horse behind. Guess that was one more bit of proof—as if she needed another—that buying the horse had been a big mistake.

Finally, the car was full. She stretched her back to ease the kinks, and debated whether she should try to get a couple of hours sleep, or whether she should simply make a pot of coffee and power through.

She'd left the foyer door open, and through it she could hear the grandfather clock strike 4:00 a.m. She double-checked her watch—she hadn't realized it had grown so late. But the grandfather clock was right, as always.

Only two hours or so till dawn. She intended to leave at first light, so that answered her question. It would be coffee, not sleep.

At night, the colorful stained glass around

the foyer looked gorgeous from the outside, but when she entered the house and shut the door, the colors disappeared. In here, the glass simply looked scarred and black.

The only thing she hadn't packed yet was the small silver box of her mother's pictures. But she mustn't forget it. She plucked it from the foyer table and started to go upstairs. A shower would be nice. Then coffee.

But suddenly, as she put her foot on the first step, the stairs loomed as steep as a mountain—far too difficult to climb. She sank down on the second step, the box in her lap, and leaned her head against the handrail.

She shut her eyes, overwhelmed all at once by a warm, black tide of sadness. She turned her face toward the wall, the rail pressing painfully into her forehead. She couldn't remember feeling this lost and alone since the night her mother died.

Died right here on this spot. Rowena placed her palms against the weathered wood of the stairs and tried to feel whatever lingered there.

"If you're here, Mom, this would be a good time to give me a sign. I'll be gone in a couple of hours, and I'm never coming back."

Silence throbbed around her, and nothing

else. She shook her head slowly, aware that she was too tired to think straight. Why else would she be talking to ghosts who couldn't even be bothered to answer?

She had a simultaneous urge to cry and yawn. She chose to yawn. She was so tired. So tired. It might be smart to nap, at least, so that she didn't drive into a ravine on the way to Texas. She let her shoulders relax. And gradually her awareness of her own body, her own physical surroundings, softened, the way it did right before sleep overtook her.

And in that absence of boundaries, she had the lovely, inexplicable sense of her mother, sitting down beside her on the stairs. Her body warmed, and the perfume of red roses filled the air.

"I miss you, Mamma," she said softly. Or maybe she just thought it. It didn't seem to be an important distinction. "And I'm so sorry I didn't protect you."

No voice disturbed the silence. No motion touched the air.

But in her heart, as she floated over the threshold to oblivion, she heard her mother speak.

And when she did, a jagged boulder of pain rushed out of her in one powerful, healing flood. Because these were the words she'd waited so long to hear.

Don't be afraid, Rowena. I love you very much.

She woke with a start, to the sound of something crashing to the floor. She lifted her head from the railing, her blood rushing fast, her skin shimmering with fear. But nothing was there. It was daylight, not dawn, but bright midmorning light, and the sun threw the familiar rectangles of color onto the floor.

Right in the center of the brightest, greenest rectangle lay her little silver box, on its side, its lid ajar. Clearly it had tumbled from her lap as she slept, causing the noise that woke her.

She stood, relieved, and climbed down to retrieve it. One of the photos had been knocked free. Just one. She put out her hand, but she paused, as if frozen, when she saw her mother's happy, loving face smiling up at her.

The shivers started again. But they didn't last long. Whatever this was—a dream, her subconscious offering up advice or something more otherworldly than that—it was nothing to be afraid of.

In fact, she felt calmer, and stronger, than

she had in a long time. She glanced out at the packed car, and tried to imagine getting in it and driving away. She tried to imagine looking in her rearview mirror and seeing Bell River get smaller and smaller, until it finally disappeared.

That was the last glimpse she'd had of her home, fifteen years ago, when Ruth drove them to the airport after her mother's funeral, and it was burned into her heart. At that terrible moment, the small, rectangular section of Bell River's ranch house was somehow the visual representation of all the loss and pain and loneliness in the world.

It had felt as if something was being torn away, some piece of her soul removed. No matter what she'd been telling herself in the years since that day, Bell River was the only place on earth she'd ever truly belonged.

When she was ripped away fifteen years ago, she had no choice.

But she had a choice now.

All she needed was courage. The courage to admit that she cared, that she needed and wanted something…someone….

The courage to give other people the power to tell her no. To rebuff her dreams. To reject her love. To break her heart.

But they had that power already, didn't they? She hadn't ever really been as free as she told herself she was. She hadn't been able to put down roots anywhere else, because her heart already belonged here. Her connections were too deep for even time and distance— and a staggering amount of denial—to sever.

Connections to her mother, and her sisters, and this land. Even to the man she had called her father, as deeply flawed and tormented as he was.

And, now, to Dallas, although she couldn't be sure he felt the same. And to his lonely son, whose heart was so fragile. If she did this, if she stayed and told the truth about her feelings, it would have to be forever. No claustrophobia, no "commitment issues," as Bree would say.

No running away out of fear or pain or guilt.

Was she strong enough to dare all that?

Of course she was. Or, if she wasn't yet, she would learn to be. Slowly, perhaps. Baby steps forward, and maybe even the occasional giant step back. But she would learn to love herself, and to be brave.

And here was where she would start.

She walked to the foyer table and picked

up her cell phone with shaking fingers. Surprised to realize that she actually knew Bree's Boston number by heart, she punched it in.

Bree answered immediately, her greeting as crisp and friendly as ever. "Hello?"

"Hello, Bree, it's—" Rowena coughed, her voice failing suddenly.

Bree said again, with a touch of impatience, "Hello? Can you hear me?"

Shutting her eyes, Rowena took a deep breath, in which she imagined the velvet scent of roses, and began.

"Bree, it's me. I hope I haven't caught you at a bad time, because I have things—*so many things*—to tell you."

Chapter Twenty-Four

The birthday party was almost over, thank God.

Dallas had done his best to compartmentalize his emotions. Anger and despair about Rowena over there, in a locked box he wasn't allowed to open. Fun and joy for Alec's ninth birthday on public display, front and center.

But he had a feeling that, in spite of the balloons and the gifts and the music and the twenty giggling third-graders who attended, his strategy hadn't worked very well.

It hadn't helped that Alec, too, was clearly struggling with Rowena's departure. Though he didn't pout, for which Dallas gave him a lot of credit, he was pale and subdued, clearly just going through the birthday party motions.

And then, of course, there was the headache called Allyson and her demon twins.

By the time Mrs. B. brought out the blazing cake, which had been re-iced, Alec didn't even have the heart to make the easy joke. Dallas had fully expected him to bust out with a quick puking sound, maybe using a cough to cover it.

But nothing. Not even a split second of innocent vulgarity. *Wow.* That said something about a nine-year-old boy's mood.

He was almost glad when Jackie Freeman's mother asked him if he could help her extricate her SUV from a crowded driveway. She had a hair appointment, she explained apologetically. But she'd be back in time to pick Jackie up.

No apology necessary! Dallas had meant it sincerely. He was grateful as hell for the chance to escape the noise and failure in here.

He was just nosing his truck back into an empty space when he saw another car drive past. It was half-hidden by all the SUVs and trucks parked along the street by their party guests, but he saw enough to know it was a nondescript sedan, brownish-muddish, whatever that color was the dealers loved so much these days.

Because apparently fate loved to poke him in the nose, it was very similar to Rowena's car. If he hadn't known hers was probably halfway to Albuquerque by now, he might have wondered....

The car found an open spot two houses down, and took a couple minutes parallel parking. He got out of the truck, but he waited, pretending that it was the good host thing to do. Really, though, he dreaded going back inside. Opening presents always followed eating cake, and it would be painful to watch Alec fake delight over every single book and toy and bike bell.

He put his keys in his pocket, and watched as the new guests got out of their cars. No, only one guest.

But...wait...

That wasn't a guest. That was Rowena. The wind picked up her loose hair and fanned it briefly before letting it rest again on her shoulders. She leaned into the car and pulled out a wrapped present.

Oh. The ridiculous hope that had almost picked up his heart and carried it into the clouds lost air and sank. She hadn't changed her mind. She'd succumbed to guilt about disappointing Alec on his birthday. She'd probably spent the morning shopping for the perfect book or toy or bike bell.

Even so, he was masochistic enough to be glad she had come. He'd rather have to lose her all over again an hour from now than have missed a chance to see her.

He moved out onto the sidewalk, and when she saw him waiting there she began to hold herself self-consciously. Perhaps she thought he was positioned to prevent her from coming in. He smiled to himself. She couldn't guess that he was actually just trying to stop himself from swooping her into his arms and making love to her until the neighbors blushed.

When she got within a few yards, close enough that the green of her eyes reached him like a blow to the solar plexus, she smiled. A hesitant smile.

"Hi," she said. "Is the party already over? Am I too late?"

He shook his head. She could show up at the end of the world, or the moment of death, and he would still be glad to see her. He felt a knife slide between his ribs and stab his heart. How in hell was he going to live without her?

"I think they're still opening presents," he said, trying to remember how normal people talked. People who didn't have knives in their hearts.

"Good." She shifted the box in her hands, studying it instead of looking at him. "But you and I should talk first, Dallas. Before I go in, I mean. I have something I want to tell you. And you have the right to decide, after that, whether you want me to go in at all."

"*He* would want you to," Dallas said simply. "That's all that really matters."

She nodded without argument. Obviously she knew how attached Alec had become to her. "Still, would it be rude of you to leave the party long enough to talk? I will make it as quick as I can. Or I could come back later, if—"

"No." He couldn't let her go before she told him whatever it was. What if she went away and changed her mind? What if, instead of coming back, she pointed her car toward Texas? "No, it's fine. It's so crowded in there they'll never miss me."

She smiled gratefully, but she glanced around dubiously, as if wondering whether she could bring herself to talk out here, where everyone could watch them.

He searched his mind quickly. Where could a person steal a minute or two of privacy?

His misspent youth came to the rescue. Between his next-door neighbor's house and the house beyond that, there was a small service lane—really just a few feet of dirt between two fences covered in ivy. But no windows overlooked it, no lights illuminated it, and he'd taken many a high school girl there, back before Rowena.

"I know a place," he said. He held out his hand, and, after a very brief hesitation, she took it. He moved quickly, and she didn't question him.

Within a minute or two, they were in the shadowy green seclusion of the service lane. It hadn't changed much, he observed. He wondered whether, someday, Alec would bring his girlfriends here. He almost laughed at his horrified reaction to the thought. He'd definitely have to install security cameras back here in a few years.

One drawback now, though—there was still nowhere to sit. Rowena took a few seconds to orient herself, and then she set the present down on a patch of wildflowers, to protect it from the dirt.

"Thanks," she said.

"For what?"

"Well...for not turning me away, for starters." She leaned against one of the leafy walls, and folded her hands in front of her. "For giving me another chance. Considering what a terrible fool I've been—"

"What do you mean, another chance? Another chance for what?"

"To tell you all the things I should have told you a long time ago." She wrinkled her nose and gave him a half smile. "Well, not *all* the things—you really would miss the party if I tried to do that. But at least to...to tell you the most important things."

He didn't take his eyes off her face. "And what are the most important things?"

She wet her lips, as if they were too dry to speak. Then she swallowed and tried to smile. "Well, the *most* important one is pretty hard. Could I start with the easiest ones first?"

He laughed. "You can start anywhere you like. It's your conversation. Your call."

She nodded, as if relieved. She put her hand in her pocket, and took out a square of paper. Photo paper, or at least that's what it looked like from here. She didn't offer to show it to him, but she held it carefully between her palms while she talked.

"The first thing is that I've discovered something about who I am. Not some psychological insight, but literally. I've discovered that I'm not Johnny Wright's biological daughter."

Of all the things he'd expected her to say...

He shook his head. "What on earth are you talking about? I know you hated him, but..."

"No. This isn't wishful thinking. I found a picture—actually, Alec found it, though he didn't realize what it was. It made me think, and..." She hesitated, as if she weren't sure how to sum up something this huge. "I had a DNA test done. Johnny was not my biological father."

He felt thickheaded, as if it were difficult to process this incredible piece of information. "You're sure?"

"I'm sure." She moved away from the wall and extended the photo she'd been holding. "I think this man may be my father. I don't know who he is, and obviously I can't be sure. But... I wanted you to see him."

He accepted the picture, though his mind was still sending out questions so fast they knocked into each other and ended up making no sense at all.

He turned it over and looked at it. He noticed Rowena's mother first, because her resemblance to Rowena was shocking. In the photo, Moira and a man were on a mountainside, in ski clothes. He could make out little of the man, except that he looked athletic, and he had dark hair.

And suddenly it hit him...how strange, how disorienting would it be to suddenly discover that you weren't who you thought you were? How empty would it feel to have only this skimpy clue to help you find out who you might be instead?

"I'm sorry," he said. "This must be very hard."

She nodded. "Most people would think I was glad, because Johnny was such an awful father. And someday, maybe I will be. But right now..."

"Right now there's just a blank where your identity used to be."

"Yes." She nodded, then nodded again, as if she were grateful to be understood. If only she knew how well he understood her...and how he hated to see her keep getting hurt.

"When did you find out?"

"I got the results on Monday. The day after we..." She flushed. "After the festival."

"I see." And he did. Her instant flight, her determination to sell everything and be rid of Silverdell once and for all—that had been the only reaction Rowena Wright was programmed to have to a shock like this.

"Do Penny and Brianna know?"

"I wasn't going to tell them," she said. "I... I already felt like enough of an outsider. But I changed my mind this morning. I called Bree first, because she was the one most likely to care."

"And what did she say?"

Rowena smiled again. "She wasn't terribly shocked. Apparently she'd had suspicions all along. She said I was lucky, and she would love to have the test done herself, just in case she could get lucky, too."

He chuckled. "That's certainly direct."

"Actually," Rowena said, "she was more concerned about the other reason I called."

"The other reason?"

"Yes." She nervously tucked her lower lip between her teeth for a moment. Then she took a breath and continued. "I told her that, whether I had Wright blood or not, I loved Bell River as much as anyone in the world.

I explained that, even though I was already packed and ready to leave, I couldn't bring myself to do it. I can't leave Bell River. Not today, and not ever."

She paused. But he was afraid to have a reaction of any kind, for fear it might make this amazing declaration somehow disappear.

She still held her hands together, palms pressed as if praying. She swallowed again, and went on. "I told her that what I want more than anything is to live here, even if she and Penny decide that the DNA test affects my inheritance, which it easily could. I asked her if she'd reconsider the dude ranch plan, and let me stay on to make it happen."

He wasn't sure he'd drawn a breath throughout that speech. If the DNA news had shocked him, this was even more incredible. It was almost impossible to imagine Rowena humbling herself before Brianna like that.

"What did she say?"

"She said that all she's ever wanted is a commitment from me that I'm in for the long haul. I gave her my word that I won't run away, no matter what happens, and she accepted it. Obviously she's still skeptical. She wants me to sign a five-year contract, but that's all right. I'd sign a five-hundred-year contract, if she asked for it."

The whole idea was so preposterous he found himself laughing. "Who are you? And what have you done with the Rowena I know?"

"I don't know who I am," she said softly. She shook her head. "I only know I'm tired of being unhappy. I'm tired of pushing life away, pushing love away, simply because it scares me. I lost Bell River once. I couldn't lose it again."

She looked suddenly very young, and bewildered. He could only imagine what courage it required for her to face her demons—the demons of pride, of fear, of guilt, of shame. How incredibly brave it was of her to admit that she needed to be loved, needed to have a home, at the very moment when she must be least sure she had a right to any of that.

He longed to take her in his arms. He could make that lost look go away. He could fill the empty place that all these changes had left inside her. He ached to fix this—to make her whole again.

She didn't have to be anyone's daughter. Or sister, either, for that matter. She didn't have to grovel for love. He had a heartful he would give her for the asking.

But she still held herself at a distance, her hands between them, like the immovable stone hands of a statue. He refused to invade that place, unless she invited him in.

Clearly she wanted to conquer her fears. She was ready, for the first time, to try. And he had to let her do it, no matter how hard it was for her—just as he had to let Alec fall off his bike, and let Mitch fall in love with a woman who might break his heart.

"And that brings me to the most important thing," Rowena said, looking at him with an expression so guarded he wondered what was coming next.

Would she ask him to stay away? To leave her alone while she fought demons and renovated ranches? Was he one challenge too many right now? Was she afraid he'd assume that staying in Silverdell meant sleeping with him?

"Okay," he said, bracing himself. "Whatever it is, I can accept it."

She opened her hands, finally. She ran her fingers through her hair, and made all the black satin lie flat behind her back.

"It's just that… Bell River wasn't the only

thing I lost, back then. I lost you, Dallas. I lost any chance of repairing the damage I'd done to you. I lost any chance of turning the stupid flirtation into something…better. Something real. And when I woke up today, and I tried to leave this town, I realized that I might not survive losing you again."

Her lips trembled, and she closed them over the last word. She had unconsciously held out her hands, palms up, so close they almost grazed his chest.

It was the invitation he'd been waiting for. His heart pounded with a primitive ferocity against his ribs, and he couldn't resist her another second.

He closed the distance between them and scooped her into his arms.

"How could you lose me? Don't you know that, when you left, you took the best part of me with you? For fifteen years, I've been waiting for you to bring it home. And yet, I would have waited another fifteen, if I had to."

"You mean…"

"I mean I love you." He realized that, though it had become an accepted reality in his own heart, he'd never spoken the words to her. "I love you more than it's possible to describe. I love your body, your heart, your mind and your soul. I love your fire, and your temper, and your laughter."

"My temper?" She let one corner of her mouth turn up wryly. For a minute she looked like the old Rowena, sassy and confident, ready to tease him.

But almost instantly she grew somber again. "I know I'm proud, and hot-tempered. I know that I'll have to work, every day, to be a better person. A calmer, less prickly person. I can't make any promises, of course, except to try."

"Don't you dare," he said, roughly. "I love you for those things, Rowena, not in spite of them. I want your fire. I need it to warm me when I'm cold, and encourage me when I'm thinking of giving up. I want your courage, too. I hope it will inspire my son to grow up to be the bravest man that he can be."

She looked at him with wide, earnest eyes.

"Alec," she said quietly, "is already very brave. He is… I love him so much, and I don't even know how, or when, it happened…."

She had to stop, as if her throat had ceased letting words through. As she gazed up at Dallas, her eyes filled with tears. She opened her lips to speak again, but no sound emerged.

And so he kissed those lips instead. He pressed her body against his, his hunger suddenly wild and raw. He tasted her sweetness, her beauty, her fire—all the things that had made him fall in love with her at the start.

When he finally released her lips, her green eyes were clouded and slightly dazed. "Does this mean you really do believe me? You trust me to stay? You trust me not to hurt you—or Alec—ever again?"

"Trust you?" He laughed, lifting her feet off the ground, and twirling her gently. "I have never met a stronger woman than you. If you say you are going to open a dude ranch, then Bell River will be the most successful dude ranch in the world. If you promise you will stay in Silverdell forever, then the only question left to ask is…"

He let her feet slide softly to the ground, enjoying the tantalizing brush of body against body. She smiled up at him, waiting for his question. For the first time he noticed flecks of amber fire that softened the vivid green of her eyes. Had those flecks only been born today?

When he didn't complete his sentence, she frowned. "Hey, you weren't finished. You said *the only question…*"

He tightened his arms around her. "The only question left to ask is…will you spend that forever with me?"

He heard her gasp softly, not in shock, for she must have known what he'd say, but as if something had caught her suddenly around the heart.

For a long, slow moment, she let her eyes drift shut. Her full lips were pink, flushed from his kiss, and her cheeks burned with an emotion so intense it apparently shot through her like a fever.

Then…because she was Rowena, and not willing to let anything be that easy…she opened her eyes, grinned and tilted her head, as if she had to consider it.

"Wait a minute. Forever with…just you?"

He bent down and kissed her neck.

"Damn straight with just me," he growled. "If you think I'm letting any other men near you, you can think again."

"Hmm." She tapped his shoulder thoughtfully, musing. "That might be a problem, because I was hoping to get the package deal. Let's say, two for one? You, of course…and maybe that wild little boy of yours?"

He grinned. "Oh, you mean the *instant family* package deal. Yes, I think we can arrange that. In fact, I know a little boy who right this minute is having the worst birthday of his life, because he thinks you're on your way to Texas."

Her eyes clouded instantly. "We should go in," she said. "I've kept you away too long. He'll be worried."

Dallas laughed, thinking of how thrilled his son would be. He caught Rowena's hand and started leading her out of their tiny green haven.

"And you know," he said, "this is really your lucky day. Today, the instant family package comes with an additional three items. An ex-wife, and her twin demon babies."

"Um…" Rowena dragged her feet and tugged at his hand. "Hang on a minute. Did you say *demon* babies?"

"Yep." He paused, and shot her a challenging glance. "What? You scared of demon babies?"

She shook her head firmly. "As you very well know, Dallas Garwood, I'm not scared of anything."

She took his arm and wrapped it around her shoulders, then looked up into his face, suddenly pale.

"Except losing you. When you walked away from Bell River yesterday, and I thought I'd never see you again..." She shivered slightly, and turned her face into his chest. "I think I'll always be afraid of losing you."

"But that," he said, his voice thick and slightly ragged, remembering how desolate he, too, had felt as he drove away from Bell River, "is the one thing that can never, ever happen."

He put his fingers under her chin, and turned her face toward his. He kissed her again, long and hard and slow, even though he knew they should hurry.

She melted against him. And when he finally lifted his mouth, she sighed.

"Yes, that was fairly convincing." Her lips spread in a devilish, intensely satisfied smile. "As long as that's settled...let's go in there and get the demon party started!"

Chapter Twenty-Five

Six months later:

Rowena had never fantasized about her wedding day, as most little girls did. Quite the opposite. She had always vowed that she would never marry. She would never let a man own her, control her, destroy her—as she'd seen her father destroy her mother.

But that was because she hadn't imagined that there could be, anywhere on this earth, a man like Dallas Garwood. He was the friend she'd always wanted, who understood her, sometimes better than she understood herself. And, at the same time, he was the lover she'd always dreamed of, in dreams so shocking she had never even admitted they existed.

He'd been at her side every day, these past six months. He gave her freedom when she needed freedom, and he tucked her against his heart when she didn't. He listened to her ideas and visions, and then found ways to make them realities. On his weekends and holidays, he always had a hammer in his hand, or a saw, or a drill.

Because of him—and Alec, Mitch, Bonnie and half a dozen other Dellians who had appeared at her door, one by one, to say they'd love to be a part of her plan—Bell River Dude Ranch was finally taking shape.

They would welcome their first guests in the spring, and they would do it as a family.

If she could just get through this ceremony without crying.

"I do," she said, realizing that the minister was waiting for her to respond to his question. Unfortunately, the words weren't altogether clear. She was nervous, and she was overflowing with emotion, which seemed determined to seep out in happy tears. It was downright embarrassing, for a woman of Rowena's reputation.

The preacher seemed inclined to ignore her

unintelligible sound, but Dallas, who stood beside her, looking like a god in his tuxedo, teasingly arched his sexy, scarred brow. "Come again?"

Alec, the ring-bearer, rolled his eyes.

"Dad," he whispered. "Don't clown around!"

"I *do*," Rowena repeated, more firmly. She widened her eyes, and squeezed Dallas's fingers, silently scolding him for making fun on such a solemn occasion.

And yet, she wouldn't have taken the silliness out of this moment for anything in the world. That was the power he had over her—the power to replace her tears with laughter.

Oh, and there was one other power, too.

"You may kiss the bride."

Dallas leaned down, his blue eyes brilliant and shining, and kissed her. And, just like that, the rest of the church disappeared. The music, the flowers, the guests, even Alec and the preacher, simply faded away into a vague, encircling cloud of stardust.

They must have kept at it too long, because she dimly heard Alec groan, and then laughter, and then a thunderous clapping. Dallas finally released her from his spell, leaving her helplessly weak in the knees and slightly disoriented.

As he straightened to smile at the applauding guests, he winked at her smugly, obviously aware of exactly what he'd done.

She growled under her breath as she turned, too, to acknowledge their cheering friends.

"I'll get you back for this," she warned, still smiling.

He grinned, lifted her hand to his lips and kissed it with a chaste innocence that made her want to laugh.

"I look forward to it eagerly, Mrs. Garwood," he said, and her knees went weak all over again.

And then, it was nothing but hugs and kisses, food and laughter and joy. Fifty people had been invited to the wedding, and sixty people had said yes. Among them were Brianna and Penny, who, now that the reception was officially underway, stood waiting for their chance to hug her.

Spotting them, Rowena smiled and held out her arms. Penny hurried up instantly, threw her arms around her sister and sobbed in unabashed joy.

"You look beautiful, Ro. I've never seen

you look this happy. You really love him, don't you?"

Rowena started to laugh, and to say something like, "Why else would I be marrying him?" But, as she so often did, she remembered her mother, and the marriage she must surely have made simply to give a name to her unborn, illegitimate child.

Did that mean that, however unwittingly, Rowena had been the reason her mother had placed herself in Johnny Wright's power? Once, that thought would have hollowed Rowena out and left her choking on guilt. But she'd learned a lot over the past six months. And one of those things was that the past was only as powerful as you allowed it to be.

So she settled for touching her handkerchief to Penny's damp cheeks and smiling. "You bet I do," she said.

She looked over at Bree and smiled, trying to show her she was welcome, too. She didn't care about the things Bree had said, back when they didn't trust each other. All that mattered was that, slowly, they were building the bridge that had been burned all those years ago.

Finally, she had sisters again. She'd stopped calling them half sisters months ago, even in her own mind. What did that mean, anyhow? No one had checked anyone's DNA when they played fairy princess out by the swimming hole, or crawled into each other's beds at night to make the monsters go away.

Brianna hesitated, but then she, too, approached, not close enough to hug, but at least close enough to touch, fingers to fingers. And Rowena saw that her eyes, too, sparkled with unshed tears.

"It really is wonderful, seeing you so happy." Bree smiled. "He loves you, too. Anyone can see that."

The little silver sparkler of happiness that Rowena seemed to carry around with her all the time now shimmered in her breast. Yes, he loved her. She was the luckiest woman in the world.

Out of the corner of her eye, she saw Bonnie standing at the rim of the room. Instinctively, Rowena felt that something was wrong. She excused herself and hurried over.

"Can I talk to you a minute?" Bonnie's eyes looked haunted, and Rowena's anxiety increased. "Alone?"

Rowena led the younger woman into the small dressing room just outside the sanctuary. She took her hands. "Honey, what's wrong?"

"I'm so sorry, Rowena," Bonnie said. Her fingers felt as cold as if she'd been dipping them into the punch bowl. "But you remember that once I told you I might have to...to leave quickly some day?"

Rowena nodded. The chill seemed to have seeped into her hands, too.

"Well, today is the day."

"Oh, no." Rowena tightened her grip. "Bonnie, there must be something we can do."

"You can trust me. You can forgive me." Bonnie suddenly looked about ten years older, and resigned to her fate. "But there's nothing else anyone can do."

Rowena heard the finality in her voice, and she respected the young woman enough to refrain from arguing. All she said was, "How soon?"

"Right now. We should have left an hour ago, but Mitch didn't want to miss the ceremony."

So Mitch was going with her. Rowena wasn't surprised. In fact, she was relieved. "Does Dallas know?"

"Mitch is talking to him now. He's sorry to have to leave without making the toast, but..."

"For heaven's sake!" Rowena shook Bonnie's cold fingers emphatically. "Do you think anything is more important to Dallas and me than your happiness and safety?"

Bonnie shook her head slowly. "No, of course not." Then she leaned in and kissed Rowena's cheek. "We have to go," she said.

But Rowena's hands still clung, reluctant to let this happen.

"You are a good person, Ro." Bonnie smiled sadly. "I want you to know that I... I will come back someday. If I can."

Rowena nodded. "I'm going to hold you to that promise," she said.

And then, before she could fully take it in, her beautiful young friend was gone.

Rowena walked blindly back into the large room, where everyone was gathered, still talking and laughing. Dallas saw her from across the room, and reached her side within seconds. He looked somber, but not terrified. She took some comfort from that.

"I—I hope she'll be all right," she said.

She'd only known Bonnie seven months—and, of course, she hadn't *really* known her at all. She suspected her real name wasn't even Bonnie. But they had become very close in those few months, and it was impossible not to worry.

Dallas's gaze lingered on the side exit, and suddenly Rowena imagined she could hear the thrum and vroom of a motorcycle vanishing in the distance.

"Mitch will take care of her," he said with a quiet conviction. And then he added, "He loves her. She's made a man of him."

As if that fact alone settled the matter.

"Dad! Dad!" Alec came screaming up to them, his earlier concern for decorum forgotten. "I'm the best man!"

"What?"

Alec waved a piece of paper up toward his father's face. "I'm the best man. Uncle Mitch said so! He said I get to give the best man's toast!"

Dallas laughed. "Awesome," he said. "I guess you *are* the best man, then."

Delighted, Alec went dancing through the crowd, shouting "I'm the best man" to anyone who would listen. Rowena watched him with a loving pride that she had once thought was reserved for biological mothers. She was fascinated by how he could affect the attitudes and arrogance of a twenty-year-old one minute, and dance around like a giddy kinder-gartner the next.

Before she knew it, someone called for the first dance. Barton James brought his guitar up to the microphone and began to strum.

Dallas put out his hand, and she took it, feeling the electric leap of sensuality that always came when they touched, skin to skin.

Behind them, Alec made a perfunctory protest.

"*I'm* the best man," he said, mildly cranky.

Dallas smiled, put his hand on the boy's head and ruffled his thick blond hair.

"I know," he said, tolerantly. "And it's great to be the best man."

Then he turned his smoldering gaze to Rowena, who shivered once more with that electric anticipation.

"But there are some things, buddy, that only the groom can do."

* * * * *